SENTIMENTAL EDUCATION

OR,

THE HISTORY OF A YOUNG MAN

BY

GUSTAVE FLAUBERT

VOLUME V.

SIMON P. MAGEE,
PUBLISHER,
CHICAGO, ILL.

CONTENTS

ILLUSTRATIONS

SENTIMENTAL EDUCATION

CHAPTER I.

A PROMISING PUPIL.

N THE 15th of September, 1840, about six o'clock in the morning, the *Ville de Montereau,* just on the point of starting, was sending forth great whirlwinds of smoke, in front of the Quai St. Bernard.

People came rushing on board in breathless haste. The traffic was obstructed by casks, cables, and baskets of linen. The sailors answered nobody. People jostled one another. Between the two paddle-boxes was piled up a heap of parcels; and the uproar was drowned in the loud hissing of the steam, which, making its way through the plates of sheet-iron, enveloped everything in a white cloud, while the bell at the prow kept ringing continuously.

At last, the vessel set out; and the two banks of the river, stocked with warehouses, timber-yards, and manufactories, opened out like two huge ribbons being unrolled.

A young man of eighteen, with long hair, holding an album under his arm, remained near the helm without moving. Through the haze he surveyed steeples, buildings of which he did not know the names; then, with a parting glance, he took in the Île St. Louis, the Cité, Nôtre Dame; and presently, as Paris disappeared from his view, he heaved a deep sigh.

Frederick Moreau, having just taken his Bachelor's degree, was returning home to Nogent-sur-Seine, where he would have to lead a languishing existence for two months, before going back to begin his legal studies. His mother had sent him, with enough to cover his expenses, to Havre to see an uncle, from whom she had expectations of his receiving an inheritance. He had returned from that place only yesterday; and he indemnified himself for not having the opportunity of spending a little time in the capital by taking the longest possible route to reach his own part of the country.

The hubbub had subsided. The passengers had all taken their places. Some of them stood warming themselves around the machinery, and the chimney spat forth with a slow, rhythmic rattle its plume of black smoke. Little drops of dew trickled over the copper plates; the deck quivered with the vibration from within; and the two paddle-wheels, rapidly turning round, lashed the water. The edges of the river were covered with sand. The vessel swept past rafts of wood which began to oscillate under the rippling of the waves, or a boat without sails in which a man sat fishing. Then the wandering haze cleared off; the sun appeared; the hill which ran along the course of the Seine to the right subsided by degrees, and another rose nearer on the opposite bank.

It was crowned with trees, which surrounded low-built houses, covered with roofs in the Italian style. They had sloping gardens divided by fresh walls, iron railings, grass-plots, hot-houses, and vases of geraniums, laid out regularly on the terraces where one could lean forward on one's elbow. More than one spectator longed, on beholding those attractive residences which looked so peaceful, to be the owner of one of them, and to dwell there till the end of his days with a good billiard-table, a sailing-boat, and a woman or some other object to dream about. The agreeable novelty of a journey by water made such outbursts natural. Already the wags on board were beginning their jokes. Many began to sing. Gaiety prevailed, and glasses of brandy were poured out.

Frederick was thinking about the apartment which he would occupy over there, on the plan of a drama, on subjects for pictures, on future passions. He found that the happiness merited by the excellence of his soul was slow in arriving. He declaimed some melancholy verses. He walked with rapid step along the deck. He went on till he reached the end at which the bell was; and, in the centre of a group of passengers and sailors, he saw a gentleman talking soft nothings to a country-woman, while fingering the gold cross which she wore over her breast. He was a jovial blade of forty with frizzled hair. His robust form was encased in a jacket of black velvet, two emeralds sparkled in his cambric shirt, and his wide, white trousers fell over odd-looking red boots of Russian leather set off with blue designs.

The presence of Frederick did not discompose him. He turned round and glanced several times at the young man with winks of enquiry. He next offered cigars to all who were standing around him. But getting tired, no doubt, of their society, he moved away from them and took a seat further up. Frederick followed him.

The conversation, at first, turned on the various kinds of tobacco, then quite naturally it glided into a discussion about women. The gentleman in the red boots gave the young man advice; he put forward theories, related anecdotes, referred to himself by way of illustration, and he gave utterance to all these things in a paternal tone, with the ingenuousness of entertaining depravity.

He was republican in his opinions. He had travelled; he was familiar with the inner life of theatres, restaurants, and newspapers, and knew all the theatrical celebrities, whom he called by their Christian names. Frederick told him confidentially about his projects; and the elder man took an encouraging view of them.

But he stopped talking to take a look at the funnel, then he went mumbling rapidly through a long calculation in order to ascertain "how much each stroke of the piston at so many times per minute would come to," etc., and having found the number, he spoke about the scenery, which he admired immensely. Then he gave expression to his delight at having got away from business.

Frederick regarded him with a certain amount of respect, and politely manifested a strong desire to know his name. The stranger, without a moment's hesitation, replied:

"Jacques Arnoux, proprietor of *L'Art Industriel*, Boulevard Montmartre."

A man-servant in a gold-laced cap came up and said:

"Would Monsieur have the kindness to go below? Mademoiselle is crying."

L'Art Industriel was a hybrid establishment, wherein the functions of an art-journal and a picture-shop were combined. Frederick had seen this title several times in the bookseller's window in his native place on big prospectuses, on which the name of Jacques Arnoux displayed itself magisterially.

The sun's rays fell perpendicularly, shedding a glittering light on the iron hoops around the masts, the plates of the barricades, and the surface of the water, which, at the prow, was cut into two furrows that spread out as far as the borders of the meadows. At each winding of the river, a screen of pale poplars presented itself with the utmost uniformity. The surrounding country at this point had an empty look. In the sky there were little white clouds which remained motionless, and the sense of weariness, which vaguely diffused itself over everything, seemed to retard the progress of the steamboat and to add to the insignificant appearance of the passengers. Putting aside a few persons of good position who were travelling first class, they were artisans or shopmen with their wives and children. As it was customary at that time to wear old clothes when travelling, they nearly all had their heads covered with shabby Greek caps or discoloured hats, thin black coats that had become quite threadbare from constant rubbing against writing-desks, or frock-coats with the casings of their buttons loose from continual service in the shop. Here and there some roll-collar waistcoat afforded a glimpse of a calico shirt stained with coffee. Pinchbeck pins were stuck into cravats that were all torn. List shoes were kept up by stitched straps.

Two or three roughs who held in their hands bamboo canes with leathern loops, kept looking askance at their fellow-passengers; and fathers of families opened their eyes wide while making enquiries. People chatted either standing up or squatting over their luggage; some went to sleep in various corners of the vessel; several occupied themselves with eating. The deck was soiled with walnut shells, butt-ends of cigars, peelings of pears, and the droppings of pork-butchers' meat, which had been carried wrapped up in paper. Three cabinet-makers in blouses took their stand in front of the bottle case; a harp-player in rags was resting with his elbows on his instrument. At intervals could be heard the sound of falling coals in the furnace, a shout, or a laugh; and the captain kept walking on the bridge from one paddle-box to the other without stopping for a moment.

Frederick, to get back to his place, pushed forward the grating leading into the part of the vessel reserved for first-class passengers, and in so doing disturbed two sportsmen with their dogs.

What he then saw was like an apparition. She was seated in the middle of a bench all alone, or, at any rate, he could see no one, dazzled as he was by her eyes. At the moment when he was passing, she raised her head; his shoulders bent involuntarily; and, when he had seated himself, some distance away, on the same side, he glanced towards her.

She wore a wide straw hat with red ribbons which fluttered in the wind behind her. Her black tresses, twining around the edges of her large brows, descended very low, and seemed amorously to press the oval of her face. Her robe of light muslin spotted with green spread out in numerous folds. She was

In the act of embroidering something; and her straight nose, her chin, her entire person was cut out on the background of the luminous air and the blue sky.

As she remained in the same attitude, he took several turns to the right and to the left to hide from her his change of position; then he placed himself close to her parasol which lay against the bench, and pretended to be looking at a sloop on the river.

Never before had he seen more lustrous dark skin, a more seductive figure, or more delicately shaped fingers than those through which the sunlight gleamed. He stared with amazement at her work-basket, as if it were something extraordinary. What was her name, her place of residence, her life, her past? He longed to become familiar with the furniture of her apartment, all the dresses that she had worn, the people whom she visited; and the desire of physical possession yielded to a deeper yearning, a painful curiosity that knew no bounds.

A negress, wearing a silk handkerchief tied round her head, made her appearance, holding by the hand a little girl already tall for her age. The child, whose eyes were swimming with tears, had just awakened. The lady took the little one on her knees. "Mademoiselle was not good, though she would soon be seven; her mother would not love her any more. She was too often pardoned for being naughty." And Frederick heard those things with delight, as if he had made a discovery, an acquisition.

He assumed that she must be of Andalusian descent, perhaps a creole: had she brought this negress across with her from the West Indian Islands?

Meanwhile his attention was directed to a long shawl with violet stripes thrown behind her back over the copper support of the bench. She must have, many a time, wrapped it around her waist, as the vessel sped through the midst of the waves; drawn it over her feet, gone to sleep in it!

Frederick suddenly noticed that with the sweep of its fringes it was slipping off, and it was on the point of falling into the water when, with a bound, he secured it. She said to him:

"Thanks, Monsieur."

Their eyes met.

"Are you ready, my dear?" cried my lord Arnoux, presenting himself at the hood of the companion-ladder.

Mademoiselle Marthe ran over to him, and, clinging to his neck, she began pulling at his moustache. The strains of a harp were heard—she wanted to see the music played; and presently the performer on the instrument, led forward by the negress, entered the place reserved for saloon passengers. Arnoux recognized in him a man who had formerly been a model, and "thou'd" him, to the astonishment of the by-standers. At length the harpist, flinging back his long hair over his shoulders, stretched out his hands and began playing.

It was an Oriental ballad all about poniards, flowers, and stars. The man in rags sang it in a sharp voice; the twanging of the harp strings broke the harmony of the tune with false notes. He played more vigorously: the chords vibrated, and their metallic sounds seemed to send forth sobs, and, as it were, the plaint of a proud and vanquished love. On both sides of the river, woods extended as far as the edge of the water. A current of fresh air swept past them, and Madame Arnoux gazed vaguely into the distance.

When the music stopped, she moved her eyes several times as if she were starting out of a dream.

The harpist approached them with an air of humility. While Arnoux was searching his pockets for money, Frederick stretched out towards the cap his closed hand, and then, opening it in a shamefaced manner, he deposited in it a louis d'or. It was not vanity that had prompted him to bestow this alms in her presence, but the idea of a blessing in which he thought she might share—an almost religious impulse of the heart.

Arnoux, pointing out the way, cordially invited him to go below. Frederick declared that he had just lunched; on the contrary, he was nearly dying of hunger; and he had not a single centime in his purse.

After that, it occurred to him that he had a perfect right, as well as anyone else, to remain in the cabin.

Ladies and gentlemen were seated before round tables, lunching, while an attendant went about serving out coffee. Monsieur and Madame Arnoux were in the far corner to the right. He took a seat on the long bench covered with velvet, having picked up a newspaper which he found there.

They would have to take the diligence at Montereau for Châlons. Their tour in Switzerland would last a month. Madame Arnoux blamed her husband for his weakness in dealing with his child. He whispered in her ear something agreeable, no doubt, for she smiled. Then, he got up to draw down the window curtain at her back. Under the low, white ceiling, a crude light filled the cabin. Frederick, sitting opposite to the place where she sat, could distinguish the shade of her eyelashes. She just moistened her lips with her glass and broke a little piece of crust between her fingers. The lapis-lazuli locket fastened by a little gold chain to her wrist made a ringing sound, every now and then, as it touched her plate. Those present, however, did not appear to notice it.

At intervals one could see, through the small portholes, the side of a boat taking away passengers or putting them on board. Those who sat round the tables stooped towards the openings, and called out the names of the various places they passed along the river.

Arnoux complained of the cooking. He grumbled particularly at the amount of the bill, and got it reduced. Then, he carried off the young man towards the forecastle to drink a glass of grog with him. But Frederick speedily came back again to gaze at Madame Arnoux, who had returned to the awning, beneath which she seated herself. She was reading a thin, grey-covered volume. From time to time, the corners of her mouth curled and a gleam of pleasure lighted up her forehead. He felt jealous of the inventor of those things which appeared to interest her so much. The more he contemplated her, the more he felt that there were yawning abysses between them. He was reflecting that he should very soon lose sight of her irrevocably, without having extracted a few words from her, without leaving her even a souvenir!

On the right, a plain stretched out. On the left, a strip of pasture-land rose gently to meet a hillock where one could see vineyards, groups of walnut-trees, a mill embedded in the grassy slopes, and, beyond that, little zigzag paths over the white mass of rocks that reached up towards the clouds. What bliss it would have been to ascend side by side with her, his arm around her waist, while her gown would sweep the yellow leaves, listening to her voice and gazing up into her glowing eyes! The steamboat might stop, and all they would have to do was to step out of it; and yet this thing, simple as it might be, was not less difficult than it would have been to move the sun.

A little further on, a château appeared with pointed roof and square turrets. A flower garden spread out in the foreground; and avenues ran, like dark archways, under the tall linden trees. He pictured her to himself passing along by this group of trees. At that moment a young lady and a young man showed themselves on the steps in front of the house, between the trunks of the orange trees. Then the entire scene vanished.

The little girl kept skipping playfully around the place where he had stationed himself on the deck. Frederick wished to kiss her. She hid herself behind her nurse. Her mother scolded her for not being nice to the gentleman who had rescued her own shawl. Was this an indirect overture?

"Is she going to speak to me?" he asked himself.

Time was flying. How was he to get an invitation to the Arnoux's house? And he could think of nothing better than to draw her attention to the autumnal hues, adding:

"We are close to winter — the season of balls and dinner-parties."

But Arnoux was entirely occupied with his luggage. They had arrived at the point of the river's bank facing Surville. The two bridges drew nearer. They passed a ropewalk, then a range of low-built houses, inside which there were pots of tar and splinters of

5—2

wood; and brats went along the sand turning head over heels. Frederick recognised a man with a sleeved waistcoat, and called out to him:

"Make haste!"

They were at the landing-place. He looked around anxiously for Arnoux amongst the crowd of passengers, and the other came and shook hands with him, saying:

"A pleasant time, dear Monsieur!"

When he was on the quay, Frederick turned around. She was standing beside the helm. He cast a look towards her into which he tried to put his whole soul. She remained motionless, as if he had done nothing. Then, without paying the slightest attentions to the obeisances of his man-servant:

"Why didn't you bring the trap down here?"

The man made excuses.

"What a clumsy fellow you are! Give me some money."

And after that he went off to get something to eat at an inn.

A quarter of an hour later, he felt an inclination to turn into the coachyard, as if by chance. Perhaps he would see her again.

"What's the use of it?" said he to himself.

The vehicle carried him off. The two horses did not belong to his mother. She had borrowed one of M. Chambrion, the tax-collector, in order to have it yoked alongside of her own. Isidore, having set forth the day before, had taken a rest at Bray until evening, and had slept at Montereau, so that the animals, with restored vigour, were trotting briskly.

Fields on which the crops had been cut stretched out in apparently endless succession; and by degrees

Villeneuve, St. Georges, Ablon, Châtillon, Corbeil, and the other places — his entire journey — came back to his recollection with such vividness that he could now recall to mind fresh details, more intimate particulars. . . . Under the lowest flounce of her gown, her foot showed itself encased in a dainty silk boot of maroon shade. The awning made of ticking formed a wide canopy over her head, and the little red tassels of the edging kept perpetually trembling in the breeze.

She resembled the women of whom he had read in romances. He would have added nothing to the charms of her person, and would have taken nothing from them. The universe had suddenly become enlarged. She was the luminous point towards which all things converged; and, rocked by the movement of the vehicle, with half-closed eyelids, and his face turned towards the clouds, he abandoned himself to a dreamy, infinite joy.

At Bray, he did not wait till the horses had got their oats; he walked on along the road ahead by himself. Arnoux had, when he spoke to her, addressed her as "Marie." He now loudly repeated the name "Marie!" His voice pierced the air and was lost in the distance.

The western sky was one great mass of flaming purple. Huge stacks of wheat, rising up in the midst of the stubble fields, projected giant shadows. A dog began to bark in a farm-house in the distance. He shivered, seized with disquietude for which he could assign no cause.

When Isidore had come up with him, he jumped up into the front seat to drive. His fit of weakness was past. He had thoroughly made up his mind to effect an introduction into the house of the Arnoux, and to become intimate with them. Their house should be amusing; besides, he liked Arnoux; then, who could tell? Thereupon a wave of blood rushed up to his face; his temples throbbed; he cracked his whip, shook the reins, and set the horses going at such a pace that the old coachman repeatedly exclaimed:

"Easy! easy now, or they'll get broken-winded!"

Gradually Frederick calmed down, and he listened to what the man was saying. Monsieur's return was impatiently awaited. Mademoiselle Louise had cried in her anxiety to go in the trap to meet him.

"Who, pray, is Mademoiselle Louise?"

"Monsieur Roque's little girl, you know."

"Ah! I had forgotten," rejoined Frederick, carelessly.

Meanwhile, the two horses could keep up the pace no longer. They were both getting lame; and nine o'clock struck at St. Laurent's when he arrived at the parade in front of his mother's house.

This house of large dimensions, with a garden looking out on the open country, added to the social importance of Madame Moreau, who was the most respected lady in the district.

She came of an old family of nobles, of which the male line was now extinct. Her husband, a plebeian whom her parents forced her to marry, met his death by a sword-thrust, during her pregnancy, leaving her an estate much encumbered. She received visitors three times a week, and from time to time, gave a fashionable dinner. But the number of wax candles was calculated beforehand, and she looked forward with some impatience to the payment of her rents.

These pecuniary embarrassments, concealed as if there were some guilt attached to them, imparted a certain gravity to her character. Nevertheless, she displayed no prudery, no sourness, in the practice of her peculiar virtue. Her most trifling charities seemed munificent alms. She was consulted about the selection of servants, the education of young girls, and the art of making preserves, and Monseigneur used to stay at her house on the occasion of his episcopal visitations.

Madame Moreau cherished a lofty ambition for her son. Through a sort of prudence grounded on the expectation of favours, she did not care to hear blame cast on the Government. He would need patronage at the start; then, with its aid, he might become a councillor of State, an ambassador, a minister. His triumphs at the college of Sens warranted this proud anticipation; he had carried off there the prize of honour.

When he entered the drawing-room, all present arose with a great racket; he was embraced; and the chairs, large and small, were drawn up in a big semi-circle around the fireplace. M. Gamblin immediately asked him what was his opinion about Madame Lafarge. This case, the rage of the period, did not fail to lead to a violent discussion. Madame Moreau stopped it, to the regret, however, of M. Gamblin. He deemed it serviceable to the young man in his character of a future lawyer, and, nettled at what had occurred, he left the drawing-room.

Nothing should have caused surprise on the part of a friend of Père Roque! The reference to Père Roque led them to talk of M. Dambreuse, who had just become the owner of the demesne of La Fortelle. But the tax-collector had drawn Frederick aside to know what he thought of M. Guizot's latest work. They were all anxious to get some information about his private affairs, and Madame Benoît went cleverly to work with that end in view by inquiring about his uncle. How was that worthy relative? They no longer heard from him. Had he not a distant cousin in America?

The cook announced that Monsieur's soup was served. The guests discreetly retired. Then, as soon as they were alone in the dining-room, his mother said to him in a low tone:

"Well?"

The old man had received him in a very cordial manner, but without disclosing his intentions.

Madame Moreau sighed.

"Where is she now?" was his thought.

The diligence was rolling along the road, and, wrapped up in the shawl, no doubt, she was leaning against the cloth of the coupé, her beautiful head nodding asleep.

He and his mother were just going up to their apartments when a waiter from the Swan of the Cross brought him a note.

"What is that, pray?"

"It is Deslauriers, who wants me," said he.

"Ha! your chum!" said Madame Moreau, with a contemptuous sneer. "Certainly it is a nice hour to select!"

Frederick hesitated. But friendship was stronger. He got his hat.

"At any rate, don't be long!" said his mother to him.

CHAPTER II.

DAMON AND PYTHIAS.

HARLES DESLAURIERS' father, an ex-captain in the line, who had left the service in 1818, had come back to Nogent, where he had married, and with the amount of the dowry bought up the business of a process-server,* which brought him barely enough to maintain him. Embittered by a long course of unjust treatment, suffering still from the effects of old wounds, and always regretting the Emperor, he vented on those around him the fits of rage that seemed to choke him. Few children received so many whackings as his son. In spite of blows, however, the brat did not yield. His mother, when she tried to interpose, was also ill-treated. Finally, the captain planted the boy in his office, and all the day long kept him bent over his desk copying documents,

---

* The French word *huissier* means a sheriff's officer, or a person whose business it is to serve writs, processes, and legal documents generally. The word "process-server" must not be understood in its colloquial English sense, for in France this business is sometimes a lucrative one.— TRANSLATOR.

with the result that his right shoulder was noticeably higher than his left.

In 1833, on the invitation of the president, the captain sold his office. His wife died of cancer. He then went to live at Dijon. After that he started in business at Troyes, where he was connected with the slave trade; and, having obtained a small scholarship for Charles, placed him at the college of Sens, where Frederick came across him. But one of the pair was twelve years old, while the other was fifteen; besides, a thousand differences of character and origin tended to keep them apart.

Frederick had in his chest of drawers all sorts of useful things — choice articles, such as a dressing-case. He liked to lie late in bed in the morning, to look at the swallows, and to read plays; and, regretting the comforts of home, he thought college life rough. To the process-server's son it seemed a pleasant life. He worked so hard that, at the end of the second year, he had got into the third form. However, owing to his poverty or to his quarrelsome disposition, he was regarded with intense dislike. But when on one occasion, in the courtyard where pupils of the middle grade took exercise, an attendant openly called him a beggar's child, he sprang at the fellow's throat, and would have killed him if three of the ushers had not intervened. Frederick, carried away by admiration, pressed him in his arms. From that day forward they became fast friends. The affection of a *grandee* no doubt flattered the vanity of the youth of meaner rank, and the other accepted as a piece of good fortune this devotion freely offered to him. During the holidays Charles's father allowed him to remain in the college. A translation of Plato which he opened by chance excited his enthusiasm. Then he became smitten with a love of metaphysical studies; and he made rapid progress, for he approached the subject with all the energy of youth and the self-confidence of an emancipated intellect. Jouffroy, Cousin, Laromiguière, Malebranche, and the Scotch metaphysicians —everything that could be found in the library dealing with this branch of knowledge passed through his hands. He found it necessary to steal the key in order to get the books.

Frederick's intellectual distractions were of a less serious description. He made sketches of the genealogy of Christ carved on a post in the Rue des Trois Rois, then of the gateway of a cathedral. After a course of mediæval dramas, he took up memoirs — Froissart, Comines, Pierre de l'Estoile, and Brantôme.

The impressions made on his mind by this kind of reading took such a hold of it that he felt a need within him of reproducing those pictures of bygone days. His ambition was to be, one day, the Walter Scott of France. Deslauriers dreamed of formulating a vast system of philosophy, which might have the most far-reaching applications.

They chatted over all these matters at recreation hours, in the playground, in front of the moral inscription painted under the clock. They kept whispering to each other about them in the chapel, even with St. Louis staring down at them. They dreamed about them in the dormitory, which looked out on a burial-ground. On walking-days they took up a position behind the others, and talked without stopping.

They spoke of what they would do later, when they had left college. First of all, they would set out on a long voyage with the money which Frederick would take out of his own fortune on reaching his majority. Then they would come back to Paris; they would work together, and would never part; and, as a relaxation from their labours, they would have love-affairs with princesses in boudoirs lined with satin, or dazzling orgies with famous courtesans. Their rapturous expectations were followed by doubts. After a crisis of verbose gaiety, they would often lapse into profound silence.

On summer evenings, when they had been walking for a long time over stony paths which bordered on vineyards, or on the high-road in the open country, and when they saw the wheat waving in the sunlight, while the air was filled with the fragrance of angelica, a sort of suffocating sensation took possession of them, and they stretched themselves on their backs, dizzy, intoxicated. Meanwhile the other lads, in their shirt-sleeves, were playing at base or flying kites. Then, as the usher called in the two companions from the playground, they would return, taking the path which led along by the gardens watered by brooklets; then they would pass through the boulevards overshadowed by the old city walls. The deserted streets rang under their tread. The grating flew back; they ascended the stairs; and they felt as sad as if they had had a great debauch.

The proctor maintained that they mutually cried up each other. Nevertheless, if Frederick worked his way up to the higher forms, it was through the exhortations of his friend; and, during the vacation in 1837, he brought Deslauriers to his mother's house.

Madame Moreau disliked the young man. He had a terrible appetite. He was fond of making republican speeches. To crown all, she got it into her head that he had been the means of leading her son into improper places. Their relations towards each other were watched. This only made their friendship grow stronger, and they bade one another adieu with heartfelt pangs when, in the following year, Deslauriers left the college in order to study law in Paris.

Frederick anxiously looked forward to the time when they would meet again. For two years they had not laid eyes on each other; and, when their embraces were over, they walked over the bridges to talk more at their ease.

The captain, who had now set up a billiard-room at Villenauxe, reddened with anger when his son called for an account of the expense of tutelage, and even cut down the cost of victuals to the lowest figure. But, as he intended to become a candidate at a later period for a professor's chair at the school, and as he had no money, Deslauriers accepted the post of principal clerk in an attorney's office at Troyes. By dint of sheer privation he spared four thousand francs; and, by not drawing upon the sum which came to him through his mother, he would always have enough to enable him to work freely for three years while he was waiting for a better position. It was necessary, therefore, to abandon their former project of living together in the capital, at least for the present.

Frederick hung down his head. This was the first of his dreams which had crumbled into dust.

"Be consoled," said the captain's son. "Life is long. We are young. We'll meet again. Think no more about it!"

He shook the other's hand warmly, and, to distract his attention, questioned him about his journey.

Frederick had nothing to tell. But, at the recollection of Madame Arnoux, his vexation disappeared. He did not refer to her, restrained by a feeling of bashfulness. He made up for it by expatiating on Arnoux, recalling his talk, his agreeable manner, his stories; and Deslauriers urged him strongly to cultivate this new acquaintance.

Frederick had of late written nothing. His literary opinions were changed. Passion was now above everything else in his estimation. He was equally enthusiastic about Werther, René, Franck, Lara, Lélia, and other ideal creations of less merit. Sometimes it seemed to him that music alone was capable of giving expression to his internal agitation. Then, he dreamed of symphonies; or else the surface of things seized hold of him, and he longed to paint. He had, however, composed verses. Deslauriers considered them beautiful, but did not ask him to write another poem.

As for himself, he had given up metaphysics. Social economy and the French Revolution absorbed all his attention. Just now he was a tall fellow of twenty-two, thin, with a wide mouth, and a resolute look. On this particular evening, he wore a poor-looking paletot of lasting; and his shoes were white with dust, for he had come all the way from Ville-nauxe on foot for the express purpose of seeing Frederick.

Isidore arrived while they were talking. Madame begged of Monsieur to return home, and, for fear of his catching cold, she had sent him his cloak.

"Wait a bit!" said Deslauriers. And they continued walking from one end to the other of the two bridges which rest on the narrow islet formed by the canal and the river.

When they were walking on the side towards Nogent, they had, exactly in front of them, a block of houses which projected a little. At the right might be seen the church, behind the mills in the wood, whose sluices had been closed up; and, at the left, the hedges covered with shrubs, along the skirts of the wood, formed a boundary for the gardens, which could scarcely be distinguished. But on the side towards Paris the high road formed a sheer descending line, and the meadows lost themselves in the distance under the vapours of the night. Silence reigned along this road, whose white track clearly showed itself through the surrounding gloom. Odours of damp leaves ascended towards them. The waterfall, where the stream had been diverted from its course a hundred paces further away, kept rumbling with that deep harmonious sound which waves make in the night time.

Deslauriers stopped, and said:

"'Tis funny to have these worthy folks sleeping so quietly! Patience! A new '89 is in preparation. People are tired of constitutions, charters, subtleties, lies! Ah, if I had a newspaper, or a platform, how I would shake off all these things! But, in order to undertake anything whatever, money is required. What a curse it is to be a tavern-keeper's son, and to waste one's youth in quest of bread!"

He hung down his head, bit his lips, and shivered under his threadbare overcoat.

Frederick flung half his cloak over his friend's shoulder. They both wrapped themselves up in it; and, with their arms around each other's waists, they walked down the road side by side.

"How do you think I can live over there without you?" said Frederick.

The bitter tone of his friend had brought back his own sadness.

"I would have done something with a woman who loved me. What are you laughing at? Love is the feeding-ground, and, as it were, the atmosphere of genius. Extraordinary emotions produce sublime works. As for seeking after her whom I want, I give that up! Besides, if I should ever find her, she will repel me. I belong to the race of the disinherited, and I shall be extinguished with a treasure that will be of paste or of diamond—I know not which."

Somebody's shadow fell across the road, and at the same time they heard these words:

"Excuse me, gentlemen!"

The person who had uttered them was a little man attired in an ample brown frock-coat, and with a cap on his head which under its peak afforded a glimpse of a sharp nose.

"Monsieur Roque?" said Frederick.

"The very man!" returned the voice.

This resident in the locality explained his presence by stating that he had come back to inspect the wolf-traps in his garden near the water-side.

"And so you are back again in the old spot? Very good! I ascertained the fact through my little girl. Your health is good, I hope? You are not going away again?"

Then he left them, repelled, probably, by Frederick's chilling reception.

Madame Moreau, indeed, was not on visiting terms with him. Père Roque lived in peculiar relations with his servant-girl, and was held in very slight esteem, although he was the vice-president at elections, and M. Dambreuse's manager.

"The banker who resides in the Rue d'Anjou," observed Deslauriers. "Do you know what you ought to do, my fine fellow?"

Isidore once more interrupted. His orders were positive not to go back without Frederick. Madame would be getting uneasy at his absence.

"Well, well, he will go back," said Deslauriers. "He's not going to stay out all night."

And, as soon as the man-servant had disappeared:

"You ought to ask that old chap to introduce you to the Dambreuses. There's nothing so useful as to be a visitor at a rich man's house. Since you have a black coat and white gloves, make use of them. You must mix in that set. You can introduce me into it later. Just think!—a man worth millions! Do all you can to make him like you, and his wife, too. Become her lover!"

Frederick uttered an exclamation by way of protest.

"Why, I can quote classical examples for you on that point, I rather think! Remember Rastignac in the *Comédie Humaine*. You will succeed, I have no doubt."

Frederick had so much confidence in Deslauriers that he felt his firmness giving way, and forgetting Madame Arnoux, or including her in the prediction made with regard to the other, he could not keep from smiling.

The clerk added:

"A last piece of advice: pass your examinations. It is always a good thing to have a handle to your name: and, without more ado, give up your Catholic and Satanic poets, whose philosophy is as old as the twelfth century! Your despair is silly. The very greatest men have had more difficult beginnings, as in the case of Mirabeau. Besides, our separation will not be so long. I will make that pickpocket of a father of mine disgorge. It is time for me to be going back. Farewell! Have you got a hundred sous to pay for my dinner?"

Frederick gave him ten francs, what was left of those he had got that morning from Isidore.

Meanwhile, some forty yards away from the bridges, a light shone from the garret-window of a low-built house.

Deslauriers noticed it. Then he said emphatically, as he took off his hat:

"Your pardon, Venus, Queen of Heaven, but Penury is the mother of wisdom. We have been slandered enough for that—so have mercy."

This allusion to an adventure in which they had both taken part, put them into a jovial mood. They laughed loudly as they passed through the streets.

Then, having settled his bill at the inn, Deslauriers walked back with Frederick as far as the crossway near the Hôtel-Dieu, and after a long embrace, the two friends parted.

CHAPTER III.

TWO months later, Frederick, having debarked one morning in the Rue Coq-Heron, immediately thought of paying his great visit.

Chance came to his aid. Père Roque had brought him a roll of papers and requested him to deliver them up himself to M. Dambreuse; and the worthy man accompanied the package with an open letter of introduction in behalf of his young fellow-countryman.

Madame Moreau appeared surprised at this proceeding. Frederick concealed the delight that it gave him.

M. Dambreuse's real name was the Count d'Ambreuse; but since 1825, gradually abandoning his title of nobility and his party, he had turned his attention to business; and with his ears open in every office, his hand in every enterprise, on the watch for every opportunity, as subtle as a Greek and as laborious as a native of Auvergne, he had amassed a fortune which might be called considerable. Furthermore, he was an officer of the Legion of Honour, a member of the General Council of the Aube, a deputy, and one of these days would be a peer of France. However,

5—3

affable as he was in other respects, he wearied the Minister by his continual applications for relief, for crosses, and licences for tobacconists' shops; and in his complaints against authority he was inclined to join the Left Centre.

His wife, the pretty Madame Dambreuse, of whom mention was made in the fashion journals, presided at charitable assemblies. By wheedling the duchesses, she appeased the rancours of the aristocratic faubourg, and led the residents to believe that M. Dambreuse might yet repent and render them some services.

The young man was agitated when he called on them.

"I should have done better to take my dress-coat with me. No doubt they will give me an invitation to next week's ball. What will they say to me?"

His self-confidence returned when he reflected that M. Dambreuse was only a person of the middle class, and he sprang out of the cab briskly on the pavement of the Rue d'Anjou.

When he had pushed forward one of the two gateways he crossed the courtyard, mounted the steps in front of the house, and entered a vestibule paved with coloured marble. A straight double staircase, with red carpet, fastened with copper rods, rested against the high walls of shining stucco. At the end of the stairs there was a banana-tree, whose wide leaves fell down over the velvet of the baluster. Two bronze candelabra, with porcelain globes, hung from little chains; the atmosphere was heavy with the fumes exhaled by the vent-holes of the hot-air stoves; and all that could be heard was the ticking of a big clock fixed at the other end of the vestibule, under a suit of armour.

A bell rang; a valet made his appearance, and introduced Frederick into a little apartment, where one could observe two strong boxes, with pigeon-holes filled with pieces of pasteboard. In the centre of it, M. Dambreuse was writing at a roll-top desk.

He ran his eye over Père Roque's letter, tore open the canvas in which the papers had been wrapped, and examined them.

At some distance, he presented the appearance of being still young, owing to his slight figure. But his thin white hair, his feeble limbs, and, above all, the extraordinary pallor of his face, betrayed a shattered constitution. There was an expression of pitiless energy in his sea-green eyes, colder than eyes of glass. His cheek-bones projected, and his finger-joints were knotted.

At length, he arose and addressed to the young man a few questions with regard to persons of their acquaintance at Nogent and also with regard to his studies, and then dismissed him with a bow. Frederick went out through another lobby, and found himself at the lower end of the courtyard near the coach-house.

A blue brougham, to which a black horse was yoked, stood in front of the steps before the house. The carriage door flew open, a lady sprang in, and the vehicle, with a rumbling noise, went rolling along the gravel. Frederick had come up to the courtyard gate from the other side at the same moment. As there was not room enough to allow him to pass, he was compelled to wait. The young lady, with her head thrust forward past the carriage blind, talked to the door-keeper in a very low tone. All he could see was her back, covered with a violet mantle. However, he took a glance into the interior of the carriage, lined with blue rep, with silk lace and fringes. The lady's ample robes filled up the space within. He stole away from this little padded box with its perfume of iris, and, so to speak, its vague odour of feminine elegance. The coachman slackened the reins, the horse brushed abruptly past the starting-point, and all disappeared.

Frederick returned on foot, following the track of the boulevard.

He regretted not having been able to get a proper view of Madame Dambreuse. A little higher than the Rue Montmartre, a regular jumble of vehicles made him turn round his head, and on the opposite side, facing him, he read on a marble plate:

'JACQUES ARNOUX."

How was it that he had not thought about her sooner? It was Deslauriers' fault; and he approached the shop, which, however, he did not enter. He was waiting for *her* to appear.

The high, transparent plate-glass windows presented to one's gaze statuettes, drawings, engravings, catalogues and numbers of *L'Art Industriel,* arranged in a skilful fashion; and the amounts of the subscription were repeated on the door, which was decorated in the centre with the publisher's initials. Against the walls could be seen large pictures whose varnish had a shiny look, two chests laden with porcelain, bronze, alluring curiosities; a little staircase separated them, shut off at the top by a Wilton portière; and a lustre of old Saxe, a green carpet on the floor, with a table of marqueterie, gave to this interior the appearance rather of a drawing-room than of a shop.

Frederick pretended to be examining the drawings. After hesitating for a long time, he went in. A clerk lifted the portière, and in reply to a question, said that Monsieur would not be in the shop before five o'clock. But if the message could be conveyed——

"No! I'll come back again," Frederick answered blandly.

The following days were spent in searching for lodgings; and he fixed upon an apartment in a second story of a furnished mansion in the Rue Hyacinthe.

With a fresh blotting-case under his arm, he set forth to attend the opening lecture of the course. Three hundred young men, bare-headed, filled an amphitheatre, where an old man in a red gown was delivering a discourse in a monotonous voice. Quill pens went scratching over the paper. In this hall he found once more the dusty odour of the school, a reading-desk of similar shape, the same wearisome monotony! For a fortnight he regularly continued his attendance at law lectures. But he left off the study of the Civil Code before getting as far as Article 3, and he gave up the Institutes at the *Summa Divisio Personarum*.

The pleasures that he had promised himself did not come to him; and when he had exhausted a circulating library, gone over the collections in the Louvre, and been at the theatre a great many nights in succession, he sank into the lowest depths of idleness.

His depression was increased by a thousand fresh annoyances. He found it necessary to count his linen and to bear with the door keeper, a bore with the figure of a male hospital nurse who came in the morning to make up his bed, smelling of alcohol and grunting. He did not like his apartment, which was ornamented with an alabaster time-piece. The partitions were thin; he could hear the students making punch, laughing and singing.

Tired of this solitude, he sought out one of his old schoolfellows named Baptiste Martinon; and he discovered this friend of his boyhood in a middle-class boarding-house in the Rue Saint-Jacques, cramming up legal procedure before a coal fire. A woman in a print dress sat opposite him darning his socks.

Martinon was what people call a very fine man — big, chubby, with a regular physiognomy, and blue eyes far up in his face. His father, an extensive landowner, had destined him for the magistracy; and wishing already to present a grave exterior, he wore his beard cut like a collar round his neck.

As there was no rational foundation for Frederick's complaints, and as he could not give evidence of any misfortune, Martinon was unable in any way to understand his lamentations about existence. As for him, he went every morning to the school, after that took a walk in the Luxembourg, in the evening swallowed his half-cup of coffee; and with fifteen hundred francs a year, and the love of this work-woman, he felt perfectly happy.

"What happiness!" was Frederick's internal comment.

At the school he had formed another acquaintance, a youth of aristocratic family, who on account of his dainty manners, suggested a resemblance to a young lady.

M. de Cisy devoted himself to drawing, and loved the Gothic style. They frequently went together to admire the Sainte-Chapelle and Nôtre Dame. But the young patrician's rank and pretensions covered an intellect of the feeblest order. Everything took him by surprise. He laughed immoderately at the most trifling joke, and displayed such utter simplicity that Frederick at first took him for a wag, and finally regarded him as a booby.

The young man found it impossible, therefore, to be effusive with anyone; and he was constantly looking forward to an invitation from the Dambreuses.

On New Year's Day, he sent them visiting-cards, but received none in return.

He made his way back to the office of *L'Art Industriel*.

A third time he returned to it, and at last saw Arnoux carrying on an argument with five or six persons around him. He scarcely responded to the young man's bow; and Frederick was wounded by this reception. None the less he cogitated over the best means of finding his way to her side.

His first idea was to come frequently to the shop on the pretext of getting pictures at low prices. Then he conceived the notion of slipping into the letter-box of the journal a few "very strong" articles, which might lead to friendly relations. Perhaps it would be better to go straight to the mark at once, and declare his love? Acting on this impulse, he wrote a letter covering a dozen pages, full of lyric movements and apostrophes; but he tore it up, and did nothing, attempted nothing — bereft of motive power by his want of success.

Above Arnoux's shop, there were, on the first floor, three windows which were lighted up every evening. Shadows might be seen moving about behind them, especially one; this was hers; and he went very far out of his way in order to gaze at these windows and to contemplate this shadow.

A negress who crossed his path one day in the
Tuileries, holding a little girl by the hand, recalled to
his mind Madame Arnoux's negress. She was sure
to come there, like the others; every time he passed
through the Tuileries, his heart began to beat with
the anticipation of meeting her. On sunny days he
continued his walk as far as the end of the Champs-
Élysées.

Women seated with careless ease in open carriages, and with their veils floating in the wind, filed
past close to him, their horses advancing at a steady
walking pace, and with an unconscious see-saw
movement that made the varnished leather of the
harness crackle. The vehicles became more numerous, and, slackening their motion after they had
passed the circular space where the roads met, they
took up the entire track. The horses' manes and the
carriage lamps were close to each other. The steel
stirrups, the silver curbs and the brass rings, flung,
here and there, luminous points in the midst of the
short breeches, the white gloves, and the furs, falling
over the blazonry of the carriage doors. He felt as if
he were lost in some far-off world. His eyes wandered along the rows of female heads, and certain
vague resemblances brought back Madame Arnoux to
his recollection. He pictured her to himself, in the
midst of the others, in one of those little broughams
like Madame Dambreuse's brougham.

But the sun was setting, and the cold wind raised
whirling clouds of dust. The coachmen let their
chins sink into their neckcloths; the wheels began to
revolve more quickly; the road-metal grated; and all
the equipages descended the long sloping avenue at
a quick trot, touching, sweeping past one another, get-

ting out of one another's way; then, at the Place de la
Concorde, they went off in different directions. Behind the Tuileries, there was a patch of slate-coloured
sky. The trees of the garden formed two enormous
masses violet-hued at their summits. The gas-lamps
were lighted; and the Seine, green all over, was torn
into strips of silver moire, near the piers of the
bridges.

He went to get a dinner for forty-three sous in a
restaurant in the Rue de la Harpe. He glanced disdainfully at the old mahogany counter, the soiled
napkins, the dingy silver-plate, and the hats hanging
up on the wall.

Those around him were students like himself.
They talked about their professors, and about their
mistresses. Much he cared about professors! Had he
a mistress? To avoid being a witness of their enjoyment, he came as late as possible. The tables
were all strewn with remnants of food. The two
waiters, worn out with attendance on customers,
lay asleep, each in a corner of his own; and an odour
of cooking, of an argand lamp, and of tobacco, filled
the deserted dining-room. Then he slowly toiled up
the streets again. The gas lamps vibrated, casting on
the mud long yellowish shafts of flickering light.
Shadowy forms surmounted by umbrellas glided along
the footpaths. The pavement was slippery: the fog
grew thicker, and it seemed to him that the moist
gloom, wrapping him around, descended into the
depths of his heart.

He was smitten with a vague remorse. He renewed his attendance at lectures. But as he was
entirely ignorant of the matters which formed the
subject of explanation, things of the simplest descrip-

tion puzzled him. He set about writing a novel entitled *Sylvio, the Fisherman's Son*. The scene of the story was Venice. The hero was himself, and Madame Arnoux was the heroine. She was called Antonia; and, to get possession of her, he assassinated a number of noblemen, and burned a portion of the city; after which achievements he sang a serenade under her balcony, where fluttered in the breeze the red damask curtains of the Boulevard Montmartre.

The reminiscences, far too numerous, on which he dwelt produced a disheartening effect on him; he went no further with the work, and his mental vacuity redoubled.

After this, he begged of Deslauriers to come and share his apartment. They might make arrangements to live together with the aid of his allowance of two thousand francs; anything would be better than this intolerable existence. Deslauriers could not yet leave Troyes. He urged his friend to find some means of distracting his thoughts, and, with that end in view, suggested that he should call on Sénécal.

Sénécal was a mathematical tutor, a hard-headed man with republican convictions, a future Saint-Just, according to the clerk. Frederick ascended the five flights, up which he lived, three times in succession, without getting a visit from him in return. He did not go back to the place.

He now went in for amusing himself. He attended the balls at the Opera House. These exhibitions of riotous gaiety froze him the moment he had passed the door. Besides, he was restrained by the fear of being subjected to insult on the subject of money, his notion being that a supper with a domino, entailing considerable expense, was rather a big adventure.

It seemed to him, however, that he must needs love her. Sometimes he used to wake up with his heart full of hope, dressed himself carefully as if he were going to keep an appointment, and started on interminable excursions all over Paris. Whenever a woman was walking in front of him, or coming in his direction, he would say: "Here she is!" Every time it was only a fresh disappointment. The idea of Madame Arnoux strengthened these desires. Perhaps he might find her on his way; and he conjured up dangerous complications, extraordinary perils from which he would save her, in order to get near her.

So the days slipped by with the same tiresome experiences, and enslavement to contracted habits. He turned over the pages of pamphlets under the arcades of the Odéon, went to read the *Revue des Deux Mondes* at the café, entered the hall of the Collége de France, and for an hour stopped to listen to a lecture on Chinese or political economy. Every week he wrote long letters to Deslauriers, dined from time to time with Martinon, and occasionally saw M. de Cisy. He hired a piano and composed German waltzes.

One evening at the theatre of the Palais-Royal, he perceived, in one of the stage-boxes, Arnoux with a woman by his side. Was it she? The screen of green taffeta, pulled over the side of the box, hid her face. At length, the curtain rose, and the screen was drawn aside. She was a tall woman of about thirty, rather faded, and, when she laughed, her thick lips uncovered a row of shining teeth. She chatted familiarly with Arnoux, giving him, from time to time, taps, with her fan, on the fingers. Then a fair-haired young girl with eyelids a little red, as if she had just been weeping, seated herself between them. Arnoux after that remained stooped over her shoulder, pouring forth a stream of talk to which she listened without replying. Frederick taxed his ingenuity to find out the social position of these women, modestly attired in gowns of sober hue with flat, turned-up collars.

At the close of the play, he made a dash for the passages. The crowd of people going out filled them up. Arnoux, just in front of him, was descending the staircase step by step, with a woman on each arm.

Suddenly a gas-burner shed its light on him. He wore a crape hat-band. She was dead, perhaps? This idea tormented Frederick's mind so much, that he hurried, next day, to the office of *L'Art Industriel*, and paying, without a moment's delay, for one of the engravings exposed in the window for sale, he asked the shop-assistant how was Monsieur Arnoux.

The shop-assistant replied:

"Why, quite well!"

Frederick, growing pale, added:

"And Madame?"

"Madame, also."

Frederick forgot to carry off his engraving.

The winter drew to an end. He was less melancholy in the spring time, and began to prepare for his examination. Having passed it indifferently, he started immediately afterwards for Nogent.

He refrained from going to Troyes to see his friend, in order to escape his mother's comments. Then, on his return to Paris at the end of the vacation, he left his lodgings, and took two rooms on the Quai Napoléon which he furnished. He had given up all hope of getting an invitation from the Dambreuses. His great passion for Madame Arnoux was beginning to die out.

CHAPTER IV.

The Inexpressible She!

ONE morning, in the month of December, while going to attend a law lecture, he thought he could observe more than ordinary animation in the Rue Saint-Jacques. The students were rushing precipitately out of the cafés, where, through the open windows, they were calling one another from one house to the other. The shop keepers in the middle of the footpath were looking about them anxiously; the window-shutters were fastened; and when he reached the Rue Soufflot, he perceived a large assemblage around the Panthéon.

Young men in groups numbering from five to a dozen walked along, arm in arm, and accosted the larger groups, which had stationed themselves here and there. At the lower end of the square, near the railings, men in blouses were holding forth, while policemen, with their three-cornered hats drawn over their ears, and their hands behind their backs, were strolling up and down beside the walls making the flags ring under the tread of their heavy boots. All wore a mysterious, wondering look; they were evi-

(39)

dently expecting something to happen. Each held
back a question which was on the edge of his lips.

Frederick found himself close to a fair-haired young
man with a prepossessing face and a moustache and
a tuft of beard on his chin, like a dandy of Louis
XIII.'s time. He asked the stranger what was the
cause of the disorder.

"I haven't the least idea," replied the other, "nor
have they, for that matter! 'Tis their fashion just
now! What a good joke!"

And he burst out laughing. The petitions for Reform, which had been signed at the quarters of the
National Guard, together with the property-census of
Humann and other events besides, had, for the past
six months, led to inexplicable gatherings of riotous
crowds in Paris, and so frequently had they broken
out anew, that the newspapers had ceased to refer to
them.

"This lacks graceful outline and colour," continued
Frederick's neighbour. "I am convinced, messire, that
we have degenerated. In the good epoch of Louis
XI., and even in that of Benjamin Constant, there
was more mutinousness amongst the students. I find
them as pacific as sheep, as stupid as greenhorns, and
only fit to be grocers. Gadzooks! And these are
what we call the youth of the schools!"

He held his arms wide apart after the fashion of
Frederick Lemaître in *Robert Macaire*.

"Youth of the schools, I give you my blessing!"

After this, addressing a rag picker, who was moving a heap of oyster-shells up against the wall of a
wine-merchant's house:

"Do you belong to them—the youth of the
schools?"

The old man lifted up a hideous countenance in which one could trace, in the midst of a grey beard, a red nose and two dull eyes, bloodshot from drink.

"No, you appear to me rather one of those men with patibulary faces whom we see, in various groups, liberally scattering gold. Oh, scatter it, my patriarch, scatter it! Corrupt me with the treasures of Albion! Are you English? I do not reject the presents of Artaxerxes! Let us have a little chat about the union of customs!"

Frederick felt a hand laid on his shoulder. It was Martinon, looking exceedingly pale.

"Well!" said he with a big sigh, "another riot!"

He was afraid of being compromised, and uttered complaints. Men in blouses especially made him feel uneasy, suggesting a connection with secret societies.

"You mean to say there are secret societies," said the young man with the moustaches. "That is a worn-out dodge of the Government to frighten the middle-class folk!"

Martinon urged him to speak in a lower tone, for fear of the police.

"You believe still in the police, do you? As a matter of fact, how do you know, Monsieur, that I am not myself a police spy?"

And he looked at him in such a way, that Martinon, much discomposed, was, at first, unable to see the joke. The people pushed them on, and they were all three compelled to stand on the little staircase which led, by one of the passages, to the new amphitheatre.

The crowd soon broke up of its own accord. Many heads could be distinguished. They bowed towards the distinguished Professor Samuel Rondelot, who, wrapped in his big frock-coat, with his silver spectacles held up high in the air, and breathing hard from his asthma, was advancing at an easy pace, on his way to deliver his lecture. This man was one of the judicial glories of the nineteenth century, the rival of the Zachariæs and the Ruhdorffs. His new dignity of peer of France had in no way modified his external demeanour. He was known to be poor, and was treated with profound respect.

Meanwhile, at the lower end of the square, some persons cried out:

"Down with Guizot!"

"Down with Pritchard!"

"Down with the sold ones!"

"Down with Louis Philippe!"

The crowd swayed to and fro, and, pressing against the gate of the courtyard, which was shut, prevented the professor from going further. He stopped in front of the staircase. He was speedily observed on the lowest of three steps. He spoke; the loud murmurs of the throng drowned his voice. Although at another time they might love him, they hated him now, for he was the representative of authority. Every time he tried to make himself understood, the outcries recommenced. He gesticulated with great energy to induce the students to follow him. He was answered by vociferations from all sides. He shrugged his shoulders disdainfully, and plunged into the passage. Martinon profited by his situation to disappear at the same moment.

"What a coward!" said Frederick.

"He was prudent," returned the other.

There was an outburst of applause from the crowd, from whose point of view this retreat, on the part of the professor, appeared in the light of a victory. From every window, faces, lighted with curiosity, looked out. Some of those in the crowd struck up the "Marseillaise;" others proposed to go to Béranger's house.

"To Laffitte's house!"

"To Chateaubriand's house!"

"To Voltaire's house!" yelled the young man with the fair moustaches.

The policemen tried to pass around, saying in the mildest tones they could assume:

"Move on, messieurs! Move on! Take yourselves off!"

Somebody exclaimed:

"Down with the slaughterers!"

This was a form of insult usual since the troubles of the month of September. Everyone echoed it. The guardians of public order were hooted and hissed. They began to grow pale. One of them could endure it no longer, and, seeing a low-sized young man approaching too close, laughing in his teeth, pushed him back so roughly, that he tumbled over on his back some five paces away, in front of a wine-merchant's shop. All made way; but almost immediately afterwards the policeman rolled on the ground himself, felled by a blow from a species of Hercules, whose hair hung down like a bundle of tow under an oilskin cap. Having stopped for a few minutes at the corner of the Rue Saint-Jacques, he had very quickly laid down a large case, which he had been carrying, in order to make a spring at the policeman, and, holding down that functionary, punched his face unmercifully. The other policemen rushed to the rescue of their comrade. The terrible shop-assistant

5—4

was so powerfully built that it took four of them at
least to get the better of him. Two of them shook
him, while keeping a grip on his collar; two others
dragged his arms; a fifth gave him digs of the knee
in the ribs; and all of them called him "brigand,"
"assassin," "rioter." With his breast bare, and his
clothes in rags, he protested that he was innocent; he
could not, in cold blood, look at a child receiving a
beating.

"My name is Dussardier. I'm employed at Messieurs Valincart Brothers' lace and fancy warehouse,
in the Rue de Cléry. Where's my case? I want my
case!"

He kept repeating:

"Dussardier, Rue de Cléry. My case!"

However, he became quiet, and, with a stoical air,
allowed himself to be led towards the guard-house in
the Rue Descartes. A flood of people came rushing
after him. Frederick and the young man with the
moustaches walked immediately behind, full of admiration for the shopman, and indignant at the violence of power.

As they advanced, the crowd became less thick.

The policemen from time to time turned round,
with threatening looks; and the rowdies, no longer
having anything to do, and the spectators not having
anything to look at, all drifted away by degrees.
The passers-by, who met the procession, as they
came along, stared at Dussardier, and in loud tones,
gave vent to abusive remarks about him. One old
woman, at her own door, bawled out that he had
stolen a loaf of bread from her. This unjust accusation increased the wrath of the two friends. At
length, they reached the guard-house. Only about

twenty persons were now left in the attenuated crowd, and the sight of the soldiers was enough to disperse them.

Frederick and his companion boldly asked to have the man who had just been imprisoned delivered up. The sentinel threatened, if they persisted, to ram them into jail too. They said they required to see the commander of the guard-house, and stated their names, and the fact that they were law-students, declaring that the prisoner was one also.

They were ushered into a room perfectly bare, in which, amid an atmosphere of smoke, four benches might be seen lining the roughly-plastered walls. At the lower end there was an open wicket. Then appeared the sturdy face of Dussardier, who, with his hair all tousled, his honest little eyes, and his broad snout, suggested to one's mind in a confused sort of way the physiognomy of a good dog.

"Don't you recognise us?" said Hussonnet.

This was the name of the young man with the moustaches.

"Why——" stammered Dussardier.

"Don't play the fool any further," returned the other. "We know that you are, just like ourselves, a law-student."

In spite of their winks, Dussardier failed to understand. He appeared to be collecting his thoughts; then, suddenly:

"Has my case been found?"

Frederick raised his eyes, feeling much discouraged. Hussonnet, however, said promptly:

"Ha! your case, in which you keep your notes of lectures? Yes, yes, make your mind easy about it!"

They made further pantomimic signs with redoubled

energy, till Dussardier at last realised that they had
come to help him; and he held his tongue, fearing
that he might compromise them. Besides, he experienced a kind of shamefacedness at seeing himself
raised to the social rank of student, and to an equality
with those young men who had such white hands.

"Do you wish to send any message to anyone?"
asked Frederick.

"No, thanks, to nobody."

"But your family?"

He lowered his head without replying; the poor
fellow was a bastard. The two friends stood quite
astonished at his silence.

"Have you anything to smoke?" was Frederick's
next question.

He felt about, then drew forth from the depths of
one of his pockets the remains of a pipe—a beautiful
pipe, made of white talc with a shank of blackwood,
a silver cover, and an amber mouthpiece.

For the last three years he had been engaged in
completing this masterpiece. He had been careful to
keep the bowl of it constantly thrust into a kind
of sheath of chamois, to smoke it as slowly as possible, without ever letting it lie on any cold stone
substance, and to hang it up every evening over the
head of his bed. And now he shook out the fragments of it into his hand, the nails of which were
covered with blood, and with his chin sunk on his
chest, his pupils fixed and dilated, he contemplated
this wreck of the thing that had yielded him such delight with a glance of unutterable sadness.

"Suppose we give him some cigars, eh?" said
Hussonnet in a whisper, making a gesture as if he
were reaching them out.

Frederick had already laid down a cigar-holder, filled, on the edge of the wicket.

"Pray take this. Good-bye! Cheer up!"

Dussardier flung himself on the two hands that were held out towards him. He pressed them frantically, his voice choked with sobs.

"What? For me!—for me!"

The two friends tore themselves away from the effusive display of gratitude which he made, and went off to lunch together at the Café Tabourey, in front of the Luxembourg.

While cutting up the beefsteak, Hussonnet informed his companion that he did work for the fashion journals, and manufactured catchwords for *L'Art Industriel*.

"At Jacques Arnoux's establishment?" said Frederick.

"Do you know him?"

"Yes!—no!—that is to say, I have seen him—I have met him."

He carelessly asked Hussonnet if he sometimes saw Arnoux's wife.

"From time to time," the Bohemian replied.

Frederick did not venture to follow up his enquiries. This man henceforth would fill up a large space in his life. He paid the lunch-bill without any protest on the other's part.

There was a bond of mutual sympathy between them; they gave one another their respective addresses, and Hussonnet cordially invited Frederick to accompany him to the Rue de Fleurus.

They had reached the middle of the garden, when Arnoux's clerk, holding his breath, twisted his features into a hideous grimace, and began to crow like a cock. Thereupon all the cocks in the vicinity responded with prolonged "cock-a-doodle-doos."

"It is a signal," explained Hussonnet.

They stopped close to the Théâtre Bobino, in front of a house to which they had to find their way through an alley. In the skylight of a garret, between the nasturtiums and the sweet peas, a young woman showed herself, bare-headed, in her stays, her two arms resting on the edge of the roof-gutter.

"Good-morrow, my angel! good-morrow, ducky!" said Hussonnet, sending her kisses.

He made the barrier fly open with a kick, and disappeared.

Frederick waited for him all the week. He did not venture to call at Hussonnet's residence, lest it might look as if he were in a hurry to get a lunch in return for the one he had paid for. But he sought the clerk all over the Latin Quarter. He came across him one evening, and brought him to his apartment on the Quai Napoléon.

They had a long chat, and unbosomed themselves to each other. Hussonnet yearned after the glory and the gains of the theatre. He collaborated in the writing of vaudevilles which were not accepted, "had heaps of plans," could turn a couplet; he sang out for Frederick a few of the verses he had composed. Then, noticing on one of the shelves a volume of Hugo and another of Lamartine, he broke out into sarcastic criticisms of the romantic school. These poets had neither good sense nor correctness, and, above all, were not French! He plumed himself on his knowledge of the language, and analysed the most beautiful phrases with that snarling severity, that academic taste which persons of playful disposition exhibit when they are discussing serious art.

Frederick was wounded in his predilections, and he felt a desire to cut the discussion short. Why not take the risk at once of uttering the word on which his happiness depended? He asked this literary youth whether it would be possible to get an introduction into the Arnoux's house through his agency.

The thing was declared to be quite easy, and they fixed upon the following day.

Hussonnet failed to keep the appointment, and on three subsequent occasions he did not turn up. One Saturday, about four o'clock, he made his appearance. But, taking advantage of the cab into which they had got, he drew up in front of the Théâtre Français to get a box-ticket, got down at a tailor's shop, then at a dressmaker's, and wrote notes in the doorkeeper's lodge. At last they came to the Boulevard Montmartre. Frederick passed through the shop, and went up the staircase. Arnoux recognised him through the glass-partition in front of his desk, and while continuing to write he stretched out his hand and laid it on Frederick's shoulder.

Five or six persons, standing up, filled the narrow apartment, which was lighted by a single window looking out on the yard, a sofa of brown damask wool occupying the interior of an alcove between two door-curtains of similar material. Upon the chimney-piece, covered with old papers, there was a bronze Venus. Two candelabra, garnished with rose-coloured wax-tapers, supported it, one at each side. At the right, near a cardboard chest of drawers, a man, seated in an armchair, was reading the newspaper, with his hat on. The walls were hidden from view beneath the array of prints and pictures, precious engravings or sketches by contemporary masters, adorned with dedications testifying the most sincere affection for Jacques Arnoux.

"You're getting on well all this time?" said he, turning round to Frederick.

And, without waiting for an answer, he asked Hussonnet in a low tone:

"What is your friend's name?" Then, raising his voice:

"Take a cigar out of the box on the cardboard stand."

The office of *L'Art Industriel,* situated in a central position in Paris, was a convenient place of resort, a neutral ground wherein rivalries elbowed each other familiarly. On this day might be seen there Anténor Braive, who painted portraits of kings; Jules Burrieu, who by his sketches was beginning to popularise the wars in Algeria; the caricaturist Sombary, the sculptor Vourdat, and others. And not a single one of them corresponded with the student's preconceived ideas. Their manners were simple, their talk free and easy. The mystic Lovarias told an obscene story; and the inventor of Oriental landscape, the famous Dittmer, wore a knitted shirt under his waistcoat, and went home in the omnibus.

The first topic that came on the carpet was the case of a girl named Apollonie, formerly a model, whom Burrieu alleged that he had seen on the boulevard in a carriage. Hussonnet explained this metamorphosis through the succession of persons who had loved her.

"How well this sly dog knows the girls of Paris!" said Arnoux.

"After you, if there are any of them left, sire," replied the Bohemian, with a military salute, in imitation of the grenadier offering his flask to Napoleon.

Then they talked about some pictures in which Apollonie had sat for the female figures. They criticised their absent brethren, expressing astonishment at the sums paid for their works; and they were all complaining of not having been sufficiently remunerated themselves, when the conversation was interrupted by the entrance of a man of middle stature, who had his coat fastened by a single button, and whose eyes glittered with a rather wild expression.

"What a lot of shopkeepers you are!" said he. "God bless my soul! what does that signify? The old masters did not trouble their heads about the million — Correggio, Murillo ——"

"Add Pellerin," said Sombary.

But, without taking the slightest notice of the epigram, he went on talking with such vehemence, that Arnoux was forced to repeat twice to him:

"My wife wants you on Thursday. Don't forget!"

This remark recalled Madame Arnoux to Frederick's thoughts. No doubt, one might be able to reach her through the little room near the sofa. Arnoux had just opened the portière leading into it to get a pocket-handkerchief, and Frédéric had seen a washstand at the far end of the apartment.

But at this point a kind of muttering sound came from the corner of the chimney-piece; it was caused by the personage who sat in the armchair reading the newspaper. He was a man of five feet nine inches in height, with rather heavy eyelashes, a head of grey hair, and an imposing appearance; and his name was Regimbart.

"What's the matter now, citizen?" said Arnoux.

"Another fresh piece of rascality on the part of Government!"

The thing that he was referring to was the dismissal of a schoolmaster.

Pellerin again took up his parallel between Michael Angelo and Shakespeare. Dittmer was taking himself off when Arnoux pulled him back in order to put two bank notes into his hand. Thereupon Hussonnet said, considering this an opportune time:

"Couldn't you give me an advance, my dear master——?"

But Arnoux had resumed his seat, and was administering a severe reprimand to an old man of mean aspect, who wore a pair of blue spectacles.

"Ha! a nice fellow you are, Père Isaac! Here are three works cried down, destroyed! Everybody is laughing at me! People know what they are now! What do you want me to do with them? I'll have to send them off to California—or to the devil! Hold your tongue!"

The specialty of this old worthy consisted in attaching the signatures of the great masters at the bottom of these pictures. Arnoux refused to pay him, and dismissed him in a brutal fashion. Then, with an entire change of manner, he bowed to a gentleman of affectedly grave demeanour, who wore whiskers and displayed a white tie round his neck and the cross of the Legion of Honour over his breast.

With his elbow resting on the window-fastening, he kept talking to him for a long time in honeyed tones. At last he burst out:

"Ah! well, I am not bothered with brokers, Count."

The nobleman gave way, and Arnoux paid him down twenty-five louis. As soon as he had gone out:

"What a plague these big lords are!"

"A lot of wretches!" muttered Regimbart.

As it grew later, Arnoux was much more busily occupied. He classified articles, tore open letters, set out accounts in a row; at the sound of hammering in the warehouse he went out to look after the packing; then he went back to his ordinary work; and, while he kept his steel pen running over the paper, he indulged in sharp witticisms. He had an invitation to dine with his lawyer that evening, and was starting next day for Belgium.

The others chatted about the topics of the day — Cherubini's portrait, the hemicycle of the Fine Arts, and the next Exhibition. Pellerin railed at the Institute. Scandalous stories and serious discussions got mixed up together. The apartment with its low ceiling was so much stuffed up that one could scarcely move; and the light of the rose-coloured wax-tapers was obscured in the smoke of their cigars, like the sun's rays in a fog.

The door near the sofa flew open, and a tall, thin woman entered with abrupt movements, which made all the trinkets of her watch rattle under her black taffeta gown.

It was the woman of whom Frederick had caught a glimpse last summer at the Palais-Royal. Some of those present, addressing her by name, shook hands with her. Hussonnet had at last managed to extract from his employer the sum of fifty francs. The clock struck seven.

All rose to go.

Arnoux told Pellerin to remain, and accompanied Mademoiselle Vatnaz into the dressing-room.

Frederick could not hear what they said; they spoke in whispers. However, the woman's voice was raised:

"I have been waiting ever since the job was done, six months ago."

There was a long silence, and then Mademoiselle Vatnaz reappeared. Arnoux had again promised her something.

"Oh! oh! later, we shall see!"

"Good-bye! happy man," said she, as she was going out.

Arnoux quickly re-entered the dressing-room, rubbed some cosmetic over his moustaches, raised his braces, stretched his straps; and, while he was washing his hands:

"I would require two over the door at two hundred and fifty apiece, in Boucher's style. Is that understood?"

"Be it so," said the artist, his face reddening.

"Good! and don't forget my wife!"

Frederick accompanied Pellerin to the top of the Faubourg Poissonnière, and asked his permission to come to see him sometimes, a favour which was graciously accorded.

Pellerin read every work on æsthetics, in order to find out the true theory of the Beautiful, convinced that, when he had discovered it, he would produce masterpieces. He surrounded himself with every imaginable auxiliary—drawings, plaster-casts, models, engravings; and he kept searching about, eating his heart out. He blamed the weather, his nerves, his studio, went out into the street to find inspiration there, quivered with delight at the thought that he had caught it, then abandoned the work in which he was engaged, and dreamed of another which should be finer. Thus, tormented by the desire for glory, and wasting his days in discussions, believing in a thousand fooleries—in systems, in criticisms, in the importance of a regulation or a reform in the domain of Art—he had at fifty as yet turned out nothing save mere sketches. His robust pride prevented him from experiencing any discouragement, but he was always irritated, and in that state of exaltation, at the same time factitious and natural, which is characteristic of comedians.

On entering his studio one's attention was directed towards two large pictures, in which the first tones of colour laid on here and there made on the white canvas spots of brown, red, and blue. A network of lines in chalk stretched overhead, like stitches of thread repeated twenty times; it was impossible to understand what it meant. Pellerin explained the subject of these two compositions by pointing out with his thumb the portions that were lacking. The first was intended to represent "The Madness of Nebuchadnezzar," and the second "The Burning of Rome by Nero." Frederick admired them.

He admired academies of women with dishevelled hair, landscapes in which trunks of trees, twisted by the storm, abounded, and above all freaks of the pen, imitations from memory of Callot, Rembrandt, or Goya, of which he did not know the models. Pellerin no longer set any value on these works of his youth. He was now all in favour of the grand style; he dogmatised eloquently about Phidias and Winckelmann. The objects around him strengthened the force of his language; one saw a death's head on a prie-dieu, yataghans, a monk's habit. Frederick put it on.

When he arrived early, he surprised the artist in his wretched folding-bed, which was hidden from

view by a strip of tapestry; for Pellerin went to bed
late, being an assiduous frequenter of the theatres. An
old woman in tatters attended on him. He dined at
a cook-shop, and lived without a mistress. His ac-
quirements, picked up in the most irregular fashion,
rendered his paradoxes amusing. His hatred of the
vulgar and the "bourgeois" overflowed in sarcasms,
marked by a superb lyricism, and he had such religious
reverence for the masters that it raised him almost to
their level.

But why had he never spoken about Madame Arnoux? As for her son, at one time he called Pellerin
a decent fellow, at other times a charlatan. Frederick
was waiting for some disclosures on his part.

One day, while turning over one of the portfolios
in the studio, he thought he could trace in the portrait of a female Bohemian some resemblance to
Mademoiselle Vatnaz; and, as he felt interested in
this lady, he desired to know what was her exact
social position.

She had been, as far as Pellerin could ascertain,
originally a schoolmistress in the provinces. She now
gave lessons in Paris, and tried to write for the small
journals.

According to Frederick, one would imagine from
her manners with Arnoux that she was his mistress.

"Pshaw! he has others!"

Then, turning away his face, which reddened with
shame as he realised the baseness of the suggestion,
the young man added, with a swaggering air:

"Very likely his wife pays him back for it?"

"Not at all; she is virtuous."

Frederick again experienced a feeling of compunc-
tion, and the result was that his attendance at the

office of the art journal became more marked than before.

The big letters which formed the name of Arnoux on the marble plate above the shop seemed to him quite peculiar and pregnant with significance, like some sacred writing. The wide footpath, by its descent, facilitated his approach; the door almost turned of its own accord; and the handle, smooth to the touch, gave him the sensation of friendly and, as it were, intelligent fingers clasping his. Unconsciously, he became quite as punctual as Regimbart.

Every day Regimbart seated himself in the chimney corner, in his armchair, got hold of the *National*, and kept possession of it, expressing his thoughts by exclamations or by shrugs of the shoulders. From time to time he would wipe his forehead with his pocket-handkerchief, rolled up in a ball, which he usually stuck in between two buttons of his green frock-coat. He had trousers with wrinkles, bluchers, and a long cravat; and his hat, with its turned-up brim, made him easily recognised, at a distance, in a crowd.

At eight o'clock in the morning he descended the heights of Montmartre, in order to imbibe white wine in the Rue Nôtre Dame des Victoires. A late breakfast, following several games of billiards, brought him on to three o'clock. He then directed his steps towards the Passage des Panoramas, where he had a glass of absinthe. After the sitting in Arnoux's shop, he entered the Bordelais smoking-divan, where he swallowed some bitters; then, in place of returning home to his wife, he preferred to dine alone in a little café in the Rue Gaillon, where he desired them to serve up to him "household dishes, natural things." Finally, he made his way to another billiard-room, and remained there till midnight, in fact, till one o'clock in the morning, up till the last moment, when, the gas being put out and the window-shutters fastened, the master of the establishment, worn out, begged of him to go.

And it was not the love of drinking that attracted Citizen Regimbart to these places, but the inveterate habit of talking politics at such resorts. With advancing age, he had lost his vivacity, and now exhibited only a silent moroseness. One would have said, judging from the gravity of his countenence, that he was turning over in his mind the affairs of the whole world. Nothing, however, came from it; and nobody, even amongst his own friends, knew him to have any occupation, although he gave himself out as being up to his eyes in business.

Arnoux appeared to have a very great esteem for him. One day he said to Frederick:

"He knows a lot, I assure you. He is an able man."

On another occasion Regimbart spread over his desk papers relating to the kaolin mines in Brittany. Arnoux referred to his own experience on the subject.

Frederick showed himself more ceremonious towards Regimbart, going so far as to invite him from time to time to take a glass of absinthe; and, although he considered him a stupid man, he often remained a full hour in his company solely because he was Jacques Arnoux's friend.

After pushing forward some contemporary masters in the early portions of their career, the picture-dealer, a man of progressive ideas, had tried, while clinging to his artistic ways, to extend his pecuniary profits. His object was to emancipate the fine arts, to get the

sublime at a cheap rate. Over every industry associated with Parisian luxury he exercised an influence
which proved fortunate with respect to little things,
but fatal with respect to great things. With his mania
for pandering to public opinion, he made clever artists
swerve from their true path, corrupted the strong, exhausted the weak, and got distinction for those of
mediocre talent; he set them up with the assistance
of his connections and of his magazine. Tyros in
painting were ambitious of seeing their works in his
shop-window, and upholsterers brought specimens of
furniture to his house. Frederick regarded him, at the
same time, as a millionaire, as a *dilettante,* and as a
man of action. However, he found many things that
filled him with astonishment, for my lord Arnoux
was rather sly in his commercial transactions.

He received from the very heart of Germany or of
Italy a picture purchased in Paris for fifteen hundred
francs, and, exhibiting an invoice that brought the
price up to four thousand, sold it over again through
complaisance for three thousand five hundred. One
of his usual tricks with painters was to exact as a
drink-allowance an abatement in the purchase-money
of their pictures, under the pretence that he would
bring out an engraving of it. He always, when selling such pictures, made a profit by the abatement;
but the engraving never appeared. To those who
complained that he had taken an advantage of them,
he would reply by a slap on the stomach. Generous
in other ways, he squandered money on cigars for
his acquaintances, "thee'd" and "thou'd" persons
who were unknown, displayed enthusiasm about a
work or a man; and, after that, sticking to his
opinion, and, regardless of consequences, spared no

expense in journeys, correspondence, and advertising.
He looked upon himself as very upright, and, yielding
to an irresistible impulse to unbosom himself, ingen-
uously told his friends about certain indelicate acts of
which he had been guilty. Once, in order to annoy
a member of his own trade who inaugurated another
art journal with a big banquet, he asked Frederick to
write, under his own eyes, a little before the hour
fixed for the entertainment, letters to the guests recalling the invitations.

"This impugns nobody's honour, do you understand?"

And the young man did not dare to refuse the
service.

Next day, on entering with Hussonnet M. Arnoux's
office, Frederick saw through the door (the one opening on the staircase) the hem of a lady's dress dis-
appearing.

"A thousand pardons!" said Hussonnet. "If I
had known that there were women——"

"Oh! as for that one, she is my own," replied
Arnoux. "She just came in to pay me a visit as she
was passing."

"You don't say so!" said Frederick.

"Why, yes; she is going back home again."

The charm of the things around him was suddenly
withdrawn. That which had seemed to him to be
diffused vaguely through the place had now vanished
—or, rather, it had never been there. He experienced
an infinite amazement, and, as it were, the painful
sensation of having been betrayed.

Arnoux, while rummaging about in his drawer, began to smile. Was he laughing at him? The clerk
laid down a bundle of moist papers on the table.

"Ha! the placards," exclaimed the picture-dealer. "I am not ready to dine this evening."

Regimbart took up his hat.

"What, are you leaving me?"

"Seven o'clock," said Regimbart.

Frederick followed him.

At the corner of the Rue Montmartre, he turned round. He glanced towards the windows of the first floor, and he laughed internally with self-pity as he recalled to mind with what love he had so often contemplated them. Where, then, did she reside? How was he to meet her now? Once more around the object of his desire a solitude opened more immense than ever!

"Are you coming to take it?" asked Regimbart.

"To take what?"

"The absinthe."

And, yielding to his importunities, Frederick allowed himself to be led towards the Bordelais smoking-divan. Whilst his companion, leaning on his elbow, was staring at the decanter, he was turning his eyes to the right and to the left. But he caught a glimpse of Pellerin's profile on the footpath outside; the painter gave a quick tap at the window-pane, and he had scarcely sat down when Regimbart asked him why they no longer saw him at the office of *L'Art Industriel*.

"May I perish before ever I go back there again. The fellow is a brute, a mere tradesman, a wretch, a downright rogue!"

These insulting words harmonised with Frederick's present angry mood. Nevertheless, he was wounded, for it seemed to him that they hit at Madame Arnoux more or less.

"Why, what has he done to you?" said Regimbart.

Pellerin stamped with his foot on the ground, and his only response was an energetic puff.

He had been devoting himself to artistic work of a kind that he did not care to connect his name with, such as portraits for two crayons, or pasticcios from the great masters for amateurs of limited knowledge; and, as he felt humiliated by these inferior productions, he preferred to hold his tongue on the subject as a general rule. But "Arnoux's dirty conduct" exasperated him too much. He had to relieve his feelings.

In accordance with an order, which had been given in Frederick's very presence, he had brought Arnoux two pictures. Thereupon the dealer took the liberty of criticising them. He found fault with the composition, the colouring, and the drawing — above all the drawing; he would not, in short, take them at any price. But, driven to extremities by a bill falling due, Pellerin had to give them to the Jew Isaac; and, a fortnight later, Arnoux himself sold them to a Spaniard for two thousand francs.

"Not a sou less! What rascality! and, faith, he has done many other things just as bad. One of these mornings we'll see him in the dock!"

"How you exaggerate!" said Frederick, in a timid voice.

"Come, now, that's good; I exaggerate!" exclaimed the artist, giving the table a great blow with his fist.

This violence had the effect of completely restoring the young man's self-command. No doubt he might have acted more nicely; still, if Arnoux found these two pictures ——

"Bad! say it out! Are you a judge of them? Is this your profession? Now, you know, my youngster, I don't allow this sort of thing on the part of mere amateurs."

"Ah! well, it's not my business," said Frederick.

"Then, what interest have you in defending him?" returned Pellerin, coldly.

The young man faltered:

"But—since I am his friend——"

"Go, and give him a hug for me. Good evening!"

And the painter rushed away in a rage, and, of course, without paying for his drink.

Frederick, whilst defending Arnoux, had convinced himself. In the heat of his eloquence, he was filled with tenderness towards this man, so intelligent and kind, whom his friends calumniated, and who had now to work all alone, abandoned by them. He could not resist a strange impulse to go at once and see him again. Ten minutes afterwards he pushed open the door of the picture-warehouse.

Arnoux was preparing, with the assistance of his clerks, some huge placards for an exhibition of pictures.

"Halloa! what brings you back again?"

This question, simple though it was, embarrassed Frederick, and, at a loss for an answer, he asked whether they had happened to find a notebook of his —a little notebook with a blue leather cover.

"The one that you put your letters to women in?" said Arnoux.

Frederic, blushing like a young girl, protested against such an assumption.

"Your verses, then?" returned the picture-dealer.

He handled the pictorial specimens that were to be exhibited, discovering their form, colouring, and frames; and Frederick felt more and more irritated by his air of abstraction, and particularly by the appearance of his hands—large hands, rather soft, with flat nails. **At length, M. Arnoux arose, and saying,** "That's disposed of!" he chucked the young man familiarly under the chin. Frederick was offended at this liberty, and recoiled a pace or two; then he made a dash for the shop-door, and passed out through it, as he imagined, for the last time in his life. Madame Arnoux herself had been lowered by the vulgarity of her husband.

During the same week he got a letter from Deslauriers, informing him that the clerk would be in Paris on the following Thursday. Then he flung himself back violently on this affection as one of a more solid and lofty character. A man of this sort was worth all the women in the world. He would no longer have any need of Regimbart, of Pellerin, of Hussonnet, of anyone! In order to provide his friend with as comfortable lodgings as possible, he bought an iron bedstead and a second armchair, and stripped off some of his own bed-covering to garnish this one properly. On Thursday morning he was dressing himself to go to meet Deslauriers when there was a ring at the door.

Arnoux entered.

"Just one word. Yesterday I got a lovely trout from Geneva. We expect you by-and-by—at seven o'clock sharp. The address is the Rue de Choiseul 24 *bis*. Don't forget!"

Frederick was obliged to sit down; his knees were tottering under him. He repeated to himself,

"At last! at last!" Then he wrote to his tailor, to his hatter, and to his bootmaker; and he despatched these three notes by three different messengers.

The key turned in the lock, and the door-keeper appeared with a trunk on his shoulder.

Frederick, on seeing Deslauriers, began to tremble like an adulteress under the glance of her husband.

"What has happened to you?" said Deslauriers. "Surely you got my letter?"

Frederick had not enough energy left to lie. He opened his arms, and flung himself on his friend's breast.

Then the clerk told his story. His father thought to avoid giving an account of the expense of tutelage, fancying that the period limited for rendering such accounts was ten years; but, well up in legal procedure, Deslauriers had managed to get the share coming to him from his mother into his clutches — seven thousand francs clear — which he had there with him in an old pocket-book.

"'Tis a reserve fund, in case of misfortune. I must think over the best way of investing it, and find quarters for myself to-morrow morning. To-day I'm perfectly free, and am entirely at your service, my old friend."

"Oh! don't put yourself about," said Frederick. "If you had anything of importance to do this evening——"

"Come, now! I would be a selfish wretch——"

This epithet, flung out at random, touched Frederick to the quick, like a reproachful hint.

The door-keeper had placed on the table close to the fire some chops, cold meat, a large lobster, some sweets for dessert, and two bottles of Bordeaux.

Deslauriers was touched by these excellent preparations to welcome his arrival.

"Upon my word, you are treating me like a king!"

They talked about their past and about the future; and, from time to time, they grasped each other's hands across the table, gazing at each other tenderly for a moment.

But a messenger came with a new hat. Deslauriers, in a loud tone, remarked that this head-gear was very showy. Next came the tailor himself to fit on the coat, to which he had given a touch with the smoothing-iron.

"One would imagine you were going to be married," said Deslauriers.

An hour later, a third individual appeared on the scene, and drew forth from a big black bag a pair of shining patent leather boots. While Frederick was trying them on, the bootmaker slyly drew attention to the shoes of the young man from the country.

"Does Monsieur require anything?"

"Thanks," replied the clerk, pulling behind his chair his old shoes fastened with strings.

This humiliating incident annoyed Frederick. At length he exclaimed, as if an idea had suddenly taken possession of him:

"Ha! deuce take it! I was forgetting."

"What is it, pray?"

"I have to dine in the city this evening."

"At the Dambreuses'? Why did you never say anything to me about them in your letters?"

"It is not at the Dambreuses', but at the Arnoux's."

"You should have let me know beforehand," said Deslauriers. "I would have come a day later."

"Impossible," returned Frederick, abruptly. "I only got the invitation this morning, a little while ago."

And to redeem his error and distract his friend's mind from the occurrence, he proceeded to unfasten the tangled cords round the trunk, and to arrange all his belongings in the chest of drawers, expressed his willingness to give him his own bed, and offered to sleep himself in the dressing-room bedstead. Then, as soon as it was four o'clock, he began the preparations for his toilet.

"You have plenty of time," said the other.

At last he was dressed and off he went.

"That's the way with the rich," thought Deslauriers.

And he went to dine in the Rue Saint-Jacques, at a little restaurant kept by a man he knew.

Frederick stopped several times while going up the stairs, so violently did his heart beat. One of his gloves, which was too tight, burst, and, while he was fastening back the torn part under his shirt-cuff, Arnoux, who was mounting the stairs behind him, took his arm and led him in.

The anteroom, decorated in the Chinese fashion, had a painted lantern hanging from the ceiling, and bamboos in the corners. As he was passing into the drawing-room, Frederick stumbled against a tiger's skin. The place had not yet been lighted up, but two lamps were burning in the boudoir in the far corner.

Mademoiselle Marthe came to announce that her mamma was dressing. Arnoux raised her as high as his mouth in order to kiss her; then, as he wished to go to the cellar himself to select certain bottles of wine, he left Frederick with the little girl.

She had grown much larger since the trip in the steamboat. Her dark hair descended in long ringlets, which curled over her bare arms. Her dress, more puffed out than the petticoat of a *danseuse*, allowed her rosy calves to be seen, and her pretty childlike form had all the fresh odour of a bunch of flowers. She received the young gentleman's compliments with a coquettish air, fixed on him her large, dreamy eyes, then slipping on the carpet amid the furniture, disappeared like a cat.

After this he no longer felt ill at ease. The globes of the lamps, covered with a paper lace-work, sent forth a white light, softening the colour of the walls, hung with mauve satin. Through the fender-bars, as through the slits in a big fan, the coal could be seen in the fireplace, and close beside the clock there was a little chest with silver clasps. Here and there things lay about which gave the place a look of home—a doll in the middle of the sofa, a fichu against the back of a chair, and on the work-table a knitted woollen vest, from which two ivory needles were hanging with their points downwards. It was altogether a peaceful spot, suggesting the idea of propriety and innocent family life.

Arnoux returned, and Madame Arnoux appeared at the other doorway. As she was enveloped in shadow, the young man could at first distinguish only her head. She wore a black velvet gown, and in her hair she had fastened a long Algerian cap, in a red silk net, which coiling round her comb, fell over her left shoulder.

Arnoux introduced Frederick.

"Oh! I remember Monsieur perfectly well," she responded.

Then the guests arrived, nearly all at the same time—Dittmer, Lovarias, Burrieu, the composer Rosenwald, the poet Théophile Lorris, two art critics, colleagues of Hussonnet, a paper manufacturer, and in the rear the illustrious Pierre Paul Meinsius, the last representative of the grand school of painting, who blithely carried along with his glory his forty-five years and his big paunch.

When they were passing into the dining-room, Madame Arnoux took his arm. A chair had been left vacant for Pellerin. Arnoux, though he took advantage of him, was fond of him. Besides, he was afraid of his terrible tongue, so much so, that, in order to soften him, he had given a portrait of him in *L'Art Industriel,* accompanied by exaggerated eulogies; and Pellerin, more sensitive about distinction than about money, made his appearance about eight o'clock quite out of breath. Frederick fancied that they had been a long time reconciled.

He liked the company, the dishes, everything. The dining-room, which resembled a mediæval parlour, was hung with stamped leather. A Dutch whatnot faced a rack for chibouks, and around the table the Bohemian glasses, variously coloured, had, in the midst of the flowers and fruits, the effect of an illumination in a garden.

He had to make his choice between ten sorts of mustard. He partook of daspachio, of curry, of ginger, of Corsican blackbirds, and a species of Roman macaroni called lasagna; he drank extraordinary wines, lip-fraeli and tokay. Arnoux indeed prided himself on entertaining people in good style. With an eye to the procurement of eatables, he paid court to mail-coach drivers, and was in league with the cooks of great houses, who communicated to him the secrets of rare sauces.

But Frederick was particularly amused by the conversation. His taste for travelling was tickled by Dittmer, who talked about the East; he gratified his curiosity about theatrical matters by listening to Rosenwald's chat about the opera; and the atrocious existence of Bohemia assumed for him a droll aspect when seen through the gaiety of Hussonnet, who related, in a picturesque fashion, how he had spent an entire winter with no food except Dutch cheese. Then, a discussion between Lovarias and Burrieu about the Florentine School gave him new ideas with regard to masterpieces, widened his horizon, and he found difficulty in restraining his enthusiasm when Pellerin exclaimed:

"Don't bother me with your hideous reality! What does it mean—reality? Some see things black, others blue—the multitude sees them brute-fashion. There is nothing less natural than Michael Angelo; there is nothing more powerful! The anxiety about external truth is a mark of contemporary baseness; and art will become, if things go on that way, a sort of poor joke as much below religion as it is below poetry, and as much below politics as it is below business. You will never reach its end—yes, its end! —which is to cause within us an impersonal exaltation, with petty works, in spite of all your finished execution. Look, for instance, at Bassolier's pictures: they are pretty, coquettish, spruce, and by no means dull. You might put them into your pocket, bring them with you when you are travelling. Notaries buy them for twenty thousand francs, while pictures of the ideal type are sold for three sous. But, without ideality, there is no grandeur; without grandeur there is no beauty. Olympus is a mountain. The most swagger monument will always be the Pyramids. Exuberance is better than taste; the desert is better than a street-pavement, and a savage is better than a hairdresser!"

Frederick, as these words fell upon his ear, glanced towards Madame Arnoux. They sank into his soul like metals falling into a furnace, added to his passion, and supplied the material of love.

His chair was three seats below hers on the same side. From time to time, she bent forward a little, turning aside her head to address a few words to her little daughter; and as she smiled on these occasions, a dimple took shape in her cheek, giving to her face an expression of more dainty good-nature.

As soon as the time came for the gentlemen to take their wine, she disappeared. The conversation became more free and easy. M. Arnoux shone in it, and Frederick was astonished at the cynicism of men. However, their preoccupation with woman established between them and him, as it were, an equality, which raised him in his own estimation.

When they had returned to the drawing-room, he took up, to keep himself in countenance, one of the albums which lay about on the table. The great artists of the day had illustrated them with drawings, had written in them snatches of verse or prose, or their signatures simply. In the midst of famous names he found many that he had never heard of before, and original thoughts appeared only underneath a flood of nonsense. All these effusions contained a more or less direct expression of homage towards Madame Arnoux. Frederick would have been afraid to write a line beside them.

She went into her boudoir to look at the little chest with silver clasps which he had noticed on the mantel-shelf. It was a present from her husband, a work of the Renaissance. Arnoux's friends complimented him, and his wife thanked him. His tender emotions were aroused, and before all the guests he gave her a kiss.

After this they all chatted in groups here and there. The worthy Meinsius was with Madame Arnoux on an easy chair close beside the fire. She was leaning forward towards his ear; their heads were just touching, and Frederick would have been glad to become deaf, infirm, and ugly if, instead, he had an illustrious name and white hair—in short, if he only happened to possess something which would install him in such intimate association with her. He began once more to eat out his heart, furious at the idea of being so young a man.

But she came into the corner of the drawing-room in which he was sitting, asked him whether he was acquainted with any of the guests, whether he was fond of painting, how long he had been a student in Paris. Every word that came out of her mouth seemed to Frederick something entirely new, an exclusive appendage of her personality. He gazed attentively at the fringes of her head-dress, the ends of which caressed her bare shoulder, and he was unable to take away his eyes; he plunged his soul into the whiteness of that feminine flesh, and yet he did not venture to raise his eyelids to glance at her higher, face to face.

Rosenwald interrupted them, begging of Madame Arnoux to sing something. He played a prelude, she waited, her lips opened slightly, and a sound, pure, long-continued, silvery, ascended into the air.

Frederick did not understand a single one of the Italian words. The song began with a grave measure, something like church music, then in a more animated strain, with a crescendo movement, it broke into repeated bursts of sound, then suddenly subsided, and the melody came back again in a tender fashion with a wide and easy swing.

She stood beside the keyboard with her arms hanging down and a far-off look on her face. Sometimes, in order to read the music, she advanced her forehead for a moment and her eyelashes moved to and fro. Her contralto voice in the low notes took a mournful intonation which had a chilling effect on the listener, and then her beautiful head, with those great brows of hers, bent over her shoulder; her bosom swelled; her eyes were wide apart; her neck, from which roulades made their escape, fell back as if under aërial kisses. She flung out three sharp notes, came down again, cast forth one higher still, and, after a silence, finished with an organ-point.

Rosenwald did not leave the piano. He continued playing, to amuse himself. From time to time a guest stole away. At eleven o'clock, as the last of them were going off, Arnoux went out along with Pellerin, under the pretext of seeing him home. He was one of those people who say that they are ill when they do not "take a turn" after dinner. Madame Arnoux had made her way towards the anteroom. Dittmer and Hussonnet bowed to her. She stretched out her hand to them. She did the same to Frederick; and he felt, as it were, something penetrating every particle of his skin.

He quitted his friends. He wished to be alone. His heart was overflowing. Why had she offered him her hand? Was it a thoughtless act, or an encouragement? "Come now! I am mad!" Besides, what did it matter, when he could now visit her entirely at his ease, live in the very atmosphere she breathed?

The streets were deserted. Now and then a heavy wagon would roll past, shaking the pavements. The houses came one after another with their grey fronts, their closed windows; and he thought with disdain of all those human beings who lived behind those walls without having seen her, and not one of whom dreamed of her existence. He had no consciousness of his surroundings, of space, of anything, and striking the ground with his heel, rapping with his walking-stick on the shutters of the shops, he kept walking on continually at random, in a state of excitement, carried away by his emotions. Suddenly he felt himself surrounded by a circle of damp air, and found that he was on the edge of the quays.

The gas-lamps shone in two straight lines, which ran on endlessly, and long red flames flickered in the depths of the water. The waves were slate-coloured, while the sky, which was of clearer hue, seemed to be supported by vast masses of shadow that rose on each side of the river. The darkness was intensified by buildings whose outlines the eye could not distinguish. A luminous haze floated above the roofs further on. All the noises of the night had melted into a single monotonous hum.

He stopped in the middle of the Pont Neuf, and, taking off his hat and exposing his chest, he drank in the air. And now he felt as if something that was inexhaustible were rising up from the very depths of his being, an afflux of tenderness that enervated him, like the motion of the waves under his eyes. A church-clock slowly struck one, like a voice calling out to him.

Then, he was seized with one of those shuddering sensations of the soul in which one seems to be transported into a higher world. He felt, as it were, endowed with some extraordinary faculty, the aim of which he could not determine. He seriously asked himself whether he would be a great painter or a great poet; and he decided in favour of painting, for the exigencies of this profession would bring him into contact with Madame Arnoux. So, then, he had found his vocation! The object of his existence was now perfectly clear, and there could be no mistake about the future.

When he had shut his door, he heard some one snoring in the dark closet near his apartment. It was his friend. He no longer bestowed a thought on him.

His own face presented itself to his view in the glass. He thought himself handsome, and for a minute he remained gazing at himself.

5—6

CHAPTER V.

"Love Knoweth No Laws."

BEFORE twelve o'clock next day he had bought a box of colours, paint-brushes, and an easel. Pellerin consented to give him lessons, and Frederick brought him to his lodgings to see whether anything was wanting among his painting utensils.

Deslauriers had come back, and the second arm-chair was occupied by a young man. The clerk said, pointing towards him:

"'Tis he! There he is! Sénécal!" Frederick disliked this young man. His forehead was heightened by the way in which he wore his hair, cut straight like a brush. There was a certain hard, cold look in his grey eyes; and his long black coat, his entire costume, savoured of the pedagogue and the ecclesiastic.

They first discussed topics of the hour, amongst others the *Stabat* of Rossini. Sénécal, in answer to a question, declared that he never went to the theatre.

Pellerin opened the box of colours.

"Are these all for you?" said the clerk.

"Why, certainly!"

"Well, really! What a notion!" And he leaned across the table, at which the mathematical tutor was turning over the leaves of a volume of Louis Blanc. He had brought it with him, and was reading passages from it in low tones, while Pellerin and Frederick were examining together the palette, the knife, and the bladders; then the talk came round to the dinner at Arnoux's.

"The picture-dealer, is it?" asked Sénécal. "A nice gentleman, truly!"

"Why, now?" said Pellerin. Sénécal replied:

"A man who makes money by political turpitude!"

And he went on to talk about a well-known lithograph, in which the Royal Family was all represented as being engaged in edifying occupations: Louis Philippe had a copy of the Code in his hand; the Queen had a Catholic prayer-book; the Princesses were embroidering; the Duc de Nemours was girding on a sword; M. de Joinville was showing a map to his young brothers; and at the end of the apartment could be seen a bed with two divisions. This picture, which was entitled "A Good Family," was a source of delight to commonplace middle-class people, but of grief to patriots.

Pellerin, in a tone of vexation, as if he had been the producer of this work himself, observed by way of answer that every opinion had some value. Sénécal protested: Art should aim exclusively at promoting morality amongst the masses! The only subjects that ought to be reproduced were those which impelled people to virtuous actions; all others were injurious.

"But that depends on the execution," cried Pellerin. "I might produce masterpieces."

"So much the worse for you, then; you have no right——"

"What?"

"No, monsieur, you have no right to excite my interest in matters of which I disapprove. What need have we of laborious trifles, from which it is impossible to derive any benefit—those Venuses, for instance, with all your landscapes? I see there no instruction for the people! Show us rather their miseries! arouse enthusiasm in us for their sacrifices! Ah, my God! there is no lack of subjects—the farm, the workshop——"

Pellerin stammered forth his indignation at this, and, imagining that he had found an argument:

"Molière, do you accept him?"

"Certainly!" said Sénécal. "I admire him as the precursor of the French Revolution."

"Ha! the Revolution! What art! Never was there a more pitiable epoch!"

"None greater, Monsieur!"

Pellerin folded his arms, and looking at him straight in the face:

"You have the appearance of a famous member of the National Guard!"

His opponent, accustomed to discussions, responded:

"I am not, and I detest it just as much as you. But with such principles we corrupt the crowd. This sort of thing, however, is profitable to the Government. It would not be so powerful but for the complicity of a lot of rogues of that sort."

The painter took up the defence of the picture-dealer, for Sénécal's opinions exasperated him. He even went so far as to maintain that Arnoux was really a man with a heart of gold, devoted to his friends, deeply attached to his wife.

"Oho! if you offered him a good sum, he would not refuse to let her serve as a model."

Frederick turned pale.

"So then, he has done you some great injury, Monsieur?"

"Me? no! I saw him once at a café with a friend. That's all."

Sénécal had spoken truly. But he had his teeth daily set on edge by the announcements in *L'Art Industriel*. Arnoux was for him the representative of a world which he considered fatal to democracy. An austere Republican, he suspected that there was something corrupt in every form of elegance, and the more so as he wanted nothing and was inflexible in his integrity.

They found some difficulty in resuming the conversation. The painter soon recalled to mind his appointment, the tutor his pupils; and, when they had gone, after a long silence, Deslauriers asked a number of questions about Arnoux.

"You will introduce me there later, will you not, old fellow?"

"Certainly," said Frederick. Then they thought about settling themselves. Deslauriers had without much trouble obtained the post of second clerk in a solicitor's office; he had also entered his name for the terms at the Law School, and bought the indispensable books; and the life of which they had dreamed now began.

It was delightful, owing to their youth, which made everything assume a beautiful aspect. As Deslauriers had said nothing as to any pecuniary arrangement, Frederick did not refer to the subject. He helped to defray all the expenses, kept the cupboard

well stocked, and looked after all the household require-
ments; but if it happened to be desirable to give
the doorkeeper a rating, the clerk took that on his
own shoulders, still playing the part, which he had
assumed in their college days, of protector and senior.

Separated all day long, they met again in the
evening. Each took his place at the fireside and set
about his work. But ere long it would be interrupted. Then would follow endless outpourings, unaccountable bursts of merriment, and occasional disputes
about the lamp flaring too much or a book being
mislaid, momentary ebullitions of anger which subsided in hearty laughter.

While in bed they left open the door of the little
room where Deslauriers slept, and kept chattering to
each other from a distance.

In the morning they walked in their shirt-sleeves
on the terrace. The sun rose; light vapours passed
over the river. From the flower-market close beside
them the noise of screaming reached their ears; and
the smoke from their pipes whirled round in the clear
air, which was refreshing to their eyes still puffed
from sleep. While they inhaled it, their hearts swelled
with great expectations.

When it was not raining on Sunday they went
out together, and, arm in arm, they sauntered through
the streets. The same reflection nearly always occurred to them at the same time, or else they would go
on chatting without noticing anything around them.
Deslauriers longed for riches, as a means for gaining
power over men. He was anxious to possess an influence over a vast number of people, to make a great
noise, to have three secretaries under his command,
and to give a big political dinner once a month.

Frederick would have furnished for himself a palace in the Moorish fashion, to spend his life reclining on cashmere divans, to the murmur of a jet of water, attended by negro pages. And these things, of which he had only dreamed, became in the end so definite that they made him feel as dejected as if he had lost them.

"What is the use of talking about all these things," said he, "when we'll never have them?"

"Who knows?" returned Deslauriers.

In spite of his democratic views, he urged Frederick to get an introduction into the Dambreuses' house.

The other, by way of objection, pointed to the failure of his previous attempts.

"Bah! go back there. They'll give you an invitation!"

Towards the close of the month of March, they received amongst other bills of a rather awkward description that of the restaurant-keeper who supplied them with dinners. Frederick, not having the entire amount, borrowed a hundred crowns from Deslauriers. A fortnight afterwards, he renewed the same request, and the clerk administered a lecture to him on the extravagant habits to which he gave himself up in the Arnoux's society.

As a matter of fact, he put no restraint upon himself in this respect. A view of Venice, a view of Naples, and another of Constantinople occupying the centre of three walls respectively, equestrian subjects by Alfred de Dreux here and there, a group by Pradier over the mantelpiece, numbers of *L'Art Industriel* lying on the piano, and works in boards on the floor in the corners, encumbered the apartment which he occupied to such an extent that it was hard to find a place to lay a book on, or to move one's elbows about freely. Frederick maintained that he needed all this for his painting.

He pursued his art-studies under Pellerin. But when he called on the artist, the latter was often out, being accustomed to attend at every funeral and public occurrence of which an account was given in the newspapers, and so it was that Frederick spent entire hours alone in the studio. The quietude of this spacious room, which nothing disturbed save the scampering of the mice, the light falling from the ceiling, or the hissing noise of the stove, made him sink into a kind of intellectual ease. Then his eyes, wandering away from the task at which he was engaged, roamed over the shell-work on the wall, around the objects of virtù on the whatnot, along the torsos on which the dust that had collected made, as it were, shreds of velvet; and, like a traveller who has lost his way in the middle of a wood, and whom every path brings back to the same spot, continually, he found underlying every idea in his mind the recollection of Madame Arnoux.

He selected days for calling on her. When he had reached the second floor, he would pause on the threshold, hesitating as to whether he ought to ring or not. Steps drew nigh, the door opened, and the announcement "Madame is gone out," a sense of relief would come upon him, as if a weight had been lifted from his heart. He met her, however. On the first occasion there were three other ladies with her; the next time it was in the afternoon, and Mademoiselle Marthe's writing-master came on the scene. Besides, the men whom Madame Arnoux received were not very punctilious about paying visits. For the sake of prudence he deemed it better not to call again.

But he did not fail to present himself regularly at the office of *L'Art Industriel* every Wednesday in order to get an invitation to the Thursday dinners, and he remained there after all the others, even longer than Regimbart, up to the last moment, pretending to be looking at an engraving or to be running his eye through a newspaper. At last Arnoux would say to him, "Shall you be disengaged to-morrow evening?" and, before the sentence was finished, he would give an affirmative answer. Arnoux appeared to have taken a fancy to him. He showed him how to become a good judge of wines, how to make hot punch, and how to prepare a woodcock ragoût. Frederick followed his advice with docility, feeling an attachment to everything connected with Madame Arnoux —her furniture, her servants, her house, her street.

During these dinners he scarcely uttered a word; he kept gazing at her. She had a little mole close to her temple. Her head-bands were darker than the rest of her hair, and were always a little moist at the edges; from time to time she stroked them with only two fingers. He knew the shape of each of her nails. He took delight in listening to the rustle of her silk skirt as she swept past doors; he stealthily inhaled the perfume that came from her handkerchief; her comb, her gloves, her rings were for him things of special interest, important as works of art, almost endowed with life like individuals; all took possession of his heart and strengthened his passion.

He had not been sufficiently self-contained to conceal it from Deslauriers. When he came home from Madame Arnoux's, he would wake up his friend, as if inadvertently. in order to have an opportunity of talking about her.

Deslauriers, who slept in the little off-room, close to where they had their water-supply, would give a great yawn. Frederick seated himself on the side of the bed. At first, he spoke about the dinner; then he referred to a thousand petty details, in which he saw marks of contempt or of affection. On one occasion, for instance, she had refused his arm, in order to take Dittmer's; and Frederick gave vent to his humiliation:

"Ah! how stupid!"

Or else she had called him her "dear friend."

"Then go after her gaily!"

"But I dare not do that," said Frederick.

"Well, then, think no more about her! Good night!"

Deslauriers thereupon turned on his side, and fell asleep. He felt utterly unable to comprehend this love, which seemed to him the last weakness of adolescence; and, as his own society was apparently not enough to content Frederick, he conceived the idea of bringing together, once a week, those whom they both recognised as friends.

They came on Saturday about nine o'clock. The three Algerine curtains were carefully drawn. The lamp and four wax-lights were burning. In the middle of the table the tobacco-pot, filled with pipes, displayed itself between the beer-bottles, the tea-pot, a flagon of rum, and some fancy biscuits.

They discussed the immortality of the soul, and drew comparisons between the different professors.

One evening Hussonnet introduced a tall young man, attired in a frock-coat, too short in the wrists, and with a look of embarrassment in his face. It was the young fellow whom they had gone to release from the guard-house the year before.

As he had not been able to restore the box of lace which he had lost in the scuffle, his employer had accused him of theft, and threatened to prosecute him. He was now a clerk in a wagon-office. Hussonnet had come across him that morning at the corner of the street, and brought him along, for Dussardier, in a spirit of gratitude, had expressed a wish to see "the other."

He stretched out towards Frederick the cigar-holder, still full, which he had religiously preserved, in the hope of being able to give it back. The young men invited him to pay them a second visit; and he was not slow in doing so.

They all had sympathies in common. At first, their hatred of the Government reached the height of an unquestionable dogma. Martinon alone attempted to defend Louis Philippe. They overwhelmed him with the commonplaces scattered through the newspapers — the "Bastillization" of Paris, the September laws, Pritchard, Lord Guizot — so that Martinon held his tongue for fear of giving offence to somebody. During his seven years at college he had never incurred the penalty of an imposition, and at the Law School he knew how to make himself agreeable to the professors. He usually wore a big frock-coat of the colour of putty, with india-rubber goloshes; but one evening he presented himself arrayed like a bridegroom, in a velvet roll-collar waistcoat, a white tie, and a gold chain.

The astonishment of the other young men was greatly increased when they learned that he had just come away from M. Dambreuse's house. In fact, the banker Dambreuse had just bought a portion of an extensive wood from Martinon senior; and, when the worthy man introduced his son, the other had invited them both to dinner.

"Was there a good supply of truffles there?" asked Deslauriers. "And did you take his wife by the waist between the two doors, *sicut decet?*"

Hereupon the conversation turned on women. Pellerin would not admit that there were beautiful women (he preferred tigers); besides the human female was an inferior creature in the æsthetic hierarchy:

"What fascinates you is just the very thing that degrades her as an idea; I mean her breasts, her hair——"

"Nevertheless," urged Frederick, "long black hair and large dark eyes——"

"Oh! we know all about that," cried Hussonnet. "Enough of Andalusian beauties on the lawn. Those things are out of date; no thank you! For the fact is, honour bright! a fast woman is more amusing than the Venus of Milo. Let us be Gallic, in Heaven's name, and after the Regency style, if we can!

'Flow, generous wines; ladies, deign to smile!'*

We must pass from the dark to the fair. Is that your opinion, Father Dussardier?"

Dussardier did not reply. They all pressed him to ascertain what his tastes were.

"Well," said he, colouring, "for my part, I would like to love the same one always!"

This was said in such a way that there was a moment of silence, some of them being surprised at this

---

* *Coulez, bons vins; femmes, deignez sourire.*

candour, and others finding in his words, perhaps, the secret yearning of their souls.

Sénécal placed his glass of beer on the mantelpiece, and declared dogmatically that, as prostitution was tyrannical and marriage immoral, it was better to practice abstinence. Deslauriers regarded women as a source of amusement—nothing more. M. de Cisy looked upon them with the utmost dread.

Brought up under the eyes of a grandmother who was a devotee, he found the society of those young fellows as alluring as a place of ill-repute and as instructive as the Sorbonne. They gave him lessons without stint; and so much zeal did he exhibit that he even wanted to smoke in spite of the qualms that upset him every time he made the experiment. Frederick paid him the greatest attention. He admired the shade of this young gentleman's cravat, the fur on his overcoat, and especially his boots, as thin as gloves, and so very neat and fine that they had a look of insolent superiority. His carriage used to wait for him below in the street.

One evening, after his departure, when there was a fall of snow, Sénécal began to complain about his having a coachman. He declaimed against kid-gloved exquisites and against the Jockey Club. He had more respect for a workman than for these fine gentlemen.

"For my part, anyhow, I work for my livelihood! I am a poor man!"

"That's quite evident," said Frederick, at length, losing patience.

The tutor conceived a grudge against him for this remark.

But, as Regimbart said he knew Sénécal pretty well, Frederick, wishing to be civil to a friend of the

Arnoux, asked him to come to the Saturday meetings;
and the two patriots were glad to be brought together in this way.

However, they took opposite views of things.

Sénécal—who had a skull of the angular type—
fixed his attention merely on systems, whereas Regimbart, on the contrary, saw in facts nothing but
facts. The thing that chiefly troubled him was the
Rhine frontier. He claimed to be an authority on the
subject of artillery, and got his clothes made by a
tailor of the Polytechnic School.

The first day, when they asked him to take some
cakes, he disdainfully shrugged his shoulders, saying
that these might suit women; and on the next few
occasions his manner was not much more gracious.
Whenever speculative ideas had reached a certain
elevation, he would mutter: "Oh! no Utopias, no
dreams!" On the subject of Art (though he used to
visit the studios, where he occasionally out of complaisance gave a lesson in fencing) his opinions were
not remarkable for their excellence. He compared the
style of M. Marast to that of Voltaire, and Mademoiselle Vatnaz to Madame de Staël, on account of an
Ode on Poland in which "there was some spirit." In
short, Regimbart bored everyone, and especially Deslauriers, for the Citizen was a friend of the Arnoux family.
Now the clerk was most anxious to visit those people
in the hope that he might there make the acquaintance
of some persons who would be an advantage to him.

"When are you going to take me there with
you?" he would say. Arnoux was either over-
burdened with business, or else starting on a journey.
Then it was not worth while, as the dinners were
coming to an end.

If he had been called on to risk his life for his friend, Frederick would have done so. But, as he was desirous of making as good a figure as possible, and with this view was most careful about his language and manners, and so attentive to his costume that he always presented himself at the office of *L'Art Industriel* irreproachably gloved, he was afraid that Deslauriers, with his shabby black coat, his attorney-like exterior, and his swaggering kind of talk, might make himself disagreeable to Madame Arnoux, and thus compromise him and lower him in her estimation. The other results would have been bad enough, but the last one would have annoyed him a thousand times more.

The clerk saw that his friend did not wish to keep his promise, and Frederick's silence seemed to him an aggravation of the insult. He would have liked to exercise absolute control over him, to see him developing in accordance with the ideal of their youth; and his inactivity excited the clerk's indignation as a breach of duty and a want of loyalty towards himself. Moreover, Frederick, with his thoughts full of Madame Arnoux, frequently talked about her husband; and Deslauriers now began an intolerable course of boredom by repeating the name a hundred times a day, at the end of each remark, like the parrot-cry of an idiot.

When there was a knock at the door, he would answer, "Come in, Arnoux!" At the restaurant he asked for a Brie cheese "in imitation of Arnoux," and at night, pretending to wake up from a bad dream, he would rouse his comrade by howling out, "Arnoux! Arnoux!" At last Frederick, worn out, said to him one day, in a piteous voice:

"Oh! don't bother me about Arnoux!"

"Never!" replied the clerk:

> "He always, everywhere, burning or icy cold,
> The pictured form of Arnoux ——"*

"Hold your tongue, I tell you!" exclaimed Frederick, raising his fist.

Then less angrily he added:

"You know well this is a painful subject to me."

"Oh! forgive me, old fellow," returned Deslauriers with a very low bow. "From this time forth we will be considerate towards Mademoiselle's nerves. Again, I say, forgive me. A thousand pardons!"

And so this little joke came to an end.

But, three weeks later, one evening, Deslauriers said to him:

"Well, I have just seen Madame Arnoux."

"Where, pray?"

"At the Palais, with Balandard, the solicitor. A dark woman, is she not, of the middle height?"

Frederick made a gesture of assent. He waited for Deslauriers to speak. At the least expression of admiration he would have been most effusive, and would have fairly hugged the other. However, Deslauriers remained silent. At last, unable to contain himself any longer, Frederick, with assumed indifference, asked him what he thought of her.

Deslauriers considered that "she was not so bad, but still nothing extraordinary."

"Ha! you think so," said Frederick.

They soon reached the month of August, the time when he was to present himself for his second ex-

---

* *Toujours lui! lui partout! ou brulante ou glacée,*
L'image de l'Arnoux.

amination.   According to the prevailing opinion, the
subjects could be made up in a fortnight.   Frederick,
having full confidence in his own powers, swallowed
up in a trice the first four books of the Code of Procedure, the first three of the Penal Code, many bits
of the system of criminal investigation, and a part of
the Civil Code, with the annotations of M. Poncelet.
The night before, Deslauriers made him run through
the whole course, a process which did not finish till
morning, and, in order to take advantage of even the
last quarter of an hour, continued questioning him
while they walked along the footpath together.

As several examinations were taking place at the
same time, there were many persons in the precincts,
and amongst others Hussonnet and Cisy: young men
never failed to come and watch these ordeals when
the fortunes of their comrades were at stake.

Frederick put on the traditional black gown; then,
followed by the throng, with three other students, he
entered a spacious apartment, into which the light
penetrated through uncurtained windows, and which
was garnished with benches ranged along the walls.
In the centre, leather chairs were drawn round a table
adorned with a green cover.   This separated the candidates from the examiners in their red gowns and
ermine shoulder-knots, the head examiners wearing
gold-laced flat caps.

Frederick found himself the last but one in the
series—an unfortunate place.   In answer to the first
question, as to the difference between a convention
and a contract, he defined the one as if it were the
other; and the professor, who was a fair sort of man,
said to him, "Don't be agitated, Monsieur! Compose
yourself!"   Then, having asked two easy questions,

5—7

which were answered in a doubtful fashion, he passed on at last to the fourth. This wretched beginning made Frederick lose his head. Deslauriers, who was facing him amongst the spectators, made a sign to him to indicate that it was not a hopeless case yet; and at the second batch of questions, dealing with the criminal law, he came out tolerably well. But, after the third, with reference to the "mystic will," the examiner having remained impassive the whole time, his mental distress redoubled; for Hussonnet brought his hands together as if to applaud, whilst Deslauriers liberally indulged in shrugs of the shoulders. Finally, the moment was reached when it was necessary to be examined on Procedure. The professor, displeased at listening to theories opposed to his own, asked him in a churlish tone:

"And so this is your view, monsieur? How do you reconcile the principle of article 1351 of the Civil Code with this application by a third party to set aside a judgment by default?"

Frederick had a great headache from not having slept the night before. A ray of sunlight, penetrating through one of the slits in a Venetian blind, fell on his face. Standing behind the seat, he kept wriggling about and tugging at his moustache.

"I am still awaiting your answer," the man with the gold-edged cap observed.

And as Frederick's movements, no doubt, irritated him:

"You won't find it in that moustache of yours!"

This sarcasm made the spectators laugh. The professor, feeling flattered, adopted a wheedling tone. He put two more questions with reference to adjournment and summary jurisdiction, then nodded his head by way of approval. The examination was over. Frederick retired into the vestibule.

While an usher was taking off his gown, to draw it over some other person immediately afterwards, his friends gathered around him, and succeeded in fairly bothering him with their conflicting opinions as to the result of his examination. Presently the announcement was made in a sonorous voice at the entrance of the hall: "The third was — put off!"

"Sent packing!" said Hussonnet. "Let us go away!"

In front of the doorkeeper's lodge they met Martinon, flushed, excited, with a smile on his face and the halo of victory around his brow. He had just passed his final examination without any impediment. All he had now to do was the thesis. Before a fortnight he would be a licentiate. His family enjoyed the acquaintance of a Minister; "a beautiful career" was opening before him.

"All the same, this puts you into a mess," said Deslauriers.

There is nothing so humiliating as to see blockheads succeed in undertakings in which we fail. Frederick, filled with vexation, replied that he did not care a straw about the matter. He had higher pretensions; and as Hussonnet made a show of leaving, Frederick took him aside, and said to him:

"Not a word about this to them, mind!"

It was easy to keep it secret, since Arnoux was starting the next morning for Germany.

When he came back in the evening the clerk found his friend singularly altered: he danced about and whistled; and the other was astonished at this capricious change of mood. Frederick declared that he did not intend to go home to his mother, as he meant to spend his holidays working.

At the news of Arnoux's departure, a feeling of delight had taken possession of him. He might present himself at the house whenever he liked without any fear of having his visits broken in upon. The consciousness of absolute security would make him self-confident. At last he would not stand aloof, he would not be separated from her! Something more powerful than an iron chain attached him to Paris; a voice from the depths of his heart called out to him to remain.

There were certain obstacles in his path. These he got over by writing to his mother: he first of all admitted that he had failed to pass, owing to alterations made in the course — a mere mischance — an unfair thing; besides, all the great advocates (he referred to them by name) had been rejected at their examinations. But he calculated on presenting himself again in the month of November. Now, having no time to lose, he would not go home this year; and he asked, in addition to the quarterly allowance, for two hundred and fifty francs, to get coached in law by a private tutor, which would be of great assistance to him; and he threw around the entire epistle a garland of regrets, condolences, expressions of endearment, and protestations of filial love.

Madame Moreau, who had been expecting him the following day, was doubly grieved. She threw a veil over her son's misadventure, and in answer told him to "come all the same." Frederick would not give way, and the result was a falling out between them. However, at the end of the week, he received the amount of the quarter's allowance together with the sum required for the payment of the private tutor,

which helped to pay for a pair of pearl-grey trousers, a white felt hat, and a gold-headed switch.
When he had procured all these things he thought:

"Perhaps this is only a hairdresser's fancy on my
part!"

And a feeling of considerable hesitation took possession of him.

In order to make sure as to whether he ought to
call on Madame Arnoux, he tossed three coins into
the air in succession. On each occasion luck was in
his favour. So then Fate must have ordained it.
He hailed a cab and drove to the Rue de Choiseul.

He quickly ascended the staircase and drew the
bell-pull, but without effect. He felt as if he were
about to faint.

Then, with fierce energy, he shook the heavy silk
tassel. There was a resounding peal which gradually
died away till no further sound was heard. Frederick
got rather frightened.

He pasted his ear to the door — not a breath! He
looked in through the key-hole, and only saw two
reed-points on the wall-paper in the midst of designs
of flowers. At last, he was on the point of going
away when he changed his mind. This time, he gave
a timid little ring. The door flew open, and Arnoux
himself appeared on the threshold, with his hair all
in disorder, his face crimson, and his features distorted
by an expression of sullen embarrassment.

"Hallo! What the deuce brings you here? Come
in!"

He led Frederick, not into the boudoir or into the
bed-room, but into the dining-room, where on the
table could be seen a bottle of champagne and two
glasses; and, in an abrupt tone:

"There is something you want to ask me, my
dear friend?"

"No! nothing! nothing!" stammered the young
man, trying to think of some excuse for his visit. At
length, he said to Arnoux that he had called to know
whether they had heard from him, as Hussonnet had
announced that he had gone to Germany.

"Not at all!" returned Arnoux. "What a feather-
headed fellow that is to take everything in the wrong
way!"

In order to conceal his agitation, Frederick kept
walking from right to left in the dining-room. Happening to come into contact with a chair, he knocked
down a parasol which had been laid across it, and the
ivory handle got broken.

"Good heavens!" he exclaimed. "How sorry I
am for having broken Madame Arnoux's parasol!"

At this remark, the picture-dealer raised his head
and smiled in a very peculiar fashion. Frederick, taking advantage of the opportunity thus offered to talk
about her, added shyly:

"Could I not see her?"

No. She had gone to the country to see her
mother, who was ill.

He did not venture to ask any questions as to the
length of time that she would be away. He merely
enquired what was Madame Arnoux's native place.

"Chartres. Does this astonish you?"

"Astonish me? Oh, no! Why should it! Not
in the least!"

After that, they could find absolutely nothing to
talk about. Arnoux, having made a cigarette for himself, kept walking round the table, puffing. Frederick,
standing near the stove, stared at the walls, the

whatnot, and the floor; and delightful pictures flitted through his memory, or, rather, before his eyes. Then he left the apartment.

A piece of a newspaper, rolled up into a ball, lay on the floor in the anteroom. Arnoux snatched it up, and, raising himself on the tips of his toes, he stuck it into the bell, in order, as he said, that he might be able to go and finish his interrupted siesta. Then, as he grasped Frederick's hand:

"Kindly tell the porter that I am not in."

And he shut the door after him with a bang.

Frederick descended the staircase step by step. The ill-success of this first attempt discouraged him as to the possible results of those that might follow. Then began three months of absolute boredom. As he had nothing to do, his melancholy was aggravated by the want of occupation.

He spent whole hours gazing from the top of his balcony at the river as it flowed between the quays, with their bulwarks of grey stone, blackened here and there by the seams of the sewers, with a pontoon of washerwomen moored close to the bank, where some brats were amusing themselves by making a water-spaniel swim in the slime. His eyes, turning aside from the stone bridge of Nôtre Dame and the three suspension bridges, continually directed their glance towards the Quai-aux-Ormes, resting on a group of old trees, resembling the linden-trees of the Montereau wharf. The Saint-Jacques tower, the Hôtel de Ville, Saint-Gervais, Saint-Louis, and Saint-Paul, rose up in front of him amid a confused mass of roofs; and the genius of the July Column glittered at the eastern side like a large gold star, whilst at the other end the dome of the Tuileries showed its outlines against the sky in one great round mass of blue. Madame Arnoux's house must be on this side in the rear!

He went back to his bedchamber; then, throwing himself on the sofa, he abandoned himself to a confused succession of thoughts — plans of work, schemes for the guidance of his conduct, attempts to divine the future. At last, in order to shake off broodings all about himself, he went out into the open air.

He plunged at random into the Latin Quarter, usually so noisy, but deserted at this particular time, for the students had gone back to join their families. The huge walls of the colleges, which the silence seemed to lengthen, wore a still more melancholy aspect. All sorts of peaceful sounds could be heard — the flapping of wings in cages, the noise made by the turning of a lathe, or the strokes of a cobbler's hammer; and the old-clothes men, standing in the middle of the street, looked up at each house fruitlessly. In the interior of a solitary café the barmaid was yawning between her two full decanters. The newspapers were left undisturbed on the tables of reading-rooms. In the ironing establishments linen quivered under the puffs of tepid wind. From time to time he stopped to look at the window of a second-hand book-shop; an omnibus which grazed the footpath as it came rumbling along made him turn round; and, when he found himself before the Luxembourg, he went no further.

Occasionally he was attracted towards the boulevards by the hope of finding there something that might amuse him. After he had passed through dark alleys, from which his nostrils were greeted by fresh moist odours, he reached vast, desolate, open spaces, dazzling with light, in which monuments cast at the side of the pavement notches of black shadow. But once more the wagons and the shops appeared, and the crowd had the effect of stunning him, especially on Sunday, when, from the Bastille to the Madeleine, it kept swaying in one immense flood over the asphalt, in the midst of a cloud of dust, in an incessant clamour. He felt disgusted at the meanness of the faces, the silliness of the talk, and the idiotic self-satisfaction that oozed through these sweating foreheads. However, the consciousness of being superior to these individuals mitigated the weariness which he experienced in gazing at them.

Every day he went to the office of *L'Art Industriel;* and in order to ascertain when Madame Arnoux would be back, he made elaborate enquiries about her mother. Arnoux's answer never varied — "the change for the better was continuing" — his wife, with his little daughter, would be returning the following week. The longer she delayed in coming back, the more uneasiness Frederick exhibited, so that Arnoux, touched by so much affection, brought him five or six times a week to dine at a restaurant.

In the long talks which they had together on these occasions Frederick discovered that the picture-dealer was not a very intellectual type of man. Arnoux might, however, take notice of his chilling manner; and now Frederick deemed it advisable to pay back, in a small measure, his polite attentions.

So, being anxious to do things on a good scale, the young man sold all his new clothes to a second-hand clothes-dealer for the sum of eighty francs, and having increased it with a hundred more francs which he had left, he called at Arnoux's house to bring him out to dine. Regimbart happened to be there, and all three of them set forth for Les Trois Frères Provençaux.

The Citizen began by taking off his surtout, and, knowing that the two others would defer to his gastronomic tastes, drew up the *menu*. But in vain did he make his way to the kitchen to speak himself to the *chef*, go down to the cellar, with every corner of which he was familiar, and send for the master of the establishment, to whom he gave "a blowing up." He was not satisfied with the dishes, the wines, or the attendance. At each new dish, at each fresh bottle, as soon as he had swallowed the first mouthful, the first draught, he threw down his fork or pushed his glass some distance away from him; then, leaning on his elbows on the table-cloth, and stretching out his arms, he declared in a loud tone that he could no longer dine in Paris! Finally, not knowing what to put into his mouth, Regimbart ordered kidney-beans dressed with oil, "quite plain," which, though only a partial success, slightly appeased him. Then he had a talk with the waiter all about the latter's predecessors at the "Provençaux": — "What had become of Antoine? And a fellow named Eugène? And Théodore, the little fellow who always used to attend down stairs? There was much finer fare in those days, and Burgundy vintages the like of which they would never see again."

Then there was a discussion as to the value of ground in the suburbs, Arnoux having speculated in that way, and looked on it as a safe thing. In the meantime, however, he would lie out of the interest on his money. As he did not want to sell out at any price, Regimbart would find out some one to whom he could let the ground; and so these two gentlemen proceeded at the close of the dessert to make calculations with a lead pencil.

They went out to get coffee in the smoking-divan on the ground-floor in the Passage du Saumon. Frederick had to remain on his legs while interminable games of billiards were being played, drenched in innumerable glasses of beer; and he lingered on there till midnight without knowing why, through want of energy, through sheer senselessness, in the vague expectation that something might happen which would give a favourable turn to his love.

When, then, would he next see her? Frederick was in a state of despair about it. But, one evening, towards the close of November, Arnoux said to him:

"My wife, you know, came back yesterday!"

Next day, at five o'clock, he made his way to her house. He began by congratulating her on her mother's recovery from such a serious illness.

"Why, no! Who told you that?"

"Arnoux!"

She gave vent to a slight "Ah!" then added that she had grave fears at first, which, however, had now been dispelled. She was seated close beside the fire in an upholstered easy-chair. He was on the sofa, with his hat between his knees; and the conversation was difficult to carry on, as it was broken off nearly every minute, so he got no chance of giving utterance to his sentiments. But, when he began to complain of having to study legal quibbles, she answered, "Oh! I understand—business!" and she let her face fall, buried suddenly in her own reflections.

He was eager to know what they were, and even did not bestow a thought on anything else. The twilight shadows gathered around them.

She rose, having to go out about some shopping; then she reappeared in a bonnet trimmed with velvet, and a black mantle edged with minever. He plucked up courage and offered to accompany her.

It was now so dark that one could scarcely see anything. The air was cold, and had an unpleasant odour, owing to a heavy fog, which partially blotted out the fronts of the houses. Frederick inhaled it with delight; for he could feel through the wadding of his coat the form of her arm; and her hand, cased in a chamois glove with two buttons, her little hand which he would have liked to cover with kisses, leaned on his sleeve. Owing to the slipperiness of the pavement, they lost their balance a little; it seemed to him as if they were both rocked by the wind in the midst of a cloud.

The glitter of the lamps on the boulevard brought him back to the realities of existence. The opportunity was a good one, there was no time to lose. He gave himself as far as the Rue de Richelieu to declare his love. But almost at that very moment, in front of a china-shop, she stopped abruptly and said to him:

"We are at the place. Thanks. On Thursday— is it not?—as usual."

The dinners were now renewed; and the more visits he paid at Madame Arnoux's, the more his love-sickness increased. The contemplation of this woman had an enervating effect upon him, like the use of a perfume that is too strong. It penetrated into the very depths of his nature, and became almost a kind of habitual sensation, a new mode of existence.

The prostitutes whom he brushed past under the gaslight, the female ballad-singers breaking into bursts of melody, the ladies rising on horseback at full gallop, the shopkeepers' wives on foot, the grisettes at their windows, all women brought her before his mental vision, either from the effect of their resemblance to her or the violent contrast to her which they presented.   As he walked along by the shops, he gazed at the cashmeres, the laces, and the jewelled eardrops, imagining how they would look draped around her figure, sewn in her corsage, or lighting up her dark hair.   In the flower-girls' baskets the bouquets blossomed for her to choose one as she passed.   In the shoemakers' show-windows the little satin slippers with swan's-down edges seemed to be waiting for her foot.   Every street led towards her house; the hackney-coaches stood in their places to carry her home the more quickly; Paris was associated with her person, and the great city, with all its noises, roared around her like an immense orchestra.

When he went into the Jardin des Plantes the sight of a palm-tree carried him off into distant countries. They were travelling together on the backs of dromedaries, under the awnings of elephants, in the cabin of a yacht amongst the blue archipelagoes, or side by side on mules with little bells attached to them who went stumbling through the grass against broken columns.   Sometimes he stopped in the Louvre before old pictures; and, his love embracing her even in vanished centuries, he substituted her for the personages in the paintings.   Wearing a hennin on her head, she was praying on bended knees before a stained-glass window.   Lady Paramount of Castile or Flanders, she remained seated in a starched ruff and a body lined with whalebone with big puffs.   Then he saw her descending some wide porphyry staircase in the midst of senators under a daïs of ostriches' feathers in a robe of brocade. At another time he dreamed of her in yellow silk trousers on the cushions of a harem — and all that was beautiful, the scintillation of the stars, certain tunes in music, the turn of a phrase, the outlines of a face, led him to think about her in an abrupt, unconscious fashion.

As for trying to make her his mistress, he was sure that any such attempt would be futile.

One evening, Dittmer, on his arrival, kissed her on the forehead; Lovarias did the same, observing:

"You give me leave — don't you? — as it is a friend's privilege?"

Frederick stammered out:

"It seems to me that we are all friends."

"Not all old friends!" she returned.

This was repelling him beforehand indirectly.

Besides, what was he to do? To tell her that he loved her? No doubt, she would decline to listen to him or else she would feel indignant and turn him out of the house. But he preferred to submit to even the most painful ordeal rather than run the horrible risk of seeing her no more. He envied pianists for their talents and soldiers for their scars. He longed for a dangerous attack of sickness, hoping in this way to make her take an interest in him.

One thing caused astonishment to himself, that he felt in no way jealous of Arnoux; and he could not picture her in his imagination undressed, so natural did her modesty appear, and so far did her sex recede into a mysterious background.

Nevertheless, he dreamed of the happiness of living with her, of "theeing" and "thouing" her, of passing his hand lingeringly over her head-bands, or remaining in a kneeling posture on the floor, with both arms clasped round her waist, so as to drink in her soul through his eyes. To accomplish this it would be necessary to conquer Fate; and so, incapable of action, cursing God, and accusing himself of being a coward, he kept moving restlessly within the confines of his passion just as a prisoner keeps moving about in his dungeon. The pangs which he was perpetually enduring were choking him. For hours he would remain quite motionless, or else he would burst into tears; and one day when he had not the strength to restrain his emotion, Deslauriers said to him:

"Why, goodness gracious! what's the matter with you?"

Frederick's nerves were unstrung. Deslauriers did not believe a word of it. At the sight of so much mental anguish, he felt all his old affection reawakening, and he tried to cheer up his friend. A man like him to let himself be depressed, what folly! It was all very well while one was young; but, as one grows older, it is only loss of time.

"You are spoiling my Frederick for me! I want him whom I knew in bygone days. The same boy as ever! I liked him! Come, smoke a pipe, old chap! Shake yourself up a little! You drive me mad!"

"It is true," said Frederick, "I am a fool!"

The clerk replied:

"Ah! old troubadour, I know well what's troubling you! A little affair of the heart? Confess it! Bah! One lost, four found instead! We console ourselves for virtuous women with the other sort. Would you like me to introduce you to some women? You have only to come to the Alhambra."

(This was a place for public balls recently opened at the top of the Champs-Elysées, which had gone down owing to a display of licentiousness somewhat ruder than is usual in establishments of the kind.)

"That's a place where there seems to be good fun. You can take your friends, if you like. I can even pass in Regimbart for you."

Frederick did not think fit to ask the Citizen to go. Deslauriers deprived himself of the pleasure of Sénécal's society. They took only Hussonnet and Cisy along with Dussardier; and the same hackney-coach set the group of five down at the entrance of the Alhambra.

Two Moorish galleries extended on the right and on the left, parallel to one another. The wall of a house opposite occupied the entire backguard; and the fourth side (that in which the restaurant was) represented a Gothic cloister with stained-glass windows. A sort of Chinese roof screened the platform reserved for the musicians. The ground was covered all over with asphalt; the Venetian lanterns fastened to posts formed, at regular intervals, crowns of many-coloured flame above the heads of the dancers. A pedestal here and there supported a stone basin, from which rose a thin streamlet of water. In the midst of the foliage could be seen plaster statues, and Hebes and Cupid, painted in oil, and presenting a very sticky appearance; and the numerous walks, garnished with sand of a deep yellow, carefully raked, made the garden look much larger than it was in reality.

Students were walking their mistresses up and down; drapers' clerks strutted about with canes in their hands; lads fresh from college were smoking their regalias; old men had their dyed beards smoothed out with combs. There were English, Russians, men from South America, and three Orientals in tarbooshes. Lorettes, grisettes, and girls of the town had come there in the hope of finding a protector, a lover, a gold coin, or simply for the pleasure of dancing; and their dresses, with tunics of water-green, cherry-red, or violet, swept along, fluttered between the ebony-trees and the lilacs. Nearly all the men's clothes were of striped material; some of them had white trousers, in spite of the coolness of the evening. The gas was lighted.

Hussonnet was acquainted with a number of the women through his connection with the fashion-journals and the smaller theatres. He sent them kisses with the tips of his fingers, and from time to time he quitted his friends to go and chat with them.

Deslauriers felt jealous of these playful familiarities. He accosted in a cynical manner a tall, fair-haired girl, in a nankeen costume. After looking at him with a certain air of sullenness, she said:

"No! I wouldn't trust you, my good fellow!" and turned on her heel.

His next attack was on a stout brunette, who apparently was a little mad; for she gave a bounce at the very first word he spoke to her, threatening, if he went any further, to call the police. Deslauriers made an effort to laugh; then, coming across a little woman sitting by herself under a gas-lamp, he asked her to be his partner in a quadrille.

The musicians, perched on the platform in the attitude of apes, kept scraping and blowing away with desperate energy. The conductor, standing up, kept beating time automatically. The dancers were much crowded and enjoyed themselves thoroughly. The

5—8

bonnet-strings, getting loose, rubbed against the cravats; the boots sank under the petticoats; and all this
bouncing went on to the accompaniment of the music.
Deslauriers hugged the little woman, and, seized with
the delirium of the cancan, whirled about, like a big
marionnette, in the midst of the dancers. Cisy and
Deslauriers were still promenading up and down. The
young aristocrat kept ogling the girls, and, in spite
of the clerk's exhortations, did not venture to talk to
them, having an idea in his head that in the resorts
of these women there was always "a man hidden
in the cupboard with a pistol who would come out
of it and force you to sign a bill of exchange."

They came back and joined Frederick. Deslauriers
had stopped dancing; and they were all asking themselves how they were to finish up the evening, when
Hussonnet exclaimed:

"Look! Here's the Marquise d'Amaëgui!"

The person referred to was a pale woman with a
retroussé nose, mittens up to her elbows, and big black
earrings hanging down her cheeks, like two dog's
ears. Hussonnet said to her:

"We ought to organise a little fête at your house
— a sort of Oriental rout. Try to collect some of your
friends here for these French cavaliers. Well, what is
annoying you? Are you going to wait for your
hidalgo?"

The Andalusian hung down her head: being well
aware of the by no means lavish habits of her friend,
she was afraid of having to pay for any refreshments
he ordered. When, at length, she let the word
"money" slip from her, Cisy offered five napoleons
— all he had in his purse; and so it was settled that
the thing should come off.

But Frederick was absent. He fancied that he had recognised the voice of Arnoux, and got a glimpse of a woman's hat; and accordingly he hastened towards an arbour which was not far off.

Mademoiselle Vatnaz was alone there with Arnoux.

"Excuse me! I am in the way?"

"Not in the least!" returned the picture-merchant.

Frederick, from the closing words of their conversation, understood that Arnoux had come to the Alhambra to talk over a pressing matter of business with Mademoiselle Vatnaz; and it was evident that he was not completely reassured, for he said to her, with some uneasiness in his manner:

"You are quite sure?"

"Perfectly certain! You are loved. Ah! what a man you are!"

And she assumed a pouting look, putting out her big lips, so red that they seemed tinged with blood. But she had wonderful eyes, of a tawny hue, with specks of gold in the pupils, full of vivacity, amorousness, and sensuality. They illuminated, like lamps, the rather yellow tint of her thin face. Arnoux seemed to enjoy her exhibition of pique. He stooped over her, saying:

"You are nice — give me a kiss!"

She caught hold of his two ears, and pressed her lips against his forehead.

At that moment the dancing stopped; and in the conductor's place appeared a handsome young man, rather fat, with a waxen complexion. He had long black hair, which he wore in the same fashion as Christ, and a blue velvet waistcoat embroidered with large gold palm-branches. He looked as proud as a peacock, and as stupid as a turkey-cock; and, having bowed to the audience, he began a ditty. A villager was supposed to be giving an account of his journey to the capital. The singer used the dialect of Lower Normandy, and played the part of a drunken man. The refrain—

> "Ah! I laughed at you there, I laughed at you there,
>   In that rascally city of Paris!" *

was greeted with enthusiastic stampings of feet. Delmas, "a vocalist who sang with expression," was too shrewd to let the excitement of his listeners cool. A guitar was quickly handed to him and he moaned forth a ballad entitled "The Albanian Girl's Brother."

The words recalled to Frederick those which had been sung by the man in rags between the paddleboxes of the steamboat. His eyes involuntarily attached themselves to the hem of the dress spread out before him.

After each couplet there was a long pause, and the blowing of the wind through the trees resembled the sound of the waves.

Mademoiselle Vatnaz blushed the moment she saw Dussardier. She soon rose, and stretching out her hand towards him:

"You do not remember me, Monsieur Auguste?"

"How do you know her?" asked Frederick.

"We have been in the same house," he replied.

Cisy pulled him by the sleeve; they went out; and, scarcely had they disappeared, when Madame Vatnaz began to pronounce a eulogy on his character. She even went so far as to add that he possessed "the genius of the heart."

----

*Ah! j'ai t'y ri, j'ai t'y ri,
    Dans ce gueusard de Paris!*

Then they chatted about Delmas, admitting that as a mimic he might be a success on the stage; and a discussion followed in which Shakespeare, the Censorship, Style, the People, the receipts of the Porte Saint-Martin, Alexandre Dumas, Victor Hugo, and Dumersan were all mixed up together.

Arnoux had known many celebrated actresses; the young men bent forward their heads to hear what he had to say about these ladies. But his words were drowned in the noise of the music; and, as soon as the quadrille or the polka was over, they all squatted round the tables, called the waiter, and laughed. Bottles of beer and of effervescent lemonade went off with detonations amid the foliage; women clucked like hens; now and then, two gentlemen tried to fight; and a thief was arrested. The dancers, in the rush of a gallop, encroached on the walks. Panting, with flushed, smiling faces, they filed off in a whirlwind which lifted up the gowns with the coat-tails. The trombones brayed more loudly; the rhythmic movement became more rapid. Behind the mediæval cloister could be heard crackling sounds; squibs went off; artificial suns began turning round; the gleam of the Bengal fires, like emeralds in colour, lighted up for the space of a minute the entire garden; and, with the last rocket, a great sigh escaped from the assembled throng.

It slowly died away. A cloud of gunpowder floated into the air. Frederick and Deslauriers were walking step by step through the midst of the crowd, when they happened to see something that made them suddenly stop: Martinon was in the act of paying some money at the place where umbrellas were left; and he was accompanying a woman of fifty, plain-looking, magnificently dressed, and of problematic social rank.

"That sly dog," said Deslauriers, "is not so simple as we imagine. But where in the world is Cisy?"

Dussardier pointed out to them the smoking-divan, where they perceived the knightly youth, with a bowl of punch before him, and a pink hat by his side, to keep him company. Hussonnet, who had been away for the past few minutes, reappeared at the same moment.

A young girl was leaning on his arm, and addressing him in a loud voice as "My little cat."

"Oh! no!" said he to her—"not in public! Call me rather 'Vicomte.' That gives you a cavalier style —Louis XIII. and dainty boots—the sort of thing I like! Yes, my good friends, one of the old *régime!* —nice, isn't she?"—and he chucked her by the chin—"Salute these gentlemen! they are all the sons of peers of France. I keep company with them in order that they may get an appointment for me as an ambassador."

"How insane you are!" sighed Mademoiselle Vatnaz. She asked Dussardier to see her as far as her own door.

Arnoux watched them going off; then, turning towards Frederick:

"Did you like the Vatnaz? At any rate, you're not quite frank about these affairs. I believe you keep your amours hidden."

Frederick, turning pale, swore that he kept nothing hidden.

"Can it be possible you don't know what it is to have a mistress?" said Arnoux.

Frederick felt a longing to mention a woman's name at random. But the story might be repeated to her. So he replied that as a matter of fact he had no mistress.

The picture-dealer reproached him for this.

"This evening you had a good opportunity! Why didn't you do like the others, each of whom went off with a woman?"

"Well, and what about yourself?" said Frederick, provoked by his persistency.

"Oh! myself—that's quite a different matter, my lad! I go home to my own one!"

Then he called a cab, and disappeared.

The two friends walked towards their own destination. An east wind was blowing. They did not exchange a word. Deslauriers was regretting that he had not succeeded in making a *shine* before a certain newspaper-manager, and Frederick was lost once more in his melancholy broodings. At length, breaking silence, he said that this public-house ball appeared to him a stupid affair.

"Whose fault is it? If you had not left us, to join that Arnoux of yours——"

"Bah! anything I could have done would have been utterly useless!"

But the clerk had theories of his own. All that was necessary in order to get a thing was to desire it strongly.

"Nevertheless, you yourself, a little while ago——"

"I don't care a straw about that sort of thing!" returned Deslauriers, cutting short Frederick's allusion. "Am I going to get entangled with women?"

And he declaimed against their affectations, their silly ways—in short, he disliked them.

"Don't be acting, then!" said Frederick.

Deslauriers became silent. Then, all at once:

"Will you bet me a hundred francs that I won't *do* the first woman that passes?"

"Yes—it's a bet!"

The first who passed was a hideous-looking beggar-woman, and they were giving up all hope of a chance presenting itself when, in the middle of the Rue de Rivoli, they saw a tall girl with a little bandbox in her hand.

Deslauriers accosted her under the arcades. She turned up abruptly by the Tuileries, and soon diverged into the Place du Carrousel. She glanced to the right and to the left. She ran after a hackney-coach; Deslauriers overtook her. He walked by her side, talking to her with expressive gestures. At length, she accepted his arm, and they went on together along the quays. Then, when they reached the rising ground in front of the Châtelet, they kept tramping up and down for at least twenty minutes, like two sailors keeping watch. But, all of a sudden, they passed over the Pont-au-Change, through the Flower Market, and along the Quai Napoléon. Frederick came up behind them. Deslauriers gave him to understand that he would be in their way, and had only to follow his own example.

"How much have you got still?"

"Two hundred sous pieces."

"That's enough—good night to you!"

Frederick was seized with the astonishment one feels at seeing a piece of foolery coming to a successful issue.

"He has the laugh at me," was his reflection. "Suppose I went back again?"

Perhaps Deslauriers imagined that he was envious of this paltry love! "As if I had not one a hundred times more rare, more noble, more absorbing." He felt a sort of angry feeling impelling him onward. He arrived in front of Madame Arnoux's door.

None of the outer windows belonged to her apartment. Nevertheless, he remained with his eyes pasted on the front of the house—as if he fancied he could, by his contemplation, break open the walls. No doubt, she was now sunk in repose, tranquil as a sleeping flower, with her beautiful black hair resting on the lace of the pillow, her lips slightly parted, and one arm under her head. Then Arnoux's head rose before him, and he rushed away to escape from this vision.

The advice which Deslauriers had given to him came back to his memory. It only filled him with horror. Then he walked about the streets in a vagabond fashion.

When a pedestrian approached, he tried to distinguish the face. From time to time a ray of light passed between his legs, tracing a great quarter of a circle on the pavement; and in the shadow a man appeared with his dosser and his lantern. The wind, at certain points, made the sheet-iron flue of a chimney shake. Distant sounds reached his ears, mingling with the buzzing in his brain; and it seemed to him that he was listening to the indistinct flourish of quadrille music. His movements as he walked on kept up this illusion. He found himself on the Pont de la Concorde.

Then he recalled that evening in the previous winter, when, as he left her house for the first time, he was forced to stand still, so rapidly did his heart beat with the hopes that held it in their clasp. And now they had all withered!

Dark clouds were drifting across the face of the moon. He gazed at it, musing on the vastness of space, the wretchedness of life, the nothingness of everything. The day dawned; his teeth began to chatter, and, half-asleep, wet with the morning mist, and bathed in tears, he asked himself, Why should I not make an end of it? All that was necessary was a single movement. The weight of his forehead dragged him along — he beheld his own dead body floating in the water. Frederick stooped down. The parapet was rather wide, and it was through pure weariness that he did not make the attempt to leap over it.

Then a feeling of dismay swept over him. He reached the boulevards once more, and sank down upon a seat. He was aroused by some police-officers, who were convinced that he had been indulging a little too freely.

He resumed his walk. But, as he was exceedingly hungry, and as all the restaurants were closed, he went to get a "snack" at a tavern by the fish-markets; after which, thinking it too soon to go in yet, he kept sauntering about the Hôtel de Ville till a quarter past eight.

Deslauriers had long since got rid of his wench; and he was writing at the table in the middle of his room. About four o'clock, M. de Cisy came in.

Thanks to Dussardier, he had enjoyed the society of a lady the night before; and he had even accompanied her home in the carriage with her husband to the very threshold of their house, where she had given him an assignation. He parted with her without even knowing her name.

"And what do you propose that I should do in that way?" said Frederick.

Thereupon the young gentleman began to cudgel his brains to think of a suitable woman; he mentioned Mademoiselle Vatnaz, the Andalusian, and all the rest. At length, with much circumlocution, he stated the object of his visit. Relying on the discretion of his friend, he came to aid him in taking an important step, after which he might definitely regard himself as a man; and Frederick showed no reluctance. He told the story to Deslauriers without relating the facts with reference to himself personally.

The clerk was of opinion that he was now going on very well. This respect for his advice increased his good humour. He owed to that quality his success, on the very first night he met her, with Mademoiselle Clémence Daviou, embroideress in gold for military outfits, the sweetest creature that ever lived, as slender as a reed, with large blue eyes, perpetually staring with wonder. The clerk had taken advantage of her credulity to such an extent as to make her believe that he had been decorated. At their private conversations he had his frock-coat adorned with a red ribbon, but divested himself of it in public in order, as he put it, not to humiliate his master. However, he kept her at a distance, allowed himself to be fawned upon, like a pasha, and, in a laughing sort of way, called her "daughter of the people." Every time they met, she brought him little bunches of violets. Frederick would not have cared for a love affair of this sort.

Meanwhile, whenever they set forth arm-in-arm to visit Pinson's or Barillot's circulating library, he experienced a feeling of singular depression. Frederick did not realise how much pain he had made Deslauriers endure for the past year, while brushing his nails before going out to dine in the Rue de Choiseul!

One evening, when from the commanding position in which his balcony stood, he had just been watching them as they went out together, he saw Hussonnet, some distance off, on the Pont d'Arcole. The Bohemian began calling him by making signals towards him, and, when Frederick had descended the five flights of stairs:

"Here is the thing—it is next Saturday, the 24th, Madame Arnoux's feast-day."

"How is that, when her name is Marie?"

"And Angèle also—no matter! They will entertain their guests at their country-house at Saint-Cloud. I was told to give you due notice about it. You'll find a vehicle at the magazine-office at three o'clock. So that makes matters all right! Excuse me for having disturbed you! But I have such a number of calls to make!"

Frederick had scarcely turned round when his doorkeeper placed a letter in his hand:

"Monsieur and Madame Dambreuse beg of Monsieur F. Moreau to do them the honour to come and dine with them on Saturday the 24th inst.—R.S.V.P."

"Too late!" he said to himself. Nevertheless, he showed the letter to Deslauriers, who exclaimed:

"Ha! at last! But you don't look as if you were satisfied. Why?"

After some little hesitation, Frederick said that he had another invitation for the same day.

"Be kind enough to let me run across to the Rue de Choiseul. I'm not joking! I'll answer this for you if it puts you about."

And the clerk wrote an acceptance of the invitation in the third person.

Having seen nothing of the world save through the fever of his desires, he pictured it to himself as an artificial creation discharging its functions by virtue of mathematical laws. A dinner in the city, an accidental meeting with a man in office, a smile from a pretty woman, might, by a series of actions deducing themselves from one another, have gigantic results. Certain Parisian drawing-rooms were like those machines which take a material in the rough and render it a hundred times more valuable. He believed in courtesans advising diplomatists, in wealthy marriages brought about by intrigues, in the cleverness of convicts, in the capacity of strong men for getting the better of fortune. In short, he considered it so useful to visit the Dambreuses, and talked about it so plausibly, that Frederick was at a loss to know what was the best course to take.

The least he ought to do, as it was Madame Arnoux's feast-day, was to make her a present. He naturally thought of a parasol, in order to make reparation for his awkwardness. Now he came across a shot-silk parasol with a little carved ivory handle, which had come all the way from China. But the price of it was a hundred and seventy-five francs, and he had not a sou, having in fact to live on the credit of his next quarter's allowance. However, he wished to get it; he was determined to have it; and, in spite of his repugnance to doing so, he had recourse to Deslauriers.

Deslauriers answered Frederick's first question by saying that he had no money.

"I want some," said Frederick—"I want some very badly!"

As the other made the same excuse over again, he flew into a passion.

"You might find it to your advantage some time——"

"What do you mean by that?"

"Oh! nothing."

The clerk understood. He took the sum required out of his reserve-fund, and when he had counted out the money, coin by coin:

"I am not asking you for a receipt, as I see you have a lot of expense!"

Frederick threw himself on his friend's neck with a thousand affectionate protestations. Deslauriers received this display of emotion frigidly. Then, next morning, noticing the parasol on the top of the piano:

"Ah! it was for that!"

"I will send it, perhaps," said Frederick, with an air of carelessness.

Good fortune was on his side, for that evening he got a note with a black border from Madame Dambreuse announcing to him that she had lost an uncle, and excusing herself for having to defer till a later period the pleasure of making his acquaintance. At two o'clock, he reached the office of the art journal. Instead of waiting for him in order to drive him in his carriage, Arnoux had left the city the night before, unable to resist his desire to get some fresh air.

Every year it was his custom, as soon as the leaves were budding forth, to start early in the morning and to remain away several days, making long journeys across the fields, drinking milk at the farmhouses, romping with the village girls, asking questions about the harvest, and carrying back home with him stalks of salad in his pocket-handkerchief. At length, in order to realise a long-cherished dream of his, he had bought a country-house.

While Frederick was talking to the picture-dealer's clerk, Mademoiselle Vatnaz suddenly made her appearance, and was disappointed at not seeing Arnoux. He would, perhaps, be remaining away two days longer. The clerk advised her "to go there"—she could not go there; to write a letter—she was afraid that the letter might get lost. Frederick offered to be the bearer of it himself. She rapidly scribbled off a letter, and implored of him to let nobody see him delivering it.

Forty minutes afterwards, he found himself at Saint-Cloud. The house, which was about a hundred paces farther away than the bridge, stood half-way up the hill. The garden-walls were hidden by two rows of linden-trees, and a wide lawn descended to the bank of the river. The railed entrance before the door was open, and Frederick went in.

Arnoux, stretched on the grass, was playing with a litter of kittens. This amusement appeared to absorb him completely. Mademoiselle Vatnaz's letter drew him out of his sleepy idleness.

"The deuce! the deuce!—this is a bore! She is right, though; I must go."

Then, having stuck the missive into his pocket, he showed the young man through the grounds with manifest delight. He pointed out everything—the stable, the cart-house, the kitchen. The drawing-room was at the right, on the side facing Paris, and looked out on a floored arbour, covered over with clematis. But presently a few harmonious notes burst forth above their heads: Madame Arnoux, fancying that there was nobody near, was singing to amuse herself. She executed quavers, trills, arpeggios. There were long notes which seemed to remain suspended in the air; others fell in a rushing shower like the spray of a waterfall; and her voice passing out through the Venetian blind, cut its way through the deep silence and rose towards the blue sky. She ceased all at once, when M. and Madame Oudry, two neighbours, presented themselves.

Then she appeared herself at the top of the steps in front of the house; and, as she descended, he caught a glimpse of her foot. She wore little open shoes of reddish-brown leather, with three straps crossing each other so as to draw just above her stockings a wirework of gold.

Those who had been invited arrived. With the exception of Maître Lefaucheur, an advocate, they were the same guests who came to the Thursday dinners. Each of them had brought some present — Dittmer a Syrian scarf, Rosenwald a scrap-book of ballads, Burieu a water-colour painting, Sombary one of his own caricatures, and Pellerin a charcoal-drawing, representing a kind of dance of death, a hideous fantasy, the execution of which was rather poor. Hussonnet dispensed with the formality of a present.

Frederick was waiting to offer his, after the others.

She thanked him very much for it. Thereupon, he said:

"Why, 'tis almost a debt. I have been so much annoyed——"

"At what, pray?" she returned. "I don't understand."

"Come! dinner is waiting!" said Arnoux, catching hold of his arm; then in a whisper: "You are not very knowing, certainly!"

Nothing could well be prettier than the dining-room, painted in water-green. At one end, a nymph of stone was dipping her toe in a basin formed like a shell. Through the open windows the entire garden could be seen with the long lawn flanked by an old Scotch fir, three-quarters stripped bare; groups of flowers swelled it out in unequal plots; and at the other side of the river extended in a wide semicircle the Bois de Boulogne, Neuilly, Sèvres, and Meudon. Before the railed gate in front a canoe with sail out-spread was tacking about.

They chatted first about the view in front of them, then about scenery in general; and they were beginning to plunge into discussions when Arnoux, at half-past nine o'clock, ordered the horse to be put to the carriage.

"Would you like me to go back with you?" said Madame Arnoux.

"Why, certainly!" and, making her a graceful bow: "You know well, madame, that it is impossible to live without you!"

Everyone congratulated her on having so good a husband.

"Ah! it is because I am not the only one," she replied quietly, pointing towards her little daughter.

Then, the conversation having turned once more on painting, there was some talk about a Ruysdaël, for which Arnoux expected a big sum, and Pellerin asked him if it were true that the celebrated Saul Mathias from London had come over during the past month to make him an offer of twenty-three thousand francs for it.

"'Tis a positive fact!" and turning towards Frederick: "That was the very same gentleman I brought

5—9

with me a few days ago to the Alhambra, much against my will, I assure you, for these English are by no means amusing companions."

Frederick, who suspected that Mademoiselle Vatnaz's letter contained some reference to an intrigue, was amazed at the facility with which my lord Arnoux found a way of passing it off as a perfectly honourable transaction; but his new lie, which was quite needless, made the young man open his eyes in speechless astonishment.

The picture-dealer added, with an air of simplicity:

"What's the name, by-the-by, of that young fellow, your friend?"

"Deslauriers," said Frederick quickly.

And, in order to repair the injustice which he felt he had done to his comrade, he praised him as one who possessed remarkable ability.

"Ah! indeed? But he doesn't look such a fine fellow as the other—the clerk in the wagon-office."

Frederick bestowed a mental imprecation on Dussardier. She would now be taking it for granted that he associated with the common herd.

Then they began to talk about the ornamentation of the capital—the new districts of the city—and the worthy Oudry happened to refer to M. Dambreuse as one of the big speculators.

Frederick, taking advantage of the opportunity to make a good figure, said he was acquainted with that gentleman. But Pellerin launched into a harangue against shopkeepers—he saw no difference between them, whether they were sellers of candles or of money. Then Rosenwald and Burieu talked about old china; Arnoux chatted with Madame Oudry about gardening; Sombary, a comical character of the old school, amused himself by chaffing her husband, referring to him sometimes as "Odry," as if he were the actor of that name, and remarking that he must be descended from Oudry, the dog-painter, seeing that the bump of the animals was visible on his forehead. He even wanted to feel M. Oudry's skull; but the latter excused himself on account of his wig; and the dessert ended with loud bursts of laughter.

When they had taken their coffee, while they smoked, under the linden-trees, and strolled about the garden for some time, they went out for a walk along the river.

The party stopped in front of a fishmonger's shop, where a man was washing eels. Mademoiselle Marthe wanted to look at them. He emptied the box in which he had them out on the grass; and the little girl threw herself on her knees in order to catch them, laughed with delight, and then began to scream with terror. They all got spoiled, and Arnoux paid for them.

He next took it into his head to go out for a sail in the cutter.

One side of the horizon was beginning to assume a pale aspect, while on the other side a wide strip of orange colour showed itself in the sky, deepening into purple at the summits of the hills, which were steeped in shadow. Madame Arnoux seated herself on a big stone with this glittering splendour at her back. The other ladies sauntered about here and there. Hussonnet, at the lower end of the river's bank, went making ducks and drakes over the water.

Arnoux presently returned, followed by a weather-beaten long boat, into which, in spite of the most prudent remonstrances, he packed his guests. The boat got upset, and they had to go ashore again.

By this time wax-tapers were burning in the drawing-room, all hung with chintz, and with branched candlesticks of crystal fixed close to the walls. Mère Oudry was sleeping comfortably in an armchair, and the others were listening to M. Lefaucheux expatiating on the glories of the Bar. Madame Arnoux was sitting by herself near the window. Frederick came over to her.

They chatted about the remarks which were being made in their vicinity. She admired oratory; he preferred the renown gained by authors. But, she ventured to suggest, it must give a man greater pleasure to move crowds directly by addressing them in person, face to face, than it does to infuse into their souls by his pen all the sentiments that animate his own. Such triumphs as these did not tempt Frederick much, as he had no ambition.

Then he broached the subject of sentimental adventures. She spoke pityingly of the havoc wrought by passion, but expressed indignation at hypocritical vileness, and this rectitude of spirit harmonised so well with the regular beauty of her face that it seemed indeed as if her physical attractions were the outcome of her moral nature.

She smiled, every now and then, letting her eyes rest on him for a minute. Then he felt her glances penetrating his soul like those great rays of sunlight which descend into the depths of the water. He loved her without mental reservation, without any hope of his love being returned, unconditionally; and in those silent transports, which were like outbursts of gratitude, he would fain have covered her forehead with a rain of kisses. However, an inspiration from within carried him beyond himself—he felt moved by a longing for self-sacrifice, an imperative impulse towards immediate self-devotion, and all the stronger from the fact that he could not gratify it.

He did not leave along with the rest. Neither did Hussonnet. They were to go back in the carriage; and the vehicle was waiting just in front of the steps when Arnoux rushed down and hurried into the garden to gather some flowers there. Then the bouquet having been tied round with a thread, as the stems fell down unevenly, he searched in his pocket, which was full of papers, took out a piece at random, wrapped them up, completed his handiwork with the aid of a strong pin, and then offered it to his wife with a certain amount of tenderness.

"Look here, my darling! Excuse me for having forgotten you!"

But she uttered a little scream: the pin, having been awkwardly fixed, had cut her, and she hastened up to her room. They waited nearly a quarter of an hour for her. At last, she reappeared, carried off Marthe, and threw herself into the carriage.

"And your bouquet?" said Arnoux.

"No! no—it is not worth while!" Frederick was running off to fetch it for her; she called out to him:

"I don't want it!"

But he speedily brought it to her, saying that he had just put it into an envelope again, as he had found the flowers lying on the floor. She thrust them behind the leathern apron of the carriage close to the seat, and off they started.

Frederick, seated by her side, noticed that she

was trembling frightfully. Then, when they had
passed the bridge, as Arnoux was turning to the left:
   "Why, no! you are making a mistake!—that
way, to the right!"

She seemed irritated; everything annoyed her. At
length, Marthe having closed her eyes, Madame Arnoux drew forth the bouquet, and flung it out through
the carriage-door, then caught Frederick's arm, making a sign to him with the other hand to say nothing about it.

After this, she pressed her handkerchief against
her lips, and sat quite motionless.

The two others, on the dickey, kept talking about
printing and about subscribers. Arnoux, who was
driving recklessly, lost his way in the middle of the
Bois de Boulogne. Then they plunged into narrow
paths. The horse proceeded along at a walking pace;
the branches of the trees grazed the hood. Frederick
could see nothing of Madame Arnoux save her two
eyes in the shade. Marthe lay stretched across her
lap while he supported the child's head.

"She is tiring you!" said her mother.

He replied:

"No! Oh, no!"

Whirlwinds of dust rose up slowly. They passed
through Auteuil. All the houses were closed up; a
gas-lamp here and there lighted up the angle of a
wall; then once more they were surrounded by darkness. At one time he noticed that she was shedding
tears.

Was this remorse or passion? What in the world
was it? This grief, of whose exact nature he was
ignorant, interested him like a personal matter. There
was now a new bond between them, as if, in a

sense, they were accomplices; and he said to her in the most caressing voice he could assume:

"You are ill?"

"Yes, a little," she returned.

The carriage rolled on, and the honeysuckles and the syringas trailed over the garden fences, sending forth puffs of enervating odour into the night air. Her gown fell around her feet in numerous folds. It seemed to him as if he were in communication with her entire person through the medium of this child's body which lay stretched between them. He stooped over the little girl, and spreading out her pretty brown tresses, kissed her softly on the forehead.

"You are good!" said Madame Arnoux.

"Why?"

"Because you are fond of children."

"Not all!"

He said no more, but he let his left hand hang down her side wide open, fancying that she would follow his example perhaps, and that he would find her palm touching his. Then he felt ashamed and withdrew it. They soon reached the paved street. The carriage went on more quickly; the number of gas-lights vastly increased—it was Paris. Hussonnet, in front of the lumber-room, jumped down from his seat. Frederick waited till they were in the courtyard before alighting; then he lay in ambush at the corner of the Rue de Choiseul, and saw Arnoux slowly making his way back to the boulevards.

Next morning he began working as hard as ever he could.

He saw himself in an Assize Court, on a winter's evening, at the close of the advocates' speeches, when the jurymen are looking pale, and when the panting audience make the partitions of the prætorium creak; and after having being four hours speaking, he was recapitulating all his proofs, feeling with every phrase, with every word, with every gesture, the chopper of the guillotine, which was suspended behind him, rising up; then in the tribune of the Chamber, an orator who bears on his lips the safety of an entire people, drowning his opponents under his figures of rhetoric, crushing them under a rep-artee, with thunders and musical intonations in his voice, ironical, pathetic, fiery, sublime. She would be there somewhere in the midst of the others, hiding beneath her veil her enthusiastic tears. After that they would meet again, and he would be unaffected by discouragements, calumnies, and insults, if she would only say, "Ah, that is beautiful!" while drawing her light hand across his brow.

These images flashed, like beacon-lights, on the horizon of his life. His intellect, thereby excited, be-came more active and more vigorous. He buried himself in study till the month of August, and was successful at his final examination.

Deslauriers, who had found it so troublesome to coach him once more for the second examination at the close of December, and for the third in February, was astonished at his ardour. Then the great ex-pectations of former days returned. In ten years it was probable that Frederick whould be deputy; in fifteen a minister. Why not? With his patrimony, which would soon come into his hands, he might, at first, start a newspaper; this would be the opening step in his career; after that they would see what the future would bring. As for himself, he was still ambitious of obtaining a chair in the Law School;

and he sustained his thesis for the degree of Doctor
in such a remarkable fashion that it won for him the
compliments of the professors.

Three days afterwards, Frederick took his own
degree. Before leaving for his holidays, he conceived
the idea of getting up a picnic to bring to a close
their Saturday reunions.

He displayed the utmost gaiety on the occasion.
Madame Arnoux was now with her mother at Chartres. But he would soon come across her again, and
would end by being her lover.

Deslauriers, admitted the same day to the young
advocates' pleading rehearsals at Orsay, had made a
speech which was greatly applauded. Although he
was sober, he drank a little more wine than was
good for him, and said to Dussardier at dessert:

"You are an honest fellow!—and, when I'm a
rich man, I'll make you my manager."

All were in a state of delight. Cisy was not going to finish his law-course. Martinon intended to
remain during the period before his admission to the
Bar in the provinces, where he would be nominated
a deputy-magistrate. Pellerin was devoting himself
to the production of a large picture representing
"The Genius of the Revolution." Hussonnet was, in
the following week, about to read for the Director of
Public Amusements the scheme of a play, and had no
doubt as to its success:

"As for the framework of the drama, they may
leave that to me! As for the passions, I have
knocked about enough to understand them thoroughly;
and as for witticisms, they're entirely in my line!"

He gave a spring, fell on his two hands, and thus
moved for some time around the table with his legs

in the air. This performance, worthy of a street-urchin, did not get rid of Sénécal's frowns. He had just been dismissed from the boarding-school, in which he had been a teacher, for having given a whipping to an aristocrat's son. His straitened circumstances had got worse in consequence: he laid the blame of this on the inequalities of society, and cursed the wealthy. He poured out his grievances into the sympathetic ears of Regimbart, who had become every day more and more disillusioned, saddened, and disgusted. The Citizen had now turned his attention towards questions arising out of the Budget, and blamed the Court party for the loss of millions in Algeria.

As he could not sleep without having paid a visit to the Alexandre smoking-divan, he disappeared at eleven o'clock. The rest went away some time afterwards; and Frederick, as he was parting with Hussonnet, learned that Madame Arnoux was to have come back the night before.

He accordingly went to the coach-office to change his time for starting to the next day; and, at about six o'clock in the evening, presented himself at her house. Her return, the door keeper said, had been put off for a week. Frederick dined alone, and then lounged about the boulevards.

Rosy clouds, scarf-like in form, stretched beyond the roofs; the shop-tents were beginning to be taken away; water-carts were letting a shower of spray fall over the dusty pavement; and an unexpected coolness was mingled with emanations from cafés, as one got a glimpse through their open doors, between some silver plate and gilt ware, of flowers in sheaves, which were reflected in the large sheets of glass. The crowd moved on at a leisurely pace. Groups of men were chatting in the middle of the foot-path; and women passed along with an indolent expression in their eyes and that camelia tint in their complexions which intense heat imparts to feminine flesh. Something immeasurable in its vastness seemed to pour itself out and enclose the houses. Never had Paris looked so beautiful. He saw nothing before him in the future but an interminable series of years all full of love.

He stopped in front of the theatre of the Porte Saint-Martin to look at the bill; and, for want of something to occupy him, paid for a seat and went in.

An old-fashioned dramatic version of a fairy-tale was the piece on the stage. There was a very small audience; and through the skylights of the top gallery the vault of heaven seemed cut up into little blue squares, whilst the stage lamps above the orchestra formed a single line of yellow illuminations. The scene represented a slave-market at Pekin, with hand-bells, tomtoms, sweeping robes, sharp-pointed caps, and clownish jokes. Then, as soon as the curtain fell, he wandered into the foyer all alone and gazed out with admiration at a large green landau which stood on the boulevard outside, before the front steps of the theatre, yoked to two white horses, while a coachman with short breeches held the reins.

He had just got back to his seat when, in the balcony, a lady and a gentleman entered the first box in front of the stage. The husband had a pale face with a narrow strip of grey beard round it, the rosette of a Government official, and that frigid look which is supposed to characterise diplomatists.

His wife, who was at least twenty years younger, and who was neither tall nor under-sized, neither ugly nor pretty, wore her fair hair in corkscrew curls in the

English fashion, and displayed a long-bodiced dress and a large black lace fan. To make people so fashionable as these come to the theatre at such a season one would imagine either that there was some accidental cause, or that they had got tired of spending the evening in one another's society. The lady kept nibbling at her fan, while the gentleman yawned. Frederick could not recall to mind where he had seen that face.

In the next interval between the acts, while passing through one of the lobbies, he came face to face with both of them. As he bowed in an undecided manner, M. Dambreuse, at once recognising him, came up and apologised for having treated him with unpardonable neglect. It was an allusion to the numerous visiting-cards he had sent in accordance with the clerk's advice. However, he confused the periods, supposing that Frederick was in the second year of his law-course. Then he said he envied the young man for the opportunity of going into the country. He sadly needed a little rest himself, but business kept him in Paris.

Madame Dambreuse, leaning on his arm, nodded her head slightly, and the agreeable sprightliness of her face contrasted with its gloomy expression a short time before.

"One finds charming diversions in it, nevertheless," she said, after her husband's last remark. "What a stupid play that was — was it not, Monsieur?" And all three of them remained there chatting about theatres and new pieces.

Frederick, accustomed to the grimaces of provincial dames, had not seen in any woman such ease of manner combined with that simplicity which is the essence of refinement, and in which ingenuous souls trace the expression of instantaneous sympathy.

They would expect to see him as soon as he returned. M. Dambreuse told him to give his kind remembrances to Père Roque.

Frederick, when he reached his lodgings, did not fail to inform Deslauriers of their hospitable invitation.

"Grand!" was the clerk's reply; "and don't let your mamma get round you! Come back without delay!"

On the day after his arrival, as soon as they had finished breakfast, Madame Moreau brought her son out into the garden.

She said she was happy to see him in a profession, for they were not as rich as people imagined. The land brought in little; the people who farmed it paid badly. She had even been compelled to sell her carriage. Finally, she placed their situation in its true colours before him.

During the first embarrassments which followed the death of her late husband, M. Roque, a man of great cunning, had made her loans of money which had been renewed, and left long unpaid, in spite of her desire to clear them off. He had suddenly made a demand for immediate payment, and she had gone beyond the strict terms of the agreement by giving up to him, at a contemptible figure, the farm of Presles. Ten years later, her capital disappeared through the failure of a banker at Melun. Through a horror which she had of mortgages, and to keep up appearances, which might be necessary in view of her son's future, she had, when Père Roque presented himself again, listened to him once more. But now she was free from debt. In short, there was left them an income of about ten thousand francs, of which two thousand three hundred belonged to him — his entire patrimony.

"It isn't possible!" exclaimed Frederick.

She nodded her head, as if to declare that it was perfectly possible.

But his uncle would leave him something?

That was by no means certain!

And they took a turn around the garden without exchanging a word. At last she pressed him to her heart, and in a voice choked with rising tears:

"Ah! my poor boy! I have had to give up my dreams!"

He seated himself on a bench in the shadow of the large acacia.

Her advice was that he should become a clerk to M. Prouharam, solicitor, who would assign over his office to him; if he increased its value, he might sell it again and find a good practice.

Frederick was no longer listening to her. He was gazing automatically across the hedge into the other garden opposite.

A little girl of about twelve with red hair happened to be there all alone. She had made earrings for herself with the berries of the service-tree. Her bodice, made of grey linen-cloth, allowed her shoulders, slightly gilded by the sun, to be seen. Her short white petticoat was spotted with the stains made by sweets; and there was, so to speak, the grace of a young wild animal about her entire person, at the same time, nervous and thin. Apparently, the presence of a stranger astonished her, for she had stopped abruptly with her watering-pot in her hand darting glances at him with her large bright eyes, which were of a limpid greenish-blue colour.

"That is M. Roque's daughter," said Madame Moreau. "He has just married his servant and legitimised the child that he had by her."

CHAPTER VI.

Blighted Hopes.

RUINED, stripped of everything, undermined!

He remained seated on the bench, as if stunned by a shock. He cursed Fate; he would have liked to beat somebody; and, to intensify his despair, he felt a kind of outrage, a sense of disgrace, weighing down upon him; for Frederick had been under the impression that the fortune coming to him through his father would mount up one day to an income of fifteen thousand livres, and he had so informed the Arnoux' in an indirect sort of way. So then he would be looked upon as a braggart, a rogue, an obscure blackguard, who had introduced himself to them in the expectation of making some profit out of it! And as for her—Madame Arnoux—how could he ever see her again now?

Moreover, that was completely impossible when he had only a yearly income of three thousand francs. He could not always lodge on the fourth floor, have the door keeper as a servant, and make his appearance with wretched black gloves turning blue at the ends, a greasy hat, and the same frock-coat for a whole year. No, no! never! And yet without her existence was intolerable. Many people were well able to live without any fortune, Deslauriers amongst the rest; and he thought himself a coward to attach so much importance to matters of trifling consequence. Need would perhaps multiply his faculties a hundredfold. He excited himself by thinking on the great men who had worked in garrets. A soul like that of Madame Arnoux ought to be touched at such a spectacle, and she would be moved by it to sympathetic tenderness. So, after all, this catastrophe was a piece of good fortune; like those earthquakes which unveil treasures, it had revealed to him the hidden wealth of his nature. But there was only one place in the world where this could be turned to account —Paris; for to his mind, art, science, and love (those three faces of God, as Pellerin would have said) were associated exclusively with the capital. That evening, he informed his mother of his intention to go back there. Madame Moreau was surprised and indignant. She regarded it as a foolish and absurd course. It would be better to follow her advice, namely, to remain near her in an office. Frederick shrugged his shoulders, "Come now"—looking on this proposal as an insult to himself.

Thereupon, the good lady adopted another plan. In a tender voice broken by sobs she began to dwell on her solitude, her old age, and the sacrifices she had made for him. Now that she was more unhappy than ever, he was abandoning her. Then, alluding to the anticipated close of her life:

"A little patience—good heavens! you will soon be free!"

These lamentations were renewed twenty times a day for three months; and at the same time the luxuries of a home made him effeminate. He found it enjoyable to have a softer bed and napkins that were not torn, so that, weary, enervated, overcome by the terrible force of comfort, Frederick allowed himself to be brought to Maître Prouharam's office.

He displayed there neither knowledge nor aptitude. Up to this time, he had been regarded as a young man of great means who ought to be the shining light of the Department.   The public would now come to the conclusion that he had imposed upon them.

At first, he said to himself:

"It is necessary to inform Madame Arnoux about it;" and for a whole week he kept formulating in his own mind dithyrambic letters and short notes in an eloquent and sublime style.   The fear of avowing his actual position restrained him.   Then he thought that it was far better to write to the husband. Arnoux knew life and could understand the true state of the case.   At length, after a fortnight's hesitation:

"Bah! I ought not to see them any more: let them forget me!   At any rate, I shall be cherished in her memory without having sunk in her estimation! She will believe that I am dead, and will regret me — perhaps."

As extravagant resolutions cost him little, he swore in his own mind that he would never return to Paris, and that he would not even make any enquiries about Madame Arnoux.

Nevertheless, he regretted the very smell of the gas and the noise of the omnibuses.   He mused on the things that she might have said to him, on the tone of her voice, on the light of her eyes — and, re-

5—10

garding himself as a dead man, he no longer did anything at all.

He arose very late, and looked through the window at the passing teams of wagoners. The first six months especially were hateful.

On certain days, however, he was possessed by a feeling of indignation even against her. Then he would go forth and wander through the meadows, half covered in winter time by the inundations of the Seine. They were cut up by rows of poplar-trees. Here and there arose a little bridge. He tramped about till evening, rolling the yellow leaves under his feet, inhaling the fog, and jumping over the ditches. As his arteries began to throb more vigorously, he felt himself carried away by a desire to do something wild; he longed to become a trapper in America, to attend on a pasha in the East, to take ship as a sailor; and he gave vent to his melancholy in long letters to Deslauriers.

The latter was struggling to get on. The slothful conduct of his friend and his eternal jeremiads appeared to him simply stupid. Their correspondence soon became a mere form. Frederick had given up all his furniture to Deslauriers, who stayed on in the same lodgings. From time to time his mother spoke to him. At length he one day told her about the present he had made, and she was giving him a rating for it, when a letter was placed in his hands.

"What is the matter now?" she said, "you are trembling?"

"There is nothing the matter with me," replied Frederick.

Deslauriers informed him that he had taken Sénécal under his protection, and that for the past fortnight they had been living together. So now Sénécal was exhibiting himself in the midst of things that had come from the Arnoux's shop.   He might sell them, criticise, make jokes about them.   Frederick felt wounded in the depths of his soul.   He went up to his own apartment.   He felt a yearning for death.

His mother called him to consult him about a plantation in the garden.

This garden was, after the fashion of an English park, cut in the middle by a stick fence; and the half of it belonged to Père Roque, who had another for vegetables on the bank of the river.   The two neighbours, having fallen out, abstained from making their appearance there at the same hour.   But since Frederick's return, the old gentleman used to walk about there more frequently, and was not stinted in his courtesies towards Madame Moreau's son.   He pitied the young man for having to live in a country town.   One day he told him that Madame Dambreuse had been anxious to hear from him.   On another occasion he expatiated on the custom of Champagne, where the stomach conferred nobility.

"At that time you would have been a lord, since your mother's name was De Fouvens.   And 'tis all very well to talk — never mind! there's something in a name.   After all," he added, with a sly glance at Frederick, "that depends on the Keeper of the Seals."

This pretension to aristocracy contrasted strangely with his personal appearance.   As he was small, his big chestnut-coloured frock-coat exaggerated the length of his bust.   When he took off his hat, a face almost like that of a woman with an extremely sharp nose could be seen; his hair, which was of a yellow colour, resembled a wig.   He saluted people with a very low bow, brushing against the wall.

Up to his fiftieth year, he had been content with the services of Catherine, a native of Lorraine, of the same age as himself, who was strongly marked with small-pox. But in the year 1834, he brought back with him from Paris a handsome blonde with a sheep-like type of countenance and a "queenly carriage." Ere long, she was observed strutting about with large earrings; and everything was explained by the birth of a daughter who was introduced to the world under the name of Elisabeth Olympe Louise Roque.

Catherine, in her first ebullition of jealousy, expected that she would curse this child. On the contrary, she became fond of the little girl, and treated her with the utmost care, consideration, and tenderness, in order to supplant her mother and render her odious — an easy task, inasmuch as Madame Éléonore entirely neglected the little one, preferring to gossip at the tradesmen's shops. On the day after her marriage, she went to pay a visit at the Sub-prefecture, no longer "thee'd" and "thou'd" the servants, and took it into her head that, as a matter of good form, she ought to exhibit a certain severity towards the child. She was present while the little one was at her lessons. The teacher, an old clerk who had been employed at the Mayor's office, did not know how to go about the work of instructing the girl. The pupil rebelled, got her ears boxed, and rushed away to shed tears on the lap of Catherine, who always took her part. After this the two women wrangled, and M. Roque ordered them to hold their tongues. He had married only out of tender regard for his daughter, and did not wish to be annoyed by them.

She often wore a white dress with ribbons, and pantalettes trimmed with lace; and on great festival-days she would leave the house attired like a princess, in order to mortify a little the matrons of the town, who forbade their brats to associate with her on account of her illegitimate birth.

She passed her life nearly always by herself in the garden, went see-sawing on the swing, chased butterflies, then suddenly stopped to watch the floral beetles swooping down on the rose-trees. It was, no doubt, these habits which imparted to her face an expression at the same time of audacity and dreaminess. She had, moreover, a figure like Marthe, so that Frederick said to her, at their second interview:

"Will you permit me to kiss you, mademoiselle?"

The little girl lifted up her head and replied:

"I will!"

But the stick-hedge separated them from one another.

"We must climb over," said Frederick.

"No, lift me up!"

He stooped over the hedge, and raising her off the ground with his hands, kissed her on both cheeks; then he put her back on her own side by a similar process; and this performance was repeated on the next occasions when they found themselves together.

Without more reserve than a child of four, as soon as she heard her friend coming, she sprang forward to meet him, or else, hiding behind a tree, she began yelping like a dog to frighten him.

One day, when Madame Moreau had gone out, he brought her up to his own room. She opened all the scent-bottles, and pomaded her hair plentifully; then, without the slightest embarrassment, she lay down on the bed, where she remained stretched out at full length, wide awake.

"I fancy myself your wife," she said to him.

Next day he found her all in tears. She confessed that she had been "weeping for her sins;" and, when he wished to know what they were, she hung down her head, and answered:

"Ask me no more!"

The time for first communion was at hand. She had been brought to confession in the morning. The sacrament scarcely made her wiser. Occasionally, she got into a real passion; and Frederick was sent for to appease her.

He often brought her with him in his walks. While he indulged in day-dreams as he walked along, she would gather wild poppies at the edges of the corn-fields; and, when she saw him more melancholy than usual, she tried to console him with her pretty childish prattle. His heart, bereft of love, fell back on this friendship inspired by a little girl. He gave her sketches of old fogies, told her stories, and devoted himself to reading books for her.

He began with the *Annales Romantiques,* a collection of prose and verse celebrated at the period. Then, forgetting her age, so much was he charmed by her intelligence, he read for her in succession, *Atala, Cinq-Mars,* and *Les Feuilles d' Automne.* But one night (she had that very evening heard *Macbeth* in Letourneur's simple translation) she woke up, exclaiming:

"The spot! the spot!" Her teeth chattered, she shivered, and, fixing terrified glances on her right hand, she kept rubbing it, saying:

"Always a spot!"

At last a doctor was brought, who directed that she should be kept free from violent emotions.

The townsfolk saw in this only an unfavourable prognostic for her morals. It was said that "young Moreau" wished to make an actress of her later.

Soon another event became the subject of discussion — namely, the arrival of uncle Barthélemy. Madame Moreau gave up her sleeping-apartment to him, and was so gracious as to serve up meat to him on fast-days.

The old man was not very agreeable. He was perpetually making comparisons between Havre and Nogent, the air of which he considered heavy, the bread bad, the streets ill-paved, the food indifferent, and the inhabitants very lazy. "How wretched trade is with you in this place!" He blamed his deceased brother for his extravagance, pointing out by way of contrast that he had himself accumulated an income of twenty-seven thousand livres a year. At last, he left at the end of the week, and on the footboard of the carriage gave utterance to these by no means re-assuring words:

"I am always very glad to know that you are in a good position."

"You will get nothing," said Madame Moreau as they re-entered the dining-room.

He had come only at her urgent request, and for eight days she had been seeking, on her part, for an opening — only too clearly perhaps. She repented now of having done so, and remained seated in her armchair with her head bent down and her lips tightly pressed together. Frederick sat opposite, staring at her; and they were both silent, as they had been five years before on his return home by the Montereau steamboat. This coincidence, which presented itself even to her mind, recalled Madame Arnoux to his recollection.

At that moment the crack of a whip outside the window reached their ears, while a voice was heard calling out to him.

It was Père Roque, who was alone in his tilted cart. He was going to spend the whole day at La Fortelle with M. Dambreuse, and cordially offered to drive Frederick there.

"You have no need of an invitation as long as you are with me. Don't be afraid!"

Frederick felt inclined to accept this offer. But how would he explain his fixed sojourn at Nogent? He had not a proper summer suit. Finally, what would his mother say? He accordingly decided not to go.

From that time, their neighbour exhibited less friendliness. Louise was growing tall; Madame Éléonore fell dangerously ill; and the intimacy broke off, to the great delight of Madame Moreau, who feared lest her son's prospects of being settled in life might be affected by association with such people.

She was thinking of purchasing for him the registrarship of the Court of Justice. Frederick raised no particular objection to this scheme. He now accompanied her to mass; in the evening he took a hand in a game of "all fours." He became accustomed to provincial habits of life, and allowed himself to slide into them; and even his love had assumed a character of mournful sweetness, a kind of soporific charm. By dint of having poured out his grief in his letters, mixed it up with everything he read, given full vent to it during his walks through the country, he had almost exhausted it, so that Madame Arnoux was for him, as it were, a dead woman whose tomb he wondered that he did not know, so tranquil and resigned had his affection for her now become.

One day, the 12th of December, 1845, about nine o'clock in the morning, the cook brought up a letter to his room. The address, which was in big characters, was written in a hand he was not acquainted with; and Frederick, feeling sleepy, was in no great hurry to break the seal. At length, when he did so, he read:

"Justice of the Peace at Havre,
111th Arrondissement.

"MONSIEUR,—Monsieur Moreau, your uncle, having died intestate——"

He had fallen in for the inheritance! As if a conflagration had burst out behind the wall, he jumped out of bed in his shirt, with his feet bare. He passed his hand over his face, doubting the evidence of his own eyes, believing that he was still dreaming, and in order to make his mind more clearly conscious of the reality of the event, he flung the window wide open.

There had been a fall of snow; the roofs were white, and he even recognised in the yard outside a washtub which had caused him to stumble after dark the evening before.

He read the letter over three times in succession. Could there be anything more certain? His uncle's entire fortune! A yearly income of twenty-seven thousand livres!* And he was overwhelmed with frantic joy at the idea of seeing Madame Arnoux once more. With the vividness of a hallucination he saw himself beside her, at her house, bringing her some present in silver paper, while at the door stood a tilbury—no, a brougham rather!—a black brougham, with a servant in brown livery. He could hear

---

* About £1,350.—TRANSLATOR.

his horse pawing the ground and the noise of the curb-chain mingling with the rippling sound of their kisses. And every day this was renewed indefinitely. He would receive them in his own house: the dining-room would be furnished in red leather; the boudoir in yellow silk; sofas everywhere! and such a variety of whatnots, china vases, and carpets! These images came in so tumultuous a fashion into his mind that he felt his head turning round. Then he thought of his mother; and he descended the stairs with the letter in his hand.

Madame Moreau made an effort to control her emotion, but could not keep herself from swooning. Frederick caught her in his arms and kissed her on the forehead.

"Dear mother, you can now buy back your carriage — laugh then! shed no more tears! be happy!"

Ten minutes later the news had travelled as far as the faubourgs. Then M. Benoist, M. Gamblin, M. Chambion, and other friends hurried towards the house. Frederick got away for a minute in order to write to Deslauriers. Then other visitors turned up. The afternoon passed in congratulations. They had forgotten all about "Roque's wife," who, however, was declared to be "very low."

When they were alone, the same evening, Madame Moreau said to her son that she would advise him to set up as an advocate at Troyes. As he was better known in his own part of the country than in any other, he might more easily find there a profitable connection.

"Ah, it is too hard!" exclaimed Frederick. He had scarcely grasped his good fortune in his hands when he longed to carry it to Madame Arnoux. He announced his express determination to live in Paris.

"And what are you going to do there?"

"Nothing!"

Madame Moreau, astonished at his manner, asked what he intended to become.

"A minister," was Frederick's reply. And he declared that he was not at all joking, that he meant to plunge at once into diplomacy, and that his studies and his instincts impelled him in that direction. He would first enter the Council of State under M. Dambreuse's patronage.

"So then, you know him?"

"Oh, yes — through M. Roque."

"That is singular," said Madame Moreau. He had awakened in her heart her former dreams of ambition. She internally abandoned herself to them, and said no more about other matters.

If he had yielded to his impatience, Frederick would have started that very instant. Next morning every seat in the diligence had been engaged; and so he kept eating out his heart till seven o'clock in the evening.

They had sat down to dinner when three prolonged tolls of the church-bell fell on their ears; and the housemaid, coming in, informed them that Madame Éléonore had just died.

This death, after all, was not a misfortune for anyone, not even for her child. The young girl would only find it all the better for herself afterwards.

As the two houses were close to one another, a great coming and going and a clatter of tongues could be heard; and the idea of this corpse being so near them threw a certain funereal gloom over their parting. Madame Moreau wiped her eyes two or three times. Frederick felt his heart oppressed.

When the meal was over, Catherine stopped him between two doors. Mademoiselle had peremptorily expressed a wish to see him. She was waiting for him in the garden. He went out there, strode over the hedge, and knocking more or less against the trees, directed his steps towards M. Roque's house. Lights were glittering through a window in the second story then a form appeared in the midst of the darkness, and a voice whispered:

"'Tis I!"

She seemed to him taller than usual, owing to her black dress, no doubt. Not knowing what to say to her, he contented himself with catching her hands, and sighing forth:

"Ah! my poor Louise!"

She did not reply. She gazed at him for a long time with a look of sad, deep earnestness.

Frederick was afraid of missing the coach; he fancied that he could hear the rolling of wheels some distance away, and, in order to put an end to the interview without any delay:

"Catherine told me that you had something——"

"Yes—'tis true! I wanted to tell you——"

He was astonished to find that she addressed him in the plural; and, as she again relapsed into silence:

"Well, what?"

"I don't know. I forget! Is it true that you're going away?"

"Yes, I'm starting just now."

She repeated: "Ah! just now?—for good?— we'll never see one another again?"

She was choking with sobs.

"Good-bye! good-bye! embrace me then!"

And she threw her arms about him passionately.

CHAPTER VII.

A Change of Fortune.

HEN he had taken his place behind the other passengers in the front of the diligence, and when the vehicle began to shake as the five horses started into a brisk trot all at the same time, he allowed himself to plunge into an intoxicating dream of the future. Like an architect drawing up the plan of a palace, he mapped out his life beforehand. He filled it with dainties and with splendours; it rose up to the sky; a profuse display of allurements could be seen there; and so deeply was he buried in the contemplation of these things that he lost sight of all external objects.

At the foot of the hill of Sourdun his attention was directed to the stage which they had reached in their journey. They had travelled only about five kilometres * at the most. He was annoyed at this tardy rate of travelling. He pulled down the coach-window in order to get a view of the road. He asked the conductor several times at what hour they would

---

* A little over three miles.— Translator.

reach their destination. However, he eventually regained his composure, and remained seated in his corner of the vehicle with eyes wide open.

The lantern, which hung from the postilion's seat, threw its light on the buttocks of the shaft-horses. In front, only the manes of the other horses could be seen undulating like white billows. Their breathing caused a kind of fog to gather at each side of the team. The little iron chains of the harness rang; the windows shook in their sashes; and the heavy coach went rolling at an even pace over the pavement. Here and there could be distinguished the wall of a barn, or else an inn standing by itself. Sometimes, as they entered a village, a baker's oven threw out gleams of light; and the gigantic silhouettes of the horses kept rushing past the walls of the opposite houses. At every change of horses, when the harness was unfastened, there was a great silence for a minute. Overhead, under the awning, some passenger might be heard tapping with his feet, while a woman sitting at the threshold of the door screened her candle with her hand. Then the conductor would jump on the footboard, and the vehicle would start on its way again.

At Mormans, the striking of the clocks announced that it was a quarter past one.

"So then we are in another day," he thought, "we have been in it for some time!"

But gradually his hopes and his recollections, Nogent, the Rue de Choiseul, Madame Arnoux, and his mother, all got mixed up together.

He was awakened by the dull sound of wheels passing over planks: they were crossing the Pont de Charenton — it was Paris. Then his two travelling

companions, the first taking off his cap, and the
second his silk handkerchief, put on their hats, and
began to chat.

The first, a big, red-faced man in a velvet frock-
coat, was a merchant; the second was coming up to
the capital to consult a physician; and, fearing that
he had disturbed this gentleman during the night,
Frederick spontaneously apologised to him, so much
had the young man's heart been softened by the feelings of happiness that possessed it. The wharf of
the wet dock being flooded, no doubt, they went
straight ahead; and once more they could see green
fields. In the distance, tall factory-chimneys were
sending forth their smoke. Then they turned into
Ivry. Then drove up a street: all at once, he saw
before him the dome of the Panthéon.

The plain, quite broken up, seemed a waste of
ruins. The enclosing wall of the fortifications made
a horizontal swelling there; and, on the footpath, on
the ground at the side of the road, little branchless
trees were protected by laths bristling with nails.
Establishments for chemical products and timber-
merchants' yards made their appearance alternately.
High gates, like those seen in farmhouses, afforded
glimpses, through their opening leaves, of wretched
yards within, full of filth, with puddles of dirty water
in the middle of them. Long wine-shops, of the
colour of ox's blood, displayed in the first floor, between the windows, two billiard-cues crossing one
another, with a wreath of painted flowers. Here and
there might be noticed a half-built plaster hut, which
had been allowed to remain unfinished. Then the
double row of houses was no longer interrupted; and
over their bare fronts enormous tin cigars showed

themselves at some distance from each other, indicating tobacconists' shops. Midwives' signboards represented in each case a matron in a cap rocking a doll under a counterpane trimmed with lace. The corners of the walls were covered with placards, which, three-quarters torn, were quivering in the wind like rags. Workmen in blouses, brewers' drays, laundresses' and butchers' carts passed along. A thin rain was falling. It was cold. There was a pale sky; but two eyes, which to him were as precious as the sun, were shining behind the haze.

They had to wait a long time at the barrier, for vendors of poultry, wagoners, and a flock of sheep caused an obstruction there. The sentry, with his great-coat thrown back, walked to and fro in front of his box, to keep himself warm. The clerk who collected the city-dues clambered up to the roof of the diligence, and a cornet-à-piston sent forth a flourish. They went down the boulevard at a quick trot, the whipple-trees clapping and the traces hanging loose. The lash of the whip went cracking through the moist air. The conductor uttered his sonorous shout:

"Look alive! look alive! oho!" and the scavengers drew out of the way, the pedestrians sprang back, the mud gushed against the coach-windows; they crossed dung-carts, cabs, and omnibuses. At length, the iron gate of the Jardin des Plantes came into sight.

The Seine, which was of a yellowish colour, almost reached the platforms of the bridges. A cool breath of air issued from it. Frederick inhaled it with his utmost energy, drinking in this good air of Paris, which seems to contain the effluvia of love and the emanations of the intellect. He was touched with

emotion at the first glimpse of a hackney-coach. He gazed with delight on the thresholds of the wine-merchants' shops garnished with straw, on the shoe-blacks with their boxes, on the lads who sold groceries as they shook their coffee-burners. Women hurried along at a jog-trot with umbrellas over their heads. He bent forward to try whether he could distinguish their faces — chance might have led Madame Arnoux to come out.

The shops displayed their wares. The crowd grew denser; the noise in the streets grew louder. After passing the Quai Saint-Bernard, the Quai de la Tournelle, and the Quai Montebello, they drove along the Quai Napoléon. He was anxious to see the windows there; but they were too far away from him. Then they once more crossed the Seine over the Pont-Neuf, and descended in the direction of the Louvre; and, having traversed the Rues Saint-Honoré, Croix des Petits-Champs, and Du Bouloi, he reached the Rue Coq-Héron, and entered the courtyard of the hotel.

To make his enjoyment last the longer, Frederick dressed himself as slowly as possible, and even walked as far as the Boulevard Montmartre. He smiled at the thought of presently beholding once more the beloved name on the marble plate. He cast a glance upwards; there was no longer a trace of the display in the windows, the pictures, or anything else.

He hastened to the Rue de Choiseul. M. and Madame Arnoux no longer resided there, and a woman next door was keeping an eye on the porter's lodge. Frederick waited to see the porter himself. After some time he made his appearance — it was no longer the same man. He did not know their address.

5—11

Frederick went into a café, and, while at breakfast, consulted the Commercial Directory. There were
three hundred Arnoux in it, but no Jacques Arnoux.
Where, then, were they living? Pellerin ought to
know.

He made his way to the very top of the Faubourg Poissonnière, to the artist's studio. As the
door had neither a bell nor a knocker, he rapped
loudly on it with his knuckles, and then called out —
shouted. But the only response was the echo of his
voice from the empty house.

After this he thought of Hussonnet; but where
could he discover a man of that sort? On one occasion he had waited on Hussonnet when the latter
was paying a visit to his mistress's house in the Rue
de Fleurus. Frederick had just reached the Rue de
Fleurus when he became conscious of the fact that
he did not even know the lady's name.

He had recourse to the Prefecture of Police. He
wandered from staircase to staircase, from office to
office. He found that the Intelligence Department
was closed for the day, and was told to come back
again next morning.

Then he called at all the picture-dealers' shops
that he could discover, and enquired whether they
could give him any information as to Arnoux's
whereabouts. The only answer he got was that M.
Arnoux was no longer in the trade.

At last, discouraged, weary, sickened, he returned
to his hotel, and went to bed. Just as he was
stretching himself between the sheets, an idea flashed
upon him which made him leap up with delight:

"Regimbart! what an idiot I was not to think of
him before!"

Next morning, at seven o'clock, he arrived in the Rue Notre Dame des Victoires, in front of a dram-shop, where Regimbart was in the habit of drinking white wine. It was not yet open. He walked about the neighbourhood, and at the end of about half-an-hour, presented himself at the place once more. Regimbart had left it.

Frederick rushed out into the street. He fancied that he could even notice Regimbart's hat some distance away. A hearse and some mourning coaches intercepted his progress. When they had got out of the way, the vision had disappeared.

Fortunately, he recalled to mind that the Citizen breakfasted every day at eleven o'clock sharp, at a little restaurant in the Place Gaillon. All he had to do was to wait patiently till then; and, after sauntering about from the Bourse to the Madeleine, and from the Madeleine to the Gymnase, so long that it seemed as if it would never come to an end, Frederick, just as the clocks were striking eleven, entered the restaurant in the Rue Gaillon, certain of finding Regimbart there.

"Don't know!" said the restaurant-keeper, in an unceremonious tone.

Frederick persisted: the man replied:

"I have no longer any acquaintance with him, Monsieur"—and, as he spoke, he raised his eyebrows majestically and shook his head in a mysterious fashion.

But, in their last interview, the Citizen had referred to the Alexandre smoking-divan. Frederick swallowed a cake, jumped into a cab, and asked the driver whether there happened to be anywhere on the heights of Sainte-Geneviève a certain Café Alexandre. The cabman drove him to the Rue des Francs

Bourgeois Saint-Michel, where there was an establishment of that name, and in answer to his question:

"M. Regimbart, if you please?" the keeper of the café said with an unusually gracious smile:

"We have not seen him as yet, Monsieur," while he directed towards his wife, who sat behind the counter, a look of intelligence. And the next moment, turning towards the clock:

"But he'll be here, I hope, in ten minutes, or at most a quarter of an hour. Celestin, hurry with the newspapers! What would Monsieur like to take?"

Though he did not want to take anything, Frederick swallowed a glass of rum, then a glass of kirsch, then a glass of curaçoa, then several glasses of grog, both cold and hot. He read through that day's *Siècle,* and then read it over again; he examined the caricatures in the *Charivari* down to the very tissue of the paper. When he had finished, he knew the advertisements by heart. From time to time, the tramp of boots on the footpath outside reached his ears — it was he! and some one's form would trace its outlines on the window-panes; but it invariably passed on.

In order to get rid of the sense of weariness he experienced, Frederick shifted his seat. He took up his position at the lower end of the room; then at the right; after that at the left; and he remained in the middle of the bench with his arms stretched out. But a cat, daintily pressing down the velvet at the back of the seat, startled him by giving a sudden spring, in order to lick up the spots of syrup on the tray; and the child of the house, an insufferable brat of four, played noisily with a rattle on the bar steps. His mother, a pale-faced little woman, with decayed teeth, was smiling in a stupid sort of way. What in the world could Regimbart be doing? Frederick waited for him in an exceedingly miserable frame of mind.

The rain clattered like hail on the covering of the cab. Through the opening in the muslin curtain he could see the poor horse in the street more motionless than a horse made of wood. The stream of water, becoming enormous, trickled down between two spokes of the wheels, and the coachman was nodding drowsily with the horsecloth wrapped round him for protection, but fearing lest his fare might give him the slip, he opened the door every now and then, with the rain dripping from him as if falling from a mountain torrent; and, if things could get worn out by looking at them, the clock ought to have by this time been utterly dissolved, so frequently did Frederick rivet his eyes on it. However, it kept going. "Mine host" Alexandre walked up and down repeating, "He'll come! Cheer up! he'll come!" and, in order to divert his thoughts, talked politics, holding forth at some length. He even carried civility so far as to propose a game of dominoes.

At length when it was half-past four, Frederick, who had been there since about twelve, sprang to his feet, and declared that he would not wait any longer.

"I can't understand it at all myself," replied the café-keeper, in a tone of straightforwardness. "This is the first time that M. Ledoux has failed to come!"

"What! Monsieur Ledoux?"

"Why, yes, Monsieur!"

"I said Regimbart," exclaimed Frederick, exasperated.

"Ah! a thousand pardons! You are making a mistake! Madame Alexandre, did not Monsieur say M. Ledoux?"

And, questioning the waiter: "You heard him yourself, just as I did?"

No doubt, to pay his master off for old scores, the waiter contented himself with smiling.

Frederick drove back to the boulevards, indignant at having his time wasted, raging against the Citizen, but craving for his presence as if for that of a god, and firmly resolved to drag him forth, if necessary, from the depths of the most remote cellars. The vehicle in which he was driving only irritated him the more, and he accordingly got rid of it. His ideas were in a state of confusion. Then all the names of the cafés which he had heard pronounced by that idiot burst forth at the same time from his memory like the thousand pieces of an exhibition of fireworks — the Café Gascard, the Café Grimbert, the Café Halbout, the Bordelais smoking-divan, the Havanais, the Havrais, the Bœuf à la Mode, the Brasserie Allemande, and the Mère Morel; and he made his way to all of them in succession. But in one he was told that Regimbart had just gone out; in another, that he might perhaps call at a later hour; in a third, that they had not seen him for six months; and, in another place, that he had the day before ordered a leg of mutton for Saturday. Finally, at Vautier's dining-rooms, Frederick, on opening the door, knocked against the waiter.

"Do you know M. Regimbart?"

"What, monsieur! do I know him? 'Tis I who have the honour of attending on him. He's upstairs —he is just finishing his dinner!"

And, with a napkin under his arm, the master of the establishment himself accosted him:

"You're asking him for M. Regimbart, monsieur? He was here a moment ago."

Frederick gave vent to an oath, but the proprietor of the dining-rooms stated that he would find the gentleman as a matter of certainty at Bouttevilain's.

"I assure you, on my honour, he left a little earlier than usual, for he had a business appointment with some gentlemen. But you'll find him, I tell you again, at Bouttevilain's, in the Rue Saint-Martin, No. 92, the second row of steps at the left, at the end of the courtyard — first floor — door to the right!"

At last, he saw Regimbart, in a cloud of tobacco-smoke, by himself, at the lower end of the refresh-ment-room, near the billiard-table, with a glass of beer in front of him, and his chin lowered in a thoughtful attitude.

"Ah! I have been a long time searching for you!"

Without rising, Regimbart extended towards him only two fingers, and, as if he had seen Frederick the day before, he gave utterance to a number of commonplace remarks about the opening of the session.

Frederick interrupted him, saying in the most natural tone he could assume:

"Is Arnoux going on well?"

The reply was a long time coming, as Regimbart was gargling the liquor in his throat:

"Yes, not badly."

"Where is he living now?"

"Why, in the Rue Paradis Poissonnière," the Citizen returned with astonishment.

"What number?"

1

"Thirty-seven — confound it! what a funny fellow you are!"

Frederick rose.

"What! are you going?"

"Yes, yes! I have to make a call — some business matter I had forgotten! Good-bye!"

Frederick went from the smoking-divan to the Arnoux's residence, as if carried along by a tepid wind, with a sensation of extreme ease such as people experience in dreams.

He found himself soon on the second floor in front of a door, at the ringing of whose bell a servant appeared. A second door was flung open. Madame Arnoux was seated near the fire. Arnoux jumped up, and rushed across to embrace Frederick. She had on her lap a little boy not quite three years old. Her daughter, now as tall as herself, was standing up at the opposite side of the mantelpiece.

"Allow me to present this gentleman to you," said Arnoux, taking his son up in his arms. And he amused himself for some minutes in making the child jump up in the air very high, and then catching him with both hands as he came down.

"You'll kill him! — ah! good heavens, have done!" exclaimed Madame Arnoux.

But Arnoux, declaring that there was not the slightest danger, still kept tossing up the child, and even addressed him in words of endearment such as nurses use in the Marseillaise dialect, his natal tongue: "Ah! my fine picheoun! my ducksy of a little nightingale!"

Then, he asked Frederick why he had been so long without writing to them, what he had been doing down in the country, and what brought him back.

"As for me, I am at present, my dear friend, a dealer in faïence. But let us talk about yourself!"

Frederick gave as reasons for his absence a protracted lawsuit and the state of his mother's health. He laid special stress on the latter subject in order to make himself interesting. He ended by saying that this time he was going to settle in Paris for good; and he said nothing about the inheritance, lest it might be prejudicial to his past.

The curtains, like the upholstering of the furniture, were of maroon damask wool. Two pillows were close beside one another on the bolster. On the coal-fire a kettle was boiling; and the shade of the lamp, which stood near the edge of the chest of drawers, darkened the apartment. Madame Arnoux wore a large blue merino dressing-gown. With her face turned towards the fire and one hand on the shoulder of the little boy, she unfastened with the other the child's bodice. The youngster in his shirt began to cry, while scratching his head, like the son of M. Alexandre.

Frederick expected that he would have felt spasms of joy; but the passions grow pale when we find ourselves in an altered situation; and, as he no longer saw Madame Arnoux in the environment wherein he had known her, she seemed to him to have lost some of her fascination; to have degenerated in some way that he could not comprehend — in fact, not to be the same. He was astonished at the serenity of his own heart. He made enquiries about some old friends, about Pellerin, amongst others.

"I don't see him often," said Arnoux. She added:

"We no longer entertain as we used to do formerly!"

Was the object of this to let him know that he would get no invitation from them? But Arnoux, continuing to exhibit the same cordiality, reproached him for not having come to dine with them uninvited; and he explained why he had changed his business.

"What are you to do in an age of decadence like ours? Great painting is gone out of fashion! Besides, we may import art into everything. You know that, for my part, I am a lover of the beautiful. I must bring you one of these days to see my earthenware works."

And he wanted to show Frederick immediately some of his productions in the store which he had between the ground-floor and the first floor.

Dishes, soup-tureens, and washhand-basins encumbered the floor. Against the walls were laid out large squares of pavement for bathrooms and dressing-rooms, with mythological subjects in the Renaissance style; whilst in the centre, a pair of whatnots, rising up to the ceiling, supported ice-urns, flower-pots, candelabra, little flower-stands, and large statuettes of many colours, representing a negro or a shepherdess in the Pompadour fashion. Frederick, who was cold and hungry, was bored with Arnoux's display of his wares. He hurried off to the Café Anglais, where he ordered a sumptuous supper, and while eating, said to himself:

"I was well off enough below there with all my troubles! She scarcely took any notice of me! How like a shopkeeper's wife!"

And in an abrupt expansion of healthfulness, he formed egoistic resolutions. He felt his heart as hard as the table on which his elbows rested. So then he could by this time plunge fearlessly into the vortex of society. The thought of the Dambreuses recurred to his mind. He would make use of them. Then he recalled Deslauriers to mind. "Ah! faith, so much the worse!" Nevertheless, he sent him a note by a messenger, making an appointment with him for the following day, in order that they might breakfast together.

Fortune had not been so kind to the other.

He had presented himself at the examination for a fellowship with a thesis on the law of wills, in which he maintained that the powers of testators ought to be restricted as much as possible; and, as his adversary provoked him in such a way as to make him say foolish things, he gave utterance to many of these absurdities without in any way inducing the examiners to falter in deciding that he was wrong. Then chance so willed it that he should choose by lot, as a subject for a lecture, Prescription. Thereupon, Deslauriers gave vent to some lamentable theories: the questions in dispute in former times ought to be brought forward as well as those which had recently arisen; why should the proprietor be deprived of his estate because he could furnish his title-deeds only after the lapse of thirty-one years? This was giving the security of the honest man to the inheritor of the enriched thief. Every injustice was consecrated by extending this law, which was a form of tyranny, the abuse of force! He had even exclaimed: "Abolish it; and the Franks will no longer oppress the Gauls, the English oppress the Irish, the Yankee oppress the Redskins, the Turks oppress the Arabs, the whites oppress the blacks, Poland——"

The President interrupted him: "Well! well! Monsieur, we have nothing to do with your political opinions — you will have them represented in **your** behalf by-and-by!"

Deslauriers did not wish to have his opinions represented; but this unfortunate Title XX. of **the** Third Book of the Civil Code had become a sort of mountain over which he stumbled.   He was elaborating a great work on "Prescription considered as the Basis of the Civil Law and of the Law of Nature amongst Peoples"; and he got lost in Dunod, Rogerius, Balbus, Merlin, Vazeille, Savigny, Traplong, and other weighty authorities on the subject.   In order to have more leisure for the purpose of devoting himself to this task, he had resigned his post of head-clerk. He lived by giving private tuitions and preparing theses; and at the meetings of newly-fledged barristers to rehearse legal arguments he frightened by his display of virulence those who held conservative views, all the young doctrinaires who acknowledged M. Guizot as their master — so that in a certain set he had gained a sort of celebrity, mingled, in a slight degree, with lack of confidence in him as an individual.

He came to keep the appointment in a big paletot, lined with red flannel, like the one Sénécal used to wear in former days.

Human respect on account of the passers-by prevented them from straining one another long in an embrace of friendship; and they made their way to Véfour's arm-in-arm, laughing pleasantly, though with tear-drops lingering in the depths of their eyes. Then, as soon as they were free from observation, Deslauriers exclaimed:

"Ah! damn it! we'll have a jolly time of it now!"

Frederick was not quite pleased to find Deslauriers all at once associating himself in this way with his own newly-acquired inheritance. His friend exhibited too much pleasure on account of them both, and not enough on his account alone.

After this, Deslauriers gave details about the reverse he had met with, and gradually told Frederick all about his occupations and his daily existence, speaking of himself in a stoical fashion, and of others in tones of intense bitterness. He found fault with everything; there was not a man in office who was not an idiot or a rascal. He flew into a passion against the waiter for having a glass badly rinsed, and, when Frederick uttered a reproach with a view to mitigating his wrath: "As if I were going to annoy myself with such numbskulls, who, you must know, can earn as much as six and even eight thousand francs a year, who are electors, perhaps eligible as candidates. Ah! no, no!"

Then, with a sprightly air, "But I've forgotten that I'm talking to a capitalist, to a Mondor,* for you are a Mondor now!"

And, coming back to the question of the inheritance, he gave expression to this view — that collateral successorship (a thing unjust in itself, though in the present case he was glad it was possible) would be abolished one of these days at the approaching revolution.

"Do you believe in that?" said Frederick.

"Be sure of it!" he replied. "This sort of thing cannot last. There is too much suffering. When I see into the wretchedness of men like Sénécal——"

"Always Sénécal!" thought Frederick.

---

* Mondor was a celebrated Italian charlatan, who, in the seventeenth century, settled in Paris and made a large fortune.—TRANSLATOR.

"But, at all events, tell me the news? Are you still in love with Madame Arnoux? Is it all over — eh?"

Frederick, not knowing what answer to give him, closed his eyes and hung down his head.

With regard to Arnoux, Deslauriers told him that the journal was now the property of Hussonnet, who had transformed it. It was called *"L'Art,* a literary institution — a company with shares of one hundred francs each; capital of the firm, forty thousand francs," each shareholder having the right to put into it his own contributions; for "the company has for its object to publish the works of beginners, to spare talent, perchance genius, the sad crises which drench," etc.

"You see the dodge!" There was, however, something to be effected by the change — the tone of the journal could be raised; then, without any delay, while retaining the same writers, and promising a continuation of the feuilleton, to supply the subscribers with a political organ: the amount to be advanced would not be very great.

"What do you think of it? Come! would you like to have a hand in it?"

Frederick did not reject the proposal; but he pointed out that it was necessary for him to attend to the regulation of his affairs.

"After that, if you require anything ——"

"Thanks, my boy!" said Deslauriers.

Then, they smoked puros, leaning with their elbows on the shelf covered with velvet beside the window. The sun was shining; the air was balmy. Flocks of birds, fluttering about, swooped down into the garden. The statues of bronze and marble, washed by the rain, were glistening. Nursery-maids.

wearing aprons, were seated on chairs, chatting together; and the laughter of children could be heard
mingling with the continuous plash that came from
the sheaf-jets of the fountain.

Frederick was troubled by Deslauriers' irritability;
but under the influence of the wine which circulated
through his veins, half-asleep, in a state of torpor,
with the sun shining full on his face, he was no
longer conscious of anything save a profound sense
of comfort, a kind of voluptuous feeling that stupefied
him, as a plant is saturated with heat and moisture.
Deslauriers, with half-closed eyelids, was staring va-
cantly into the distance.   His breast swelled, and he
broke out in the following strain:

"Ah! those were better days when Camille Des-
moulins, standing below there on a table, drove the
people on to the Bastille. Men really lived in those
times; they could assert themselves, and prove their
strength!   Simple   advocates   commanded   generals.
Kings were beaten by beggars; whilst now ——"

He stopped, then added all of a sudden:

"Pooh! the future is big with great things!"

And, drumming a battle-march on the window-
panes, he declaimed some verses of Barthélemy, which
ran thus:

> "'That dread Assembly shall again appear,
>   Which, after forty years, fills you with fear,
>   Marching with giant stride and dauntless soul'*

—I don't know the rest of it! But 'tis late; suppose
we go?"

---

* "Elle reparaitra, la terrible Assemblée,
     Dont, après quarante ans, votre tête est troublée,
     Colosse qui sans peur marche d'un pas puissant."

And he went on setting forth his theories in the street.

Frederick, without listening to him, was looking at certain materials and articles of furniture in the shop-windows which would be suitable for his new residence in Paris; and it was, perhaps, the thought of Madame Arnoux that made him stop before a second-hand dealer's window, where three plates made of fine ware were exposed to view. They were decorated with yellow arabesques with metallic reflections, and were worth a hundred crowns apiece. He got them put by.

"For my part, if I were in your place," said Deslauriers, "I would rather buy silver plate," revealing by this love of substantial things the man of mean extraction.

As soon as he was alone, Frederick repaired to the establishment of the celebrated Pomadère, where he ordered three pairs of trousers, two coats, a pelisse trimmed with fur, and five waistcoats. Then he called at a bootmaker's, a shirtmaker's, and a hatter's, giving them directions in each shop to make the greatest possible haste. Three days later, on the evening of his return from Havre, he found his complete wardrobe awaiting him in his Parisian abode; and impatient to make use of it, he resolved to pay an immediate visit to the Dambreuses. But it was too early yet — scarcely eight o'clock.

"Suppose I went to see the others?" said he to himself.

He came upon Arnoux, all alone, in the act of shaving in front of his glass. The latter proposed to drive him to a place where they could amuse themselves, and when M. Dambreuse was referred to,

"Ah, that's just lucky! You'll see some of his friends there. Come on, then! It will be good fun!"

Frederick asked to be excused. Madame Arnoux recognised his voice, and wished him good-day, through the partition, for her daughter was indisposed, and she was also rather unwell herself. The noise of a soup-ladle against a glass could be heard from within, and all those quivering sounds made by things being lightly moved about, which are usual in a sick-room. Then Arnoux left his dressing-room to say good-bye to his wife. He brought forward a heap of reasons for going out:

"You know well that it is a serious matter! I must go there; 'tis a case of necessity. They'll be waiting for me!"

"Go, go, my dear! Amuse yourself!"

Arnoux hailed a hackney-coach:

"Palais Royal, No. 7 Montpensier Gallery." And, as he let himself sink back in the cushions:

"Ah! how tired I am, my dear fellow! It will be the death of me! However, I can tell it to you—to you!"

He bent towards Frederick's ear in a mysterious fashion:

"I am trying to discover again the red of Chinese copper!"

And he explained the nature of the glaze and the little fire.

On their arrival at Chevet's shop, a large hamper was brought to him, which he stowed away in the hackney-coach. Then he bought for his "poor wife" pine-apples and various dainties, and directed that they should be sent early next morning.

After this, they called at a costumer's establishment; it was to a ball they were going.

5—12

Arnoux selected blue velvet breeches, a vest of the same material, and a red wig; Frederick a domino; and they went down the Rue de Laval towards a house the second floor of which was illuminated by coloured lanterns.

At the foot of the stairs they heard violins playing above.

"Where the deuce are you bringing me to?" said Frederick.

"To see a nice girl! don't be afraid!"

The door was opened for them by a groom; and they entered the anteroom, where paletots, mantles, and shawls were thrown together in a heap on some chairs. A young woman in the costume of a dragoon of Louis XIV.'s reign was passing at that moment. It was Mademoiselle Rosanette Bron, the mistress of the place.

"Well?" said Arnoux.

"'Tis done!" she replied.

"Ah! thanks, my angel!"

And he wanted to kiss her.

"Take care, now, you foolish man! You'll spoil the paint on my face!"

Arnoux introduced Frederick.

"Step in there, Monsieur; you are quite welcome!"

She drew aside a door-curtain, and cried out with a certain emphasis:

"Here's my lord Arnoux, girl, and a princely friend of his!"

Frederick was at first dazzled by the lights. He could see nothing save some silk and velvet dresses, naked shoulders, a mass of colours swaying to and fro to the accompaniment of an orchestra hidden be-

hind green foliage, between walls hung with yellow
silk, with pastel portraits here and there and crystal
chandeliers in the style of Louis XVI.'s period. High
lamps, whose globes of roughened glass resembled
snowballs, looked down on baskets of flowers placed
on brackets in the corners; and at the opposite side,
at the rear of a second room, smaller in size, one
could distinguish, in a third, a bed with twisted
posts, and at its head a Venetian mirror.

The dancing stopped, and there were bursts of applause, a hubbub of delight, as Arnoux was seen advancing with his hamper on his head; the eatables
contained in it made a lump in the centre.

"Make way for the lustre!"

Frederick raised his eyes: it was the lustre of old
Saxe that had adorned the shop attached to the office
of *L'Art Industriel.* The memory of former days
was brought back to his mind. But a foot-soldier
of the line in undress, with that silly expression of
countenance ascribed by tradition to conscripts, planted
himself right in front of him, spreading out his
two arms in order to emphasise his astonishment, and,
in spite of the hideous black moustaches, unusually
pointed, which disfigured his face, Frederick recognised his old friend Hussonnet. In a half-Alsatian,
half-negro kind of gibberish, the Bohemian loaded him
with congratulations, calling him his colonel. Frederick, put out of countenance by the crowd of personages assembled around him, was at a loss for an
answer. At a tap on the desk from a fiddlestick, the
partners in the dance fell into their places.

They were about sixty in number, the women being for the most part dressed either as village-girls or
marchionesses, and the men, who were nearly all of

mature age, being got up as wagoners, 'longshoremen, or sailors.

Frederick having taken up his position close to the wall, stared at those who were going through the quadrille in front of him.

An old beau, dressed like a Venetian Doge in a long gown of purple silk, was dancing with Mademoiselle Rosanette, who wore a green coat, laced breeches, and boots of soft leather with gold spurs. The pair in front of them consisted of an Albanian laden with yataghans and a Swiss girl with blue eyes and skin white as milk, who looked as plump as a quail with her chemise-sleeves and red corset exposed to view. In order to turn to account her hair, which fell down to her hips, a tall blonde, a walking lady in the opera, had assumed the part of a female savage; and over her brown swaddling-cloth she displayed nothing save leathern breeches, glass bracelets, and a tinsel diadem, from which rose a large sheaf of peacock's feathers. In front of her, a gentleman who had intended to represent Pritchard,* muffled up in a grotesquely big black coat, was beating time with his elbows on his snuff-box. A little Watteau shepherd in blue-and-silver, like moonlight, dashed his crook against the thyrsus of a Bacchante crowned with grapes, who wore a leopard's skin over her left side, and buskins with gold ribbons, On the other side, a Polish lady, in a spencer of nacarat-coloured velvet, made her gauze petticoat flutter over her pearl-gray stockings, which rose above her fashionable pink boots bordered with white fur.

---

*This probably refers to the English astronomer of that name. — TRANSLATOR.

She was smiling on a big-paunched man of forty, disguised as a choir-boy, who was skipping very high, lifting up his surplice with one hand, and with the other his red clerical cap. But the queen, the star, was Mademoiselle Loulou, a celebrated dancer at public halls. As she had now become wealthy, she wore a large lace collar over her vest of smooth black velvet; and her wide trousers of poppy-coloured silk, clinging closely to her figure, and drawn tight round her waist by a cashmere scarf, had all over their seams little natural white camellias. Her pale face, a little puffed, and with the nose somewhat *retroussé*, looked all the more pert from the disordered appearance of her wig, over which she had with a touch of her hand clapped a man's grey felt hat, so that it covered her right ear; and, with every bounce she made, her pumps, adorned with diamond buckles, nearly reached the nose of her neighbour, a big mediæval baron, who was quite entangled in his steel armour. There was also an angel, with a gold sword in her hand, and two swan's wings over her back, who kept rushing up and down, every minute losing her partner who appeared as Louis XIV., displaying an utter ignorance of the figures and confusing the quadrille.

Frederick, as he gazed at these people, experienced a sense of forlornness, a feeling of uneasiness. He was still thinking of Madame Arnoux and it seemed to him as if he were taking part in some plot that was being hatched against her.

When the quadrille was over, Mademoiselle Rosanette accosted him. She was slightly out of breath, and her gorget, polished like a mirror, swelled up softly under her chin.

"And you, Monsieur," said she, "don't you dance?"

Frederick excused himself; he did not know how to dance.

"Really! but with me? Are you quite sure?" And, poising herself on one hip, with her other knee a little drawn back, while she stroked with her left hand the mother-of-pearl pommel of her sword, she kept staring at him for a minute with a half-beseeching, half-teasing air. At last she said "Good night! then," made a pirouette, and disappeared.

Frederick, dissatisfied with himself, and not well knowing what to do, began to wander through the ball-room.

He entered the boudoir padded with pale blue silk, with bouquets of flowers from the fields, whilst on the ceiling, in a circle of gilt wood, Cupids, emerging out of an azure sky, played over the clouds, resembling down in appearance. This display of luxuries, which would to-day be only trifles to persons like Rosanette, dazzled him, and he admired everything — the artificial convolvuli which adorned the surface of the mirror, the curtains on the mantelpiece, the Turkish divan, and a sort of tent in a recess in the wall, with pink silk hangings and a covering of white muslin overhead. Furniture made of dark wood with inlaid work of copper filled the sleeping apartment, where, on a platform covered with swan's-down, stood the large canopied bedstead trimmed with ostrich-feathers. Pins, with heads made of precious stones, stuck into pincushions, rings trailing over trays, lockets with hoops of gold, and little silver chests, could be distinguished in the shade under the light shed by a Bohemian urn suspended from three chainlets. Through a little door, which was slightly ajar, could be seen a hot-house occupying the en-

tire breadth of a terrace, with an aviary at the other
end.

Here were surroundings specially calculated to
charm him. In a sudden revolt of his youthful blood
he swore that he would enjoy such things; he grew
bold; then, coming back to the place opening into
the drawing-room, where there was now a larger
gathering—it kept moving about in a kind of
luminous pulverulence—he stood to watch the quadrilles, blinking his eyes to see better, and inhaling the
soft perfumes of the women, which floated through
the atmosphere like an immense kiss.

But, close to him, on the other side of the door,
was Pellerin—Pellerin, in full dress, his left arm over
his breast and with his hat and a torn white glove
in his right.

"Halloa! 'Tis a long time since we saw you!
Where the deuce have you been? Gone to travel in
Italy? 'Tis a commonplace country enough—Italy,
eh? not so unique as people say it is? No matter!
Will you bring me your sketches one of these days?"

And, without giving him time to answer, the artist
began talking about himself. He had made considerable progress, having definitely satisfied himself as to
the stupidity of the line. We ought not to look so
much for beauty and unity in a work as for character
and diversity of subject.

"For everything exists in nature; therefore, everything is legitimate; everything is plastic. It is only a
question of catching the note, mind you! I have discovered the secret." and giving him a nudge,
he repeated several times, "I have discovered
the secret, you see! Just look at that little
woman with the headdress of a sphinx who is dan-

cing with a Russian postilion — that's neat, dry, fixed, all in flats and in stiff tones — indigo under the eyes, a patch of vermilion on the cheek, and bistre on the temples — pif! paf!" And with his thumb he drew, as it were, pencil-strokes in the air. "Whilst the big one over there," he went on, pointing towards a fishwife in a cherry gown with a gold cross hanging from her neck, and a lawn fichu fastened round her shoulders, "is nothing but curves. The nostrils are spread out just like the borders of her cap; the corners of the mouth are rising up; the chin sinks: all is fleshy, melting, abundant, tranquil, and sunshiny — a true Rubens! Nevertheless, they are both perfect! Where, then, is the type?" He grew warm with the subject. "What is this but a beautiful woman? What is it but the beautiful? Ah! the beautiful — tell me what that is——"

Frederick interrupted him to enquire who was the merry-andrew with the face of a he-goat, who was in the very act of blessing all the dancers in the middle of a pastourelle.

"Oh! he's not much! — a widower, the father of three boys. He leaves them without breeches, spends his whole day at the club, and lives with the servant!"

"And who is that dressed like a bailiff talking in the recess of the window to a Marquise de Pompadour?"

"The Marquise is Mademoiselle Vandael, formerly an actress at the Gymnase, the mistress of the Doge, the Comte de Palazot. They have now been twenty years living together — nobody can tell why. Had she fine eyes at one time, this woman? As for the citizen by her side, his name is Captain d'Herbigny, an

old man of the hurdy-gurdy sort that you can play
on, with nothing in the world except his Cross of the
Legion of Honour and his pension.   He passes for the
uncle of the grisettes at festival times, arranges duels,
and dines in the city."

"A rascal?" said Frederick.

"No! an honest man!"

"Ha!"

The artist was going on to mention the names of
many others, when, perceiving a gentleman who, like
Molière's physician, wore a big black serge gown
opening very wide as it descended in order to display
all his trinkets:

"The person who presents himself there before you
is Dr. Des Rogis, who, full of rage at not having
made a name for himself, has written a book of med-
ical pornography, and willingly blacks people's boots
in society, while he is at the same time discreet.
These ladies adore him.   He and his wife (that lean
châtelaine in the grey dress) trip about together at
every public place — aye, and at other places too.   In
spite of domestic embarrassments, they have a *day* —
artistic teas, at which verses are recited.   Attention!"

In fact, the doctor came up to them at that moment; and soon they formed all three, at the entrance
to the drawing-room, a group of talkers, which was
presently augmented by Hussonnet, then by the lover
of the female savage, a young poet who displayed,
under a court cloak of Francis I.'s reign, the most
pitiful of anatomies, and finally a sprightly youth disguised as a Turk of the barrier.   But his vest with
its yellow galloon had taken so many voyages on the
backs of strolling dentists, his wide trousers full of
creases, were of so faded a red, his turban, rolled

about like an eel in the Tartar fashion, was so poor
in appearance — in short, his entire costume was so
wretched and made-up, that the women did not attempt to hide their disgust. The doctor consoled
him by pronouncing eulogies on his mistress, the lady
in the dress of a 'longshorewoman. This Turk was a
banker's son.

Between two quadrilles, Rosanette advanced towards the mantelpiece, where an obese little old man,
in a maroon coat with gold buttons, had seated himself in an armchair. In spite of his withered cheeks,
which fell over his white cravat, his hair, still fair,
and curling naturally like that of a poodle, gave him
a certain frivolity of aspect.

She was listening to him with her face bent close
to his. Presently, she accommodated him with a little
glass of syrup; and nothing could be more dainty than
her hands under their laced sleeves, which passed
over the facings of her green coat. When the old
man had swallowed it, he kissed them.

"Why, that's M. Oudry, a neighbor of Arnoux!"

"He has lost her!" said Pellerin, smiling.

A Longjumeau postilion caught her by the waist.
A waltz was beginning. Then all the women, seated
round the drawing-room on benches, rose up quickly
at the same time; and their petticoats, their scarfs,
and their head-dresses went whirling round.

They whirled so close to him that Frederick could
notice the beads of perspiration on their foreheads;
and this gyral movement, more and more lively, regular, provocative of dizzy sensations, communicated to
his mind a sort of intoxication, which made other
images surge up within it, while every woman passed
with the same dazzling effect, and each of them with

a special kind of exciting influence, according to her style of beauty.

The Polish lady, surrendering herself in a languorous fashion, inspired him with a longing to clasp her to his heart while they were both spinning forward on a sledge along a plain covered with snow. Horizons of tranquil voluptuousness in a châlet at the side of a lake opened out under the footsteps of the Swiss girl, who waltzed with her bust erect and her eyelashes drooping. Then, suddenly, the Bacchante, bending back her head with its dark locks, made him dream of devouring caresses in a wood of oleanders, in the midst of a storm, to the confused accompaniment of tabours. The fishwife, who was panting from the rapidity of the music, which was far too great for her, gave vent to bursts of laughter; and he would have liked, while drinking with her in some tavern in the "Porcherons," * to rumple her fichu with both hands, as in the good old times. But the 'longshorewoman, whose light toes barely skimmed the floor, seemed to conceal under the suppleness of her limbs and the seriousness of her face all the refinements of modern love, which possesses the exactitude of a science and the mobility of a bird. Rosanette was whirling with arms akimbo; her wig, in an awkward position, bobbing over her collar, flung iris-powder around her; and, at every turn, she was near catching hold of Frederick with the ends of her gold spurs.

During the closing bar of the waltz, Mademoiselle Vatnaz made her appearance. She had an Algerian

---

* The "Porcherons" was the name given to an old quarter of Paris famous for its taverns, situated between the Rue du Faubourg Montmartre and the Rue de Saint-Lazare.— TRANSLATOR.

handkerchief on her head, a number of piastres on her forehead, antimony at the edges of her eyes, with a kind of paletot made of black cashmere falling over a petticoat of sparkling colour, with stripes of silver; and in her hand she held a tambourine.

Behind her back came a tall fellow in the classical costume of Dante, who happened to be — she now made no concealment any longer about it — the ex-singer of the Alhambra, and who, though his name was Auguste Delamare, had first called himself Anténor Delamarre, then Delmas, then Belmar, and at last Delmar, thus modifying and perfecting his name, as his celebrity increased, for he had forsaken the public-house concert for the theatre, and had even just made his *début* in a noisy fashion at the Ambigu in *Gaspardo le Pêcheur*.

Hussonnet, on seeing him, knitted his brows. Since his play had been rejected, he hated actors. It was impossible to conceive the vanity of individuals of this sort, and above all of this fellow. "What a prig! Just look at him!"

After a light bow towards Rosanette, Delmar leaned back against the mantelpiece; and he remained motionless with one hand over his heart, his left foot thrust forward, his eyes raised towards heaven, with his wreath of gilt laurels above his cowl, while he strove to put into the expression of his face a considerable amount of poetry in order to fascinate the ladies. They made, at some distance, a great circle around him.

But the Vatnaz, having given Rosanette a prolonged embrace, came to beg of Hussonnet to revise, with a view to the improvement of the style, an educational work which she intended to publish, under the title

of "The Young Ladies' Garland," a collection of literature and moral philosophy.

The man of letters promised to assist her in the
preparation of the work. Then she asked him whether
he could not in one of the prints to which he had
access give her friend a slight puff, and even assign
to him, later, some part. Hussonnet had forgotten to
take a glass of punch on account of her.

It was Arnoux who had brewed the beverage;
and, followed by the Comte's groom carrying an
empty tray, he offered it to the ladies with a self-
satisfied air.

When he came to pass in front of M. Oudry,
Rosanette stopped him.

"Well—and this little business?"

He coloured slightly; finally, addressing the old
man:

"Our fair friend tells me that you would have the
kindness——"

"What of that, neighbour? I am quite at your
service!"

And M. Dambreuse's name was pronounced. As
they were talking to one another in low tones, Frederick could only hear indistinctly; and he made his
way to the other side of the mantelpiece, where Rosanette and Delmar were chatting together.

The mummer had a vulgar countenance, made, like
the scenery of the stage, to be viewed from a distance—coarse hands, big feet, and a heavy jaw; and
he disparaged the most distinguished actors, spoke of
poets with patronising contempt, made use of the expressions "my organ," "my physique," "my powers,"
enamelling his conversation with words that were
scarcely intelligible even to himself, and for which he

had quite an affection, such as *"morbidezza,"* "analogue," and "homogeneity."

Rosanette listened to him with little nods of approbation. One could see her enthusiasm bursting out under the paint on her cheeks, and a touch of moisture passed like a veil over her bright eyes of an indefinable colour. How could such a man as this fascinate her? Frederick internally excited himself to greater contempt for him, in order to banish, perhaps, the species of envy which he felt with regard to him.

Mademoiselle Vatnaz was now with Arnoux, and, while laughing from time to time very loudly, she cast glances towards Rosanette, of whom M. Oudry did not lose sight.

Then Arnoux and the Vatnaz disappeared. The old man began talking in a subdued voice to Rosanette.

"Well, yes, 'tis settled then! Leave me alone!"

And she asked Frederick to go and give a look into the kitchen to see whether Arnoux happened to be there.

A battalion of glasses half-full covered the floor; and the saucepans, the pots, the turbot-kettle, and the frying-stove were all in a state of commotion. Arnoux was giving directions to the servants, whom he "thee'd" and "thou'd," beating up the mustard, tasting the sauces, and larking with the housemaid.

"All right," he said; "tell them 'tis ready! I'm going to have it served up."

The dancing had ceased. The women came and sat down; the men were walking about. In the centre of the drawing-room, one of the curtains stretched over a window was swelling in the wind; and the Sphinx, in spite of the observations of everyone, exposed her sweating arms to the current of air.

Where could Rosanette be? Frederick went on further to find her, even into her boudoir and her bedroom. Some, in order to be alone, or to be in pairs, had retreated into the corners. Whisperings intermingled with the shade. There were little laughs stifled under handkerchiefs, and at the sides of women's corsages one could catch glimpses of fans quivering with slow, gentle movements, like the beating of a wounded bird's wings.

As he entered the hot-house, he saw under the large leaves of a caladium near the jet d'eau, Delmar lying on his face on the sofa covered with linen cloth. Rosanette, seated beside him, had passed her fingers through his hair; and they were gazing into each other's faces. At the same moment, Arnoux came in at the opposite side — that which was near the aviary. Delmar sprang to his feet; then he went out at a rapid pace, without turning round; and even paused close to the door to gather a hibiscus flower, with which he adorned his button-hole. Rosanette hung down her head; Frederick, who caught a sight of her profile, saw that she was in tears.

"I say! What's the matter with you?" exclaimed Arnoux.

She shrugged her shoulders without replying.

"Is it on account of him?" he went on.

She threw her arms round his neck, and kissing him on the forehead, slowly:

"You know well that I will always love you, my big fellow! Think no more about it! Let us go to supper!"

A copper chandelier with forty wax tapers lighted up the dining-room, the walls of which were hidden from view under some fine old earthenware that was hung up there; and this crude light, falling perpendicularly, rendered still whiter, amid the side-dishes and the fruits, a huge turbot which occupied the centre of the tablecloth, with plates all round filled with crayfish soup. With a rustle of garments, the women, having arranged their skirts, their sleeves, and their scarfs, took their seats beside one another; the men, standing up, posted themselves at the corners. Pellerin and M. Oudry were placed near Rosanette, Arnoux was facing her. Palazot and his female companion had just gone out.

"Good-bye to them!" said she. "Now let us begin the attack!"

And the choir-boy, a facetious man with a big sign of the cross, said grace.

The ladies were scandalised, and especially the fishwife, the mother of a young girl of whom she wished to make an honest woman. Neither did Arnoux like "that sort of thing," as he considered that religion ought to be respected.

A German clock with a cock attached to it happening to chime out the hour of two, gave rise to a number of jokes about the cuckoo. All kinds of talk followed — puns, anecdotes, bragging remarks, bets, lies taken for truth, improbable assertions, a tumult of words, which soon became dispersed in the form of chats between particular individuals. The wines went round; the dishes succeeded each other; the doctor carved. An orange or a cork would every now and then be flung from a distance. People would quit their seats to go and talk to some one at another end of the table. Rosanette turned round towards Delmar, who sat motionless behind her; Pellerin kept babbling; M. Oudry smiled. Mademoiselle Vatnaz ate, almost alone, a group of crayfish, and the shells crackled under her long teeth. The angel, poised on the piano-stool — the only place on which her wings permitted her to sit down — was placidly masticating without ever stopping.

"What an appetite!" the choir-boy kept repeating in amazement, "what an appetite!"

And the Sphinx drank brandy, screamed out with her throat full, and wriggled like a demon. Suddenly her jaws swelled, and no longer being able to keep down the blood which rushed to her head and nearly choked her, she pressed her napkin against her lips, and threw herself under the table.

Frederick had seen her falling: "'Tis nothing!" And at his entreaties to be allowed to go and look after her, she replied slowly:

"Pooh! what's the good? That's just as pleasant as anything else. Life is not so amusing!"

Then, he shivered, a feeling of icy sadness taking possession of him, as if he had caught a glimpse of whole worlds of wretchedness and despair — a chafing-dish of charcoal beside a folding-bed, the corpses of the Morgue in leathern aprons, with the tap of cold water that fl ws over their heads.

Meanwhile, Hussonnet, squatted at the feet of the female savage, was howling in a hoarse voice in imitation of the actor Grassot:

"Be not cruel, O Celuta! this little family fête is charming! Intoxicate me with delight, my loves! Let us be gay! let us be gay!"

And he began kissing the women on the shoulders. They quivered under the tickling of his moustaches. Then he conceived the idea of breaking a plate against his head by rapping it there with a little energy.

5—13

Others followed his example. The broken earthen-ware flew about in bits like slates in a storm; and the 'longshorewoman exclaimed:

"Don't bother yourselves about it; these cost nothing. We get a present of them from the merchant who makes them!"

Every eye was riveted on Arnoux. He replied:

"Ha! about the invoice—allow me!" desiring, no doubt, to pass for not being, or for no longer being, Rosanette's lover.

But two angry voices here made themselves heard:

"Idiot!"

"Rascal!"

"I am at your command!"

"So am I at yours!"

It was the mediæval knight and the Russian postilion who were disputing, the latter having maintained that armour dispensed with bravery, while the other regarded this view as an insult. He desired to fight; all interposed to prevent him, and in the midst of the uproar the captain tried to make himself heard.

"Listen to me, messieurs! One word! I have some experience, messieurs!"

Rosanette, by tapping with her knife on a glass, succeeded eventually in restoring silence, and, addressing the knight, who had kept his helmet on, and then the postilion, whose head was covered with a hairy cap:

"Take off that saucepan of yours! and you, there, your wolf's head! Are you going to obey me, damn you? Pray show respect to my epaulets! I am your commanding officer!"

They complied, and everyone present applauded

exclaiming, "Long live the Maréchale! long live the Maréchale!" Then she took a bottle of champagne off the stove, and poured out its contents into the cups which they successively stretched forth to her. As the table was very large, the guests, especially the women, came over to her side, and stood erect on tiptoe on the slats of the chairs, so as to form, for the space of a minute, a pyramidal group of head-dresses, naked shoulders, extended arms, and stooping bodies; and over all these objects a spray of wine played for some time, for the merry-andrew and Arnoux, at opposite corners of the dining-room, each letting fly the cork of a bottle, splashed the faces of those around them.

The little birds of the aviary, the door of which had been left open, broke into the apartment, quite scared, flying round the chandelier, knocking against the window-panes and against the furniture, and some of them, alighting on the heads of the guests, presented the appearance there of large flowers.

The musicians had gone. The piano had been drawn out of the anteroom. The Vatnaz seated herself before it, and, accompanied by the choir-boy, who thumped his tambourine, she made a wild dash into a quadrille, striking the keys like a horse pawing the ground, and wriggling her waist about, the better to mark the time. The Maréchale dragged out Frederick; Hussonnet took the windmill; the 'longshore-woman put out her joints like a circus-clown; the merry-andrew exhibited the manœuvres of an orang-outang; the female savage, with outspread arms, imitated the swaying motion of a boat. At last, unable to go on any further, they all stopped; and a window was flung open.

The broad daylight penetrated the apartment with the cool breath of morning. There was an exclamation of astonishment, and then came silence. The yellow flames flickered, making the sockets of the candlesticks crack from time to time. The floor was strewn with ribbons, flowers, and pearls. The pier-tables were sticky with the stains of punch and syrup. The hangings were soiled, the dresses rumpled and dusty. The plaits of the women's hair hung loose over their shoulders, and the paint, trickling down with the perspiration, revealed pallid faces and red, blinking eyelids.

The Maréchale, fresh as if she had come out of a bath, had rosy cheeks and sparkling eyes. She flung her wig some distance away, and her hair fell around her like a fleece, allowing none of her uniform to be seen except her breeches, the effect thus produced being at the same time comical and pretty.

The Sphinx, whose teeth chattered as if she had the ague, wanted a shawl.

Rosanette rushed up to her own room to look for one, and, as the other came after her, she quickly shut the door in her face.

The Turk remarked, in a loud tone, that M. Oudry had not been seen going out. Nobody noticed the maliciousness of this observation, so worn out were they all.

Then, while waiting for vehicles, they managed to get on their broad-brimmed hats and cloaks. It struck seven. The angel was still in the dining-room, seated at the table with a plate of sardines and fruit stewed in melted butter in front of her, and close beside her was the fishwife, smoking cigarettes, while giving her advice as to the right way to live.

At last, the cabs having arrived, the guests took their departure. Hussonnet, who had an engagement as correspondent for the provinces, had to read through fifty-three newspapers before his breakfast. The female savage had a rehearsal at the theatre; Pellerin had to see a model; and the choir-boy had three appointments. But the angel, attacked by the preliminary symptoms of indigestion, was unable to rise. The mediæval baron carried her to the cab.

"Take care of her wings!" cried the 'longshore-woman through the window.

At the top of the stairs, Mademoiselle Vatnaz said to Rosanette:

"Good-bye, darling! That was a very nice evening party of yours."

Then, bending close to her ear: "Take care of him!"

"Till better times come," returned the Maréchale, in drawling tones, as she turned her back.

Arnoux and Frederick returned together, just as they had come. The dealer in faïence looked so gloomy that his companion wished to know if he were ill.

"I? Not at all!"

He bit his moustache, knitted his brows; and Frederick asked him, was it his business that annoyed him.

"By no means!"

Then all of a sudden:

"You know him—Père Oudry—don't you?"

And, with a spiteful expression on his countenance:

"He's rich, the old scoundrel!"

After this, Arnoux spoke about an important piece of ware-making, which had to be finished that day at his works. He wanted to see it; the train was starting in an hour.

"Meantime, I must go and embrace my wife."

"Ha! his wife!" thought Frederick. Then he made his way home to go to bed, with his head aching terribly; and, to appease his thirst, he swallowed a whole carafe of water.

Another thirst had come to him—the thirst for women, for licentious pleasure, and all that Parisian life permitted him to enjoy. He felt somewhat stunned, like a man coming out of a ship, and in the visions that haunted his first sleep, he saw the shoulders of the fishwife, the loins of the 'longshore-woman, the calves of the Polish lady, and the headdress of the female savage flying past him and coming back again continually. Then, two large black eyes, which had not been at the ball, appeared before him; and, light as butterflies, burning as torches, they came and went, ascended to the cornice and descended to his very mouth.

Frederick made desperate efforts to recognise those eyes, without succeeding in doing so. But already the dream had taken hold of him. It seemed to him that he was yoked beside Arnoux to the pole of a hackney-coach, and that the Maréchale, astride of him, was disembowelling him with her gold spurs.

CHAPTER VIII.

FREDERICK ENTERTAINS

FREDERICK found a little mansion at the corner of the Rue Rumfort, and he bought it along with the brougham, the horse, the furniture, and two flower-stands which were taken from the Arnoux's house to be placed on each side of his drawing-room door. In the rear of this apartment were a bedroom and a closet. The idea occurred to his mind to put up Deslauriers there. But how could he receive her — *her*, his future mistress? The presence of a friend would be an obstacle. He knocked down the partition-wall in order to enlarge the drawing-room, and converted the closet into a smoking-room.

He bought the works of the poets whom he loved, books of travel, atlases, and dictionaries, for he had innumerable plans of study. He hurried on the workmen, rushed about to the different shops, and in his impatience to enjoy, carried off everything without even holding out for a bargain beforehand.

From the tradesmen's bills, Frederick ascertained that he would have to expend very soon forty thousand francs, not including the succession duties, which would exceed thirty-seven thousand. As his fortune was in landed property, he wrote to the notary at Havre to sell a portion of it in order to pay off his debts, and to have some money at his disposal. Then, anxious to become acquainted at last with that vague entity, glittering and indefinable, which is known as "society," he sent a note to the Dambreuses to know whether he might be at liberty to call upon them. Madame, in reply, said she would expect a visit from him the following day.

This happened to be their reception-day. Carriages were standing in the courtyard. Two footmen rushed forward under the marquée, and a third at the head of the stairs began walking in front of him.

He was conducted through an anteroom, a second room, and then a drawing-room with high windows and a monumental mantelshelf supporting a timepiece in the form of a sphere, and two enormous porcelain vases, in each of which bristled, like a golden bush, a cluster of sconces. Pictures in the manner of Espagnolet hung on the walls. The heavy tapestry portières fell majestically, and the armchairs, the brackets, the tables, the entire furniture, which was in the style of the Second Empire, had a certain imposing and diplomatic air.

Frederick smiled with pleasure in spite of himself.

At last he reached an oval apartment wainscoted in cypress-wood, stuffed with dainty furniture, and letting in the light through a single sheet of plate-glass, which looked out on a garden. Madame Dambreuse was seated at the fireside, with a dozen persons gathered round her in a circle. With a polite greeting, she made a sign to him to take a seat, without, however, exhibiting any surprise at not having seen him for so long a time.

Just at the moment when he was entering the room, they had been praising the eloquence of the Abbé Cœur. Then they deplored the immorality of servants, a topic suggested by a theft which a *valet-de-chambre* had committed, and they began to indulge in tittle-tattle. Old Madame de Sommery had a cold; Mademoiselle de Turvisot had got married; the Montcharrons would not return before the end of January; neither would the Bretancourts, now that people remained in the country till a late period of the year. And the triviality of the conversation was, so to speak, intensified by the luxuriousness of the surroundings; but what they said was less stupid than their way of talking, which was aimless, disconnected, and utterly devoid of animation. And yet there were present men versed in life — an ex-minister, the curé of a large parish, two or three Government officials of high rank. They adhered to the most hackneyed commonplaces. Some of them resembled weary dowagers; others had the appearance of horse-jockeys; and old men accompanied their wives, of whom they were old enough to be the grandfathers.

Madame Dambreuse received all of them graciously. When it was mentioned that anyone was ill, she knitted her brows with a painful expression on her face, and when balls or evening parties were discussed, assumed a joyous air. She would ere long be compelled to deprive herself of these pleasures, for she was going to take away from a boarding-school a niece of her husband, an orphan. The guests extolled her devotedness: this was behaving like a true mother of a family.

Frederick gazed at her attentively. The dull skin of her face looked as if it had been stretched out,

and had a bloom in which there was no brilliancy;
like that of preserved fruit. But her hair, which was
in corkscrew curls, after the English fashion, was
finer than silk; her eyes of a sparkling blue; and all
her movements were dainty.   Seated at the lower
end of the apartment, on a small sofa, she kept
brushing off the red flock from a Japanese screen, no
doubt in order to let her hands be seen to greater
advantage — long narrow hands, a little thin, with
fingers tilting up at the points.   She wore a grey
moiré gown with a high-necked body, like a Puritan
lady.

Frederick asked her whether she intended to go
to La Fortelle this year. Madame Dambreuse was
unable to say. He was sure, however, of one thing,
that one would be bored to death in Nogent.

Then the visitors thronged in more quickly. There
was an incessant rustling of robes on the carpet.
Ladies, seated on the edges of chairs, gave vent to
little sneering laughs, articulated two or three words,
and at the end of five minutes left along with their
young daughters. It soon became impossible to follow the conversation, and Frederick withdrew when
Madame Dambreuse said to him:

"Every Wednesday, is it not, Monsieur Moreau?"
making up for her previous display of indifference by
these simple words.

He was satisfied.   Nevertheless, he took a deep
breath when he got out into the open air; and, need-
ing a less artificial environment, Frederick recalled to
mind that he owed the Maréchale a visit.

The door of the anteroom was open.   Two Havanese lapdogs rushed forward.   A voice exclaimed:

"Delphine! Delphine! Is that you, Felix?"

He stood there without advancing a step. The two little dogs kept yelping continually. At length Rosanette appeared, wrapped up in a sort of dressing-gown of white muslin trimmed with lace, and with her stockingless feet in Turkish slippers.

"Ah! excuse me, Monsieur! I thought it was the hairdresser. One minute; I am coming back!"

And he was left alone in the dining-room. The Venetian blinds were closed. Frederick, as he cast a glance round, was beginning to recall the hubbub of the other night, when he noticed on the table, in the middle of the room, a man's hat, an old felt hat, bruised, greasy, dirty. To whom did this hat belong? Impudently displaying its torn lining, it seemed to say:

"I have the laugh, after all! I am the master!"

The Maréchale suddenly reappeared on the scene. She took up the hat, opened the conservatory, flung it in there, shut the door again (other doors flew open and closed again at the same moment), and, having brought Frederick through the kitchen, she introduced him into her dressing-room.

It could at once be seen that this was the most frequented room in the house, and, so to speak, its true moral centre. The walls, the armchairs, and a big divan with a spring were adorned with a chintz pattern on which was traced a great deal of foliage. On a white marble table stood two large washhand-basins of fine blue earthenware. Crystal shelves, forming a whatnot overhead, were laden with phials, brushes, combs, sticks of cosmetic, and powder-boxes. The fire was reflected in a high cheval-glass. A sheet was hanging outside a bath, and odours of almond-paste and of benzoin were exhaled.

"You'll excuse the disorder. I'm dining in the city this evening."

And as she turned on her heel, she was near crushing one of the little dogs. Frederick declared that they were charming. She lifted up the pair of them, and raising their black snouts up to her face:

"Come! do a laugh—kiss the gentleman!"

A man dressed in a dirty overcoat with a fur collar here entered abruptly.

"Felix, my worthy fellow," said she, "you'll have that business of yours disposed of next Sunday without fail."

The man proceeded to dress her hair. Frederick told her he had heard news of her friends, Madame de Rochegune, Madame de Saint-Florentin, and Madame Lombard, every woman being noble, as if it were at the mansion of the Dambreuses. Then he talked about the theatres. An extraordinary performance was to be given that evening at the Ambigu.

"Shall you go?"

"Faith, no! I'm staying at home."

Delphine appeared. Her mistress gave her a scolding for having gone out without permission.

The other vowed that she was just "returning from market."

"Well, bring me your book. You have no objection, isn't that so?"

And, reading the pass-book in a low tone, Rosanette made remarks on every item. The different sums were not added up correctly.

"Hand me over four sous!"

Delphine handed the amount over to her, and, when she had sent the maid away:

"Ah! Holy Virgin! could I be more unfortunate than I am with these creatures?"

Frederick was shocked at this complaint about servants. It recalled the others too vividly to his mind, and established between the two houses a kind of vexatious equality.

When Delphine came back again, she drew close to the Maréchale's side in order to whisper something in her ear.

"Ah, no! I don't want her!"

Delphine presented herself once more.

"Madame, she insists."

"Ah, what a plague! Throw her out!"

At the same moment, an old lady, dressed in black, pushed forward the door. Frederick heard nothing, saw nothing. Rosanette rushed into her apartment to meet her.

When she reappeared her cheeks were flushed, and she sat down in one of the armchairs without saying a word. A tear fell down her face; then, turning towards the young man, softly:

"What is your Christian name?"

"Frederick."

"Ha! Federico! It doesn't annoy you when I address you in that way?"

And she gazed at him in a coaxing sort of way that was almost amorous.

All of a sudden she uttered an exclamation of delight at the sight of Mademoiselle Vatnaz.

The lady-artist had no time to lose before presiding at her *table d'hôte* at six o'clock sharp; and she was panting for breath, being completely exhausted. She first took out of her pocket a gold chain in a paper, then various objects that she had bought.

"You should know that there are in the Rue Joubert splendid Suède gloves at thirty-six sous. Your dyer wants eight days more. As for the guipure, I told you that they would dye it again. Bugneaux has got the instalment you paid. That's all, I think. You owe me a hundred and eighty-five francs."

Rosanette went to a drawer to get ten napoleons. Neither of the pair had any money. Frederick offered some.

"I'll pay you back," said the Vatnaz, as she stuffed the fifteen francs into her handbag. "But you are a naughty boy! I don't love you any longer — you didn't get me to dance with you even once the other evening! Ah! my dear, I came across a case of stuffed humming-birds which are perfect loves at a shop in the Quai Voltaire. If I were in your place, I would make myself a present of them. Look here! What do you think of it?"

And she exhibited an old remnant of pink silk which she had purchased at the Temple to make a mediæval doublet for Delmar.

"He came to-day, didn't he?"

"No."

"That's singular."

And, after a minute's silence:

"Where are you going this evening?"

"To Alphonsine's," said Rosanette, this being the third version given by her as to the way in which she was going to pass the evening.

Mademoiselle Vatnaz went on: "And what news about the old man of the mountain?"

But, with an abrupt wink, the Maréchale bade her hold her tongue; and she accompanied Frederick out as far as the anteroom to ascertain from him whether he would soon see Arnoux.

"Pray ask him to come—not before his wife, mind!"

At the top of the stairs an umbrella was placed against the wall near a pair of goloshes.

"Vatnaz's goloshes," said Rosanette. "What a foot, eh? My little friend is rather strongly built!"

And, in a melodramatic tone, making the final letter of the word roll:

"Don't tru-us-st her!"

Frederick, emboldened by a confidence of this sort, tried to kiss her on the neck.

"Oh, do it! It costs nothing!"

He felt rather light-hearted as he left her, having no doubt that ere long the Maréchale would be his mistress. This desire awakened another in him; and, in spite of the species of grudge that he owed her, he felt a longing to see Madame Arnoux.

Besides, he would have to call at her house in order to execute the commission with which he had been entrusted by Rosanette.

"But now," thought he (it had just struck six), "Arnoux is probably at home."

So he put off his visit till the following day.

She was seated in the same attitude as on the former day, and was sewing a little boy's shirt.

The child, at her feet, was playing with a wooden toy menagerie. Marthe, a short distance away, was writing.

He began by complimenting her on her children. She replied without any exaggeration of maternal silliness.

The room had a tranquil aspect. A glow of sunshine stole in through the window-panes, lighting up the angles of the different articles of furniture, and, as Madame Arnoux sat close beside the window, a large ray, falling on the curls over the nape of her neck, penetrated with liquid gold her skin, which assumed the colour of amber.

Then he said:

"This young lady here has grown very tall during the past three years! Do you remember, Mademoiselle, when you slept on my knees in the carriage?"

Marthe did not remember.

"One evening, returning from Saint-Cloud?"

There was a look of peculiar sadness in Madame Arnoux's face. Was it in order to prevent any allusion on his part to the memories they possessed in common?

Her beautiful black eyes, whose sclerotics were glistening, moved gently under their somewhat drooping lids, and her pupils revealed in their depths an inexpressible kindness of heart. He was seized with a love stronger than ever, a passion that knew no bounds. It enervated him to contemplate the object of his attachment; however, he shook off this feeling. How was he to make the most of himself? by what means? And, having turned the matter over thoroughly in his mind, Frederick could think of none that seemed more effectual than money.

He began talking about the weather, which was less cold than it had been at Havre.

"You have been there?"

"Yes; about a family matter—an inheritance."

"Ah! I am very glad," she said, with an air of such genuine pleasure that he felt quite touched, just as if she had rendered him a great service.

She asked him what he intended to do, as it was
necessary for a man to occupy himself with something.

He recalled to mind his false position, and said
that he hoped to reach the Council of State with the
help of M. Dambreuse, the secretary.

"You are acquainted with him, perhaps?"

"Merely by name."

Then, in a low tone:

"*He* brought you to the ball the other night, did
he not?"

Frederick remained silent.

"That was what I wanted to know; thanks!"

After that she put two or three discreet questions
to him about his family and the part of the country
in which he lived. It was very kind of him not to
have forgotten them after having lived so long away
from Paris.

"But could I do so?" he rejoined. "Have you
any doubt about it?"

Madame Arnoux arose: "I believe that you entertain towards us a true and solid affection. *Au
revoir!*"

And she extended her hand towards him in a sincere and virile fashion.

Was this not an engagement, a promise? Frederick felt a sense of delight at merely living; he had
to restrain himself to keep from singing. He wanted
to burst out, to do generous deeds, and to give alms.
He looked around him to see if there were anyone
near whom he could relieve. No wretch happened
to be passing by; and his desire for self-devotion
evaporated, for he was not a man to go out of his
way to find opportunities for benevolence.

Then he remembered his friends. The first of whom he thought was Hussonnet, the second, Pellerin. The lowly position of Dussardier naturally called for consideration. As for Cisy, he was glad to let that young aristocrat get a slight glimpse as to the extent of his fortune. He wrote accordingly to all four to come to a housewarming the following Sunday at eleven o'clock sharp; and he told Deslauriers to bring Sénécal.

The tutor had been dismissed from the third boarding-school in which he had been employed for not having given his consent to the distribution of prizes — a custom which he looked upon as dangerous to equality. He was now with an engine-builder, and for the past six months had been no longer living with Deslauriers. There had been nothing painful about their parting.

Sénécal had been visited by men in blouses — all patriots, all workmen, all honest fellows, but at the same time men whose society seemed distasteful to the advocate. Besides, he disliked certain ideas of his friend, excellent though they might be as weapons of warfare. He held his tongue on the subject through motives of ambition, deeming it prudent to pay deference to him in order to exercise control over him, for he looked forward impatiently to a revolutionary movement, in which he calculated on making an opening for himself and occupying a prominent position.

Sénécal's convictions were more disinterested. Every evening, when his work was finished, he returned to his garret and sought in books for something that might justify his dreams. He had annotated the *Contrat Social;* he had crammed himself with

the *Revue Indépendante;* he was acquainted with
Mably, Morelly, Fourier, Saint-Simon, Comte, Cabet,
Louis Blanc—the heavy cartload of Socialistic writers
—those who claim for humanity the dead level of
barracks, those who would like to amuse it in a
brothel or to bend it over a counter; and from a
medley of all these things he constructed an ideal of
virtuous democracy, with the double aspect of a farm
in which the landlord was to receive a share of the
produce, and a spinning-mill, a sort of American
Lacedæmon, in which the individual would only exist
for the benefit of society, which was to be more
omnipotent, absolute, infallible, and divine than the
Grand Lamas and the Nebuchadnezzars. He had no
doubt as to the approaching realisation of this ideal;
and Sénécal raged against everything that he considered hostile to it with the reasoning of a geometrician and the zeal of an Inquisitor. Titles of
nobility, crosses, plumes, liveries above all, and even
reputations that were too loud-sounding scandalised
him, his studies as well as his sufferings intensifying
every day his essential hatred of every kind of distinction and every form of social superiority.

"What do I owe to this gentleman that I should be
polite to him? If he wants me, he can come to me."

Deslauriers, however, forced him to go to Frederick's reunion.

They found their friend in his bedroom. Spring-
roller blinds and double curtains, Venetian mirrors—
nothing was wanting there. Frederick, in a velvet
vest, was lying back on an easy-chair, smoking
cigarettes of Turkish tobacco.

Sénécal wore the gloomy look of a bigot arriving
in the midst of a pleasure-party.

Deslauriers gave him a single comprehensive glance; then, with a very low bow:

"Monseigneur, allow me to pay my respects to you!"

Dussardier leaped on his neck. "So you are a rich man now. Ah! upon my soul, so much the better!"

Cisy made his appearance with crape on his hat. Since the death of his grandmother, he was in the enjoyment of a considerable fortune, and was less bent on amusing himself than on being distinguished from others — not being the same as everyone else — in short, on "having the proper stamp." This was his favourite phrase.

However, it was now midday, and they were all yawning.

Frederick was waiting for some one.

At the mention of Arnoux's name, Pellerin made a wry face. He looked on him as a renegade since he had abandoned the fine arts.

"Suppose we pass over him — what do you say to that?"

They all approved of this suggestion.

The door was opened by a man-servant in long gaiters; and the dining-room could be seen with its lofty oak plinths relieved with gold, and its two sideboards laden with plate.

The bottles of wine were heating on the stove; the blades of new knives were glittering beside oysters. In the milky tint of the enamelled glasses there was a kind of alluring sweetness; and the table disappeared from view under its load of game, fruit, and meats of the rarest quality.

These attentions were lost on Sénécal. He began by asking for household bread (the hardest that could be got), and in connection with this subject, spoke of the murders of Buzançais and the crisis arising from lack of the means of subsistence.

Nothing of this sort could have happened if agriculture had been better protected, if everything had not been given up to competition, to anarchy, and to the deplorable maxim of "Let things alone! let things go their own way!" It was in this way that the feudalism of money was established—the worst form of feudalism. But let them take care! The people in the end will get tired of it, and may make the capitalist pay for their sufferings either by bloody proscriptions or by the plunder of their houses.

Frederick saw, as if by a lightning-flash, a flood of men with bare arms invading Madame Dambreuse's drawing-room, and smashing the mirrors with blows of pikes.

Sénécal went on to say that the workman, owing to the insufficiency of wages, was more unfortunate than the helot, the negro, and the pariah, especially if he has children.

"Ought he to get rid of them by asphyxia, as some English doctor, whose name I don't remember —a disciple of Malthus—advises him?"

And, turning towards Cisy: "Are we to be obliged to follow the advice of the infamous Malthus?"

Cisy, who was ignorant of the infamy and even of the existence of Malthus, said by way of reply, that after all, much human misery was relieved, and that the higher classes——

"Ha! the higher classes!" said the Socialist, with a sneer. "In the first place, there are no higher classes. 'Tis the heart alone that makes anyone

higher than another. We want no alms, understand!
but equality, the fair division of products."

What he required was that the workman might
become a capitalist, just as the soldier might become
a colonel. The trade-wardenships, at least, in limit-
ing the number of apprentices, prevented workmen
from growing inconveniently numerous, and the sen-
timent of fraternity was kept up by means of the fêtes
and the banners.

Hussonnet, as a poet, regretted the banners; so
did Pellerin, too — a predilection which had taken
possession of him at the Café Dagneaux, while listening to the Phalansterians talking. He expressed
the opinion that Fourier was a great man.

"Come now!" said Deslauriers. "An old fool
who sees in the overthrow of governments the effects
of Divine vengeance. He is just like my lord Saint-
Simon and his church, with his hatred of the French
Revolution — a set of buffoons who would fain re-es-
tablish Catholicism."

M. de Cisy, no doubt in order to get information
or to make a good impression, broke in with this remark, which he uttered in a mild tone:

"These two men of science are not, then, of the
same way of thinking as Voltaire?"

"That fellow! I make you a present of him!"

"How is that?" Why, I thought——"

"Oh! no, he did not love the people!"

Then the conversation came down to contemporary events: the Spanish marriages, the dilapidations
of Rochefort, the new chapter-house of Saint-Denis,
which had led to the taxes being doubled. Nevertheless, according to Sénécal, they were not high
enough!

"And why are they paid? My God! to erect the palace for apes at the Museum, to make showy staff-officers parade along our squares, or to maintain a Gothic etiquette amongst the flunkeys of the Château!"

"I have read in the *Mode*," said Cisy, "that at the Tuileries ball on the feast of Saint-Ferdinand, everyone was disguised as a miser."

"How pitiable!" said the Socialist, with a shrug of his shoulders, as if to indicate his disgust.

"And the Museum of Versailles!" exclaimed Pellerin. "Let us talk about it! These idiots have fore-shortened a Delacroix and lengthened a Gros! At the Louvre they have so well restored, scratched, and made a jumble of all the canvases, that in ten years probably not one will be left. As for the errors in the catalogue, a German has written a whole volume on the subject. Upon my word, the foreigners are laughing at us."

"Yes, we are the laughing-stock of Europe," said Sénécal.

"'Tis because Art is conveyed in fee-simple to the Crown."

"As long as you haven't universal suffrage——"

"Allow me!"—for the artist, having been rejected at every *salon* for the last twenty years, was filled with rage against Power.

"Ah! let them not bother us! As for me, I ask for nothing. Only the Chambers ought to pass en-actments in the interests of Art. A chair of æsthetics should be established with a professor who, being a practical man as well as a philosopher, would suc-ceed, I hope, in grouping the multitude. You would do well, Hussonnet, to touch on this matter with a word or two in your newspaper?"

"Are the newspapers free? are we ourselves free?" said Deslauriers in an angry tone. "When one reflects that there might be as many as twenty-eight different formalities to set up a boat on the river, it makes me feel a longing to go and live amongst the cannibals! The Government is eating us up. Everything belongs to it — philosophy, law, the arts, the very air of heaven; and France, bereft of all energy, lies under the boot of the gendarme and the cassock of the devil-dodger with the death-rattle in her throat!"

The future Mirabeau thus poured out his bile in abundance. Finally he took his glass in his right hand, raised it, and with his other arm akimbo, and his eyes flashing:

"I drink to the utter destruction of the existing order of things — that is to say, of everything included in the words Privilege, Monopoly, Regulation, Hierarchy, Authority, State!" — and in a louder voice — "which I would like to smash as I do this!" dashing on the table the beautiful wine-glass, which broke into a thousand pieces.

They all applauded, and especially Dussardier.

The spectacle of injustices made his heart leap up with indignation. Everything that wore a beard claimed his sympathy. He was one of those persons who fling themselves under vehicles to relieve the horses who have fallen. His erudition was limited to two works, one entitled *Crimes of Kings,* and the other *Mysteries of the Vatican*. He had listened to the advocate with open-mouthed delight. At length, unable to stand it any longer:

"For my part, the thing I blame Louis Philippe for is abandoning the Poles!"

"One moment!" said Hussonnet. "In the first place, Poland has no existence; 'tis an invention of Lafayette! The Poles, as a general rule, all belong to the Faubourg Saint-Marceau, the real ones having been drowned with Poniatowski." In short, "he no longer gave into it;" he had "got over all that sort of thing; it was just like the sea-serpent, the revocation of the Edict of Nantes, and that antiquated humbug about the Saint-Bartholomew massacre!"

Sénécal, while he did not defend the Poles, extolled the latest remarks made by the men of letters. The Popes had been calumniated, inasmuch as they, at any rate, defended the people, and he called the League "the aurora of Democracy, a great movement in the direction of equality as opposed to the individualism of Protestants."

Frederick was a little surprised at these views. They probably bored Cisy, for he changed the conversation to the *tableaux vivants* at the Gymnase, which at that time attracted a great number of people.

Sénécal regarded them with disfavour. Such exhibitions corrupted the daughters of the proletariat. Then, it was noticeable that they went in for a display of shameless luxury. Therefore, he approved of the conduct of the Bavarian students who insulted Lola Montès. In imitation of Rousseau, he showed more esteem for the wife of a coal-porter than for the mistress of a king.

"You don't appreciate dainties," retorted Hussonnet in a majestic tone. And he took up the championship of ladies of this class in order to praise Rosanette. Then, as he happened to make an allusion to the ball at her house and to Arnoux's costume, Pellerin remarked:

"People maintain that he is becoming shaky?"

The picture-dealer had just been engaged in a lawsuit with reference to his grounds at Belleville, and he was actually in a kaolin company in Lower Brittany with other rogues of the same sort.

Dussardier knew more about him, for his own master, M. Moussinot, having made enquiries about Arnoux from the banker, Oscar Lefébvre, the latter had said in reply that he considered him by no means solvent, as he knew about bills of his that had been renewed.

The dessert was over; they passed into the drawing-room, which was hung, like that of the Maréchale, in yellow damask in the style of Louis XVI.

Pellerin found fault with Frederick for not having chosen in preference the Neo-Greek style; Sénécal rubbed matches against the hangings; Deslauriers did not make any remark.

There was a bookcase set up there, which he called "a little girl's library." The principal contemporary writers were to be found there. It was impossible to speak about their works, for Hussonnet immediately began relating anecdotes with reference to their personal characteristics, criticising their faces, their habits, their dress, glorifying fifth-rate intellects and disparaging those of the first; and all the while making it clear that he deplored modern decadence.

He instanced some village ditty as containing in itself alone more poetry than all the lyrics of the nineteenth century. He went on to say that Balzac was overrated, that Byron was effaced, and that Hugo knew nothing about the stage.

"Why, then," said Sénécal, "have you not got the volumes of the working-men poets?"

And M. de Cisy, who devoted his attention to literature, was astonished at not seeing on Frederick's table some of those new physiological studies—the physiology of the smoker, of the angler, of the man employed at the barrier.

They went on irritating him to such an extent that he felt a longing to shove them out by the shoulders.

"But they are making me quite stupid!" And then he drew Dussardier aside, and wished to know whether he could do him any service.

The honest fellow was moved. He answered that his post of cashier entirely sufficed for his wants.

After that, Frederick led Deslauriers into his own apartment, and, taking out of his escritoire two thousand francs:

"Look here, old boy, put this money in your pocket. 'Tis the balance of my old debts to you."

"But—what about the journal?" said the advocate. "You are, of course, aware that I spoke about it to Hussonnet."

And, when Frederick replied that he was "a little short of cash just now," the other smiled in a sinister fashion.

After the liqueurs they drank beer, and after the beer, grog; and then they lighted their pipes once more. At last they left, at five o'clock in the evening, and they were walking along at each others' side without speaking, when Dussardier broke the silence by saying that Frederick had entertained them in excellent style. They all agreed with him on that point.

Then Hussonnet remarked that his luncheon was too heavy. Sénécal found fault with the trivial character of his household arrangements. Cisy took the same view. It was absolutely devoid of the "proper stamp."

"For my part, I think," said Pellerin, "he might have had the grace to give me an order for a picture."

Deslauriers held his tongue, as he had the bank-notes that had been given to him in his breeches' pocket.

Frederick was left by himself. He was thinking about his friends, and it seemed to him as if a huge ditch surrounded with shade separated him from them. He had nevertheless held out his hand to them, and they had not responded to the sincerity of his heart.

He recalled to mind what Pellerin and Dussardier had said about Arnoux. Undoubtedly it must be an invention, a calumny? But why? And he had a vision of Madame Arnoux, ruined, weeping, selling her furniture. This idea tormented him all night long. Next day he presented himself at her house.

At a loss to find any way of communicating to her what he had heard, he asked her, as if in casual conversation, whether Arnoux still held possession of his building grounds at Belleville.

"Yes, he has them still."

"He is now, I believe, a shareholder in a kaolin company in Brittany."

"That's true."

"His earthenware-works are going on very well, are they not?"

"Well—I suppose so——"

And, as he hesitated:

"What is the matter with you? You frighten me!"

He told her the story about the renewals. She hung down her head, and said:

"I thought so!"

In fact, Arnoux, in order to make a good speculation, had refused to sell his grounds, had borrowed money extensively on them, and finding no purchasers, had thought of rehabilitating himself by establishing the earthenware manufactory. The expense of this had exceeded his calculations. She knew nothing more about it. He evaded all her questions, and declared repeatedly that it was going on very well.

Frederick tried to reassure her. These in all probability were mere temporary embarrassments. However, if he got any information, he would impart it to her.

"Oh! yes, will you not?" said she, clasping her two hands with an air of charming supplication.

So then, he had it in his power to be useful to her. He was now entering into her existence — finding a place in her heart.

Arnoux appeared.

"Ha! how nice of you to come to take me out to dine!"

Frederick was silent on hearing these words.

Arnoux spoke about general topics, then informed his wife that he would be returning home very late, as he had an appointment with M. Oudry.

"At his house?"

"Why, certainly, at his house."

As they went down the stairs, he confessed that, as the Maréchale had no engagement at home, they were going on a secret pleasure-party to the Moulin Rouge; and, as he always needed somebody to be the recipient of his outpourings, he got Frederick to drive him to the door.

In place of entering, he walked about on the footpath, looking up at the windows on the second floor. Suddenly the curtains parted.

"Ha! bravo! Père Oudry is no longer there! Good evening!"

Frederick did not know what to think now.

From this day forth, Arnoux was still more cordial than before; he invited the young man to dine with his mistress; and ere long Frederick frequented both houses at the same time.

Rosanette's abode furnished him with amusement. He used to call there of an evening on his way back from the club or the play. He would take a cup of tea there, or play a game of loto. On Sundays they played charades; Rosanette, more noisy than the rest, made herself conspicuous by funny tricks, such as running on all-fours or muffling her head in a cotton cap. In order to watch the passers-by through the window, she had a hat of waxed leather; she smoked chibouks; she sang Tyrolese airs. In the afternoon, to kill time, she cut out flowers in a piece of chintz and pasted them against the window-panes, smeared her two little dogs with varnish, burned pastilles, or drew cards to tell her fortune. Incapable of resisting a desire, she became infatuated about some trinket which she happened to see, and could not sleep till she had gone and bought it, then bartered it for another, sold costly dresses for little or nothing, lost her jewellery, squandered money, and would have sold her chemise for a stage-box at the theatre. Often she asked Frederick to explain to her some word she came across when reading a book, but did not pay any attention to his answer, for she jumped quickly to another idea, while heaping questions on top of each other. After spasms of gaiety came childish outbrusts of rage, or else she sat on the ground dreaming before the fire with her head down and her hands clasping her knees, more inert than a torpid adder. Without minding it, she made her toilet in his presence, drew on her silk stockings, then washed her face with great splashes of water, throwing back her figure as if she were a shivering naïad; and her laughing white teeth, her sparkling eyes, her beauty, her gaiety, dazzled Frederick, and made his nerves tingle under the lash of desire.

Nearly always he found Madame Arnoux teaching her little boy how to read, or standing behind Marthe's chair while she played her scales on the piano. When she was doing a piece of sewing, it was a great source of delight to him to pick up her scissors now and then. In all her movements there was a tranquil majesty. Her little hands seemed made to scatter alms and to wipe away tears, and her voice, naturally rather hollow, had caressing intonations and a sort of breezy lightness.

She did not display much enthusiasm about literature; but her intelligence exercised a charm by the use of a few simple and penetrating words. She loved travelling, the sound of the wind in the woods, and a walk with uncovered head under the rain.

Frederick listened to these confidences with rapture, fancying that he saw in them the beginning of a certain self-abandonment on her part.

His association with these two women made, as it were, two different strains of music in his life, the one playful, passionate, diverting, the other grave and almost religious, and vibrating both at the same time, they always increased in volume and gradually blended with one another; for if Madame Arnoux happened merely to touch him with her finger, the image of the other immediately presented itself to him as an object of desire, because from that quarter a better opportunity was thrown in his way, and, when his heart happened to be touched while in Rosanette's company, he was immediately reminded of the woman for whom he felt such a consuming passion.

This confusion was, in some measure, due to a similarity which existed between the interiors of the two houses. One of the trunks which was formerly to be seen in the Boulevard Montmartre now adorned Rosanette's dining-room. The same courses were served up for dinner in both places, and even the same velvet cap was to be found trailing over the easy-chairs; then, a heap of little presents — screens, boxes, fans — went to the mistress's house from the wife's and returned again, for Arnoux, without the slightest embarrassment, often took back from the one what he had given to her in order to make a present of it to the other.

The Maréchale laughed with Frederick at the utter disregard for propriety which his habits exhibited. One Sunday, after dinner, she led him behind the door, and showed him in the pocket of Arnoux's overcoat a bag of cakes which he had just pilfered from the table, in order, no doubt, to regale his little family with it at home. M. Arnoux gave himself up to some rogueries which bordered on vileness. It seemed to him a duty to practise fraud with regard to the city dues; he never paid when he went to the theatre, or if he took a ticket for the second seats always tried to

make his way into the first; and he used to relate
as an excellent joke that it was a custom of his at the
cold baths to put into the waiters' collection-box a
breeches' button instead of a ten-sous piece — and
this did not prevent the Maréchale from loving him.

One day, however, she said, while talking about
him:

"Ah! he's making himself a nuisance to me, at
last! I've had enough of him! Faith, so much the
better — I'll find another instead!"

Frederick believed that the other had already been
found, and that his name was M. Oudry.

"Well," said Rosanette, "what does that signify?"

Then, in a voice choked with rising tears:

"I ask very little from him, however, and he
won't give me that.

He had even promised a fourth of his profits in the
famous kaolin mines. No profit made its appearance
any more than the cashmere with which he had been
luring her on for the last six months.

Frederick immediately thought of making her a
present. Arnoux might regard it as a lesson for himself, and be annoyed at it.

For all that, he was good-natured, his wife herself
said so, but so foolish! Instead of bringing people to
dine every day at his house, he now entertained his
acquaintances at a restaurant. He bought things that
were utterly useless, such as gold chains, timepieces,
and household articles. Madame Arnoux even pointed
out to Frederick in the lobby an enormous supply of
tea-kettles, foot-warmers, and samovars. Finally, she
one day confessed that a certain matter caused her
much anxiety. Arnoux had made her sign a promissory note payable to M. Dambreuse.

5—15

Meanwhile Frederick still cherished his literary projects as if it were a point of honour with himself to do so. He wished to write a history of æsthetics, a result of his conversations with Pellerin; next, to write dramas dealing with different epochs of the French Revolution, and to compose a great comedy, an idea traceable to the indirect influence of Deslauriers and Hussonnet. In the midst of his work her face or that of the other passed before his mental vision. He struggled against the longing to see her, but was not long ere he yielded to it; and he felt sadder as he came back from Madame Arnoux's house.

One morning, while he was brooding over his melancholy thoughts by the fireside, Deslauriers came in. The incendiary speeches of Sénécal had filled his master with uneasiness, and once more he found himself without resources.

"What do you want me to do?" said Frederick.

"Nothing! I know you have no money. But it will not be much trouble for you to get him a post either through M. Dambreuse or else through Arnoux. The latter ought to have need of engineers in his establishment."

Frederick had an inspiration. Sénécal would be able to let him know when the husband was away, carry letters for him and assist him on a thousand occasions when opportunities presented themselves. Services of this sort are always rendered between man and man. Besides, he would find means of employing him without arousing any suspicion on his part. Chance offered him an auxiliary; it was a circumstance that omened well for the future, and he hastened to take advantage of it; and, with an affectation of indifference, he replied that the thing was

feasible perhaps, and that he would devote attention
to it.

And he did so at once. Arnoux took a great deal
of pains with his earthenware works. He was endeavouring to discover the copper-red of the Chinese,
but his colours evaporated in the process of baking.
In order to avoid cracks in his ware, he mixed lime
with his potter's clay; but the articles got broken for
the most part; the enamel of his paintings on the raw
material boiled away; his large plates became bulged;
and, attributing these mischances to the inferior plant
of his manufactory, he was anxious to start other
grinding-mills and other drying-rooms. Frederick recalled some of these things to mind, and, when he
met Arnoux, said that he had discovered a very able
man, who would be capable of finding his famous
red. Arnoux gave a jump; then, having listened to
what the young man had to tell him, replied that he
wanted assistance from nobody.

Frederick spoke in a very laudatory style about
Sénécal's prodigious attainments, pointing out that
he was at the same time an engineer, a chemist, and
an accountant, being a mathematician of the first rank.
The earthenware-dealer consented to see him.

But they squabbled over the emoluments. Frederick interposed, and, at the end of a week, succeeded
in getting them to come to an agreement.

But as the works were situated at Creil, Sénécal
could not assist him in any way. This thought alone
was enough to make his courage flag, as if he had
met with some misfortune. His notion was that the
more Arnoux would be kept apart from his wife the
better would be his own chance with her. Then he
proceeded to make repeated apologies for Rosanette.

He referred to all the wrongs she had sustained at
the other's hands, referred to the vague threats which
she had uttered a few days before, and even spoke
about the cashmere without concealing the fact that
she had accused Arnoux of avarice.

Arnoux, nettled at the word (and, furthermore,
feeling some uneasiness), brought Rosanette the cashmere, but scolded her for having made any complaint to Frederick. When she told him that she had
reminded him a hundred times of his promise, he
pretended that, owing to pressure of business, he had
forgotten all about it.

The next day Frederick presented himself at her
abode, and found the Maréchale still in bed, though it
was two o'clock, with Delmar beside her finishing a
pâté de foie gras at a little round table. Before he
had advanced many paces, she broke out into a cry
of delight, saying: "I have him! I have him!" Then
she seized him by the ears, kissed him on the forehead, thanked him effusively, "thee'd" and "thou'd"
him, and even wanted to make him sit down on the
bed. Her fine eyes, full of tender emotion, were
sparkling with pleasure. There was a smile on her
humid mouth. Her two round arms emerged through
the sleeveless opening of her night-dress, and, from
time to time, he could feel through the cambric the
well-rounded outlines of her form.

All this time Delmar kept rolling his eyeballs about.
"But really, my dear, my own pet . . ."

It was the same way on the occasion when he
saw her next. As soon as Frederick entered, she sat
up on a cushion in order to embrace him with more
ease, called him a darling, a "dearie," put a flower
in his button-hole, and settled his cravat. These

delicate attentions were redoubled when Delmar happened to be there. Were they advances on her part? So it seemed to Frederick.

As for deceiving a friend, Arnoux, in his place, would not have had many scruples on that score, and he had every right not to adhere to rigidly virtuous principles with regard to this man's mistress, seeing that his relations with the wife had been strictly honourable, for so he thought — or rather he would have liked Arnoux to think so, in any event, as a sort of justification of his own prodigious cowardice. Nevertheless he felt somewhat bewildered; and presently he made up his mind to lay siege boldly to the Maréchale.

So, one afternoon, just as she was stooping down in front of her chest of drawers, he came across to her, and repeated his overtures without a pause.

Thereupon, she began to cry, saying that she was very unfortunate, but that people should not despise her on that account.

He only made fresh advances. She now adopted a different plan, namely, to laugh at his attempts without stopping. He thought it a clever thing to answer her sarcasms with repartees in the same strain, in which there was even a touch of exaggeration. But he made too great a display of gaiety to convince her that he was in earnest; and their comradeship was an impediment to any outpouring of serious feeling. At last, when she said one day, in reply to his amorous whispers, that she would not take another woman's leavings, he answered.

"What other woman?"

"Ah! yes, go and meet Madame Arnoux again!"

For Frederick used to talk about her often. Arnoux, on his side, had the same mania. At last she lost patience at always hearing this woman's praises sung, and her insinuation was a kind of revenge.

Frederick resented it. However, Rosanette was beginning to excite his love to an unusual degree. Sometimes, assuming the attitude of a woman of experience, she spoke ill of love with a sceptical smile that made him feel inclined to box her ears. A quarter of an hour afterwards, it was the only thing of any consequence in the world, and, with her arms crossed over her breast, as if she were clasping some one close to her: "Oh, yes, 'tis good! 'tis good!" and her eyelids would quiver in a kind of rapturous swoon. It was impossible to understand her, to know, for instance, whether she loved Arnoux, for she made fun of him, and yet seemed jealous of him. So likewise with the Vatnaz, whom she would sometimes call a wretch, and at other times her best friend. In short, there was about her entire person, even to the very arrangement of her chignon over her head, an inexpressible something, which seemed like a challenge; and he desired her for the satisfaction, above all, of conquering her and being her master.

How was he to accomplish this? for she often sent him away unceremoniously, appearing only for a moment between two doors in order to say in a subdued voice, "I'm engaged—for the evening;" or else he found her surrounded by a dozen persons; and when they were alone, so many impediments presented themselves one after the other, that one would have sworn there was a bet to keep matters from going any further. He invited her to dinner; as a rule, she declined the invitation. On one occasion, she accepted it, but did not come.

A Machiavellian idea arose in his brain.

Having heard from Dussardier about Pellerin's complaints against himself, he thought of giving the artist an order to paint the Maréchale's portrait, a life-sized portrait, which would necessitate a good number of sittings. He would not fail to be present at all of them. The habitual incorrectness of the painter would facilitate their private conversations. So then he would urge Rosanette to get the picture executed in order to make a present of her face to her dear Arnoux. She consented, for she saw herself in the midst of the Grand Salon in the most prominent position with a crowd of people staring at her picture, and the newspapers would all talk about it, which at once would set her afloat.

As for Pellerin, he eagerly snatched at the offer. This portrait ought to place him in the position of a great man; it ought to be a masterpiece. He passed in review in his memory all the portraits by great masters with which he was acquainted, and decided finally in favour of a Titian, which would be set off with ornaments in the style of Veronese. Therefore, he would carry out his design without artificial backgrounds in a bold light, which would illuminate the flesh-tints with a single tone, and which would make the accessories glitter.

"Suppose I were to put on her," he thought, "a pink silk dress with an Oriental bournous? Oh, no! the bournous is only a rascally thing! Or suppose, rather, I were to make her wear blue velvet with a grey background, richly coloured? We might likewise give her a white guipure collar with a black fan and a scarlet curtain behind." And thus, seeking for ideas, he enlarged his conception, and regarded it with admiration.

He felt his heart beating when Rosanette, accompanied by Frederick, called at his house for the first sitting. He placed her standing up on a sort of platform in the midst of the apartment, and, finding fault with the light and expressing regret at the loss of his former studio, he first made her lean on her elbow against a pedestal, then sit down in an armchair, and, drawing away from her and coming near her again by turns in order to adjust with a fillip the folds of her dress, he watched her with eyelids half-closed, and appealed to Frederick's taste with a passing word.

"Well, no," he exclaimed; "I return to my own idea. I will set you up in the Venetian style."

She would have a poppy-coloured velvet gown with a jewelled girdle; and her wide sleeve lined with ermine would afford a glimpse of her bare arm, which was to touch the balustrade of a staircase rising behind her. At her left, a large column would mount as far as the top of the canvas to meet certain structures so as to form an arch. Underneath one would vaguely distinguish groups of orange-trees almost black, through which the blue sky, with its streaks of white cloud, would seem cut into fragments. On the baluster, covered with a carpet, there would be, on a silver dish, a bouquet of flowers, a chaplet of amber, a poniard, and a little chest of antique ivory, rather yellow with age, which would appear to be disgorging gold sequins. Some of them, falling on the ground here and there, would form brilliant splashes, as it were, in such a way as to direct one's glance towards the tip of her foot, for she would be standing on the last step but one in a natural position, as if in the act of moving under the glow of the broad sunlight.

He went to look for a picture-case, which he laid on the platform to represent the step. Then he arranged as accessories, on a stool by way of balustrade, his pea-jacket, a buckler, a sardine-box, a bundle of pens, and a knife; and when he had flung in front of Rosanette a dozen big sous, he made her assume the attitude he required.

"Just try to imagine that these things are riches, magnificent presents. The head a little on one side! Perfect! and don't stir! This majestic posture exactly suits your style of beauty."

She wore a plaid dress and carried a big muff, and only kept from laughing outright by an effort of self-control.

"As regards the headdress, we will mingle with it a circle of pearls. It always produces a striking effect with red hair."

The Maréchale burst out into an exclamation, remarking that she had not red hair.

"Nonsense! The red of painters is not that of ordinary people."

He began to sketch the position of the masses; and he was so much preoccupied with the great artists of the Renaissance that he kept talking about them persistently. For a whole hour he went on musing aloud on those splendid lives, full of genius, glory, and sumptuous displays, with triumphal entries into the cities, and galas by torchlight among half-naked women, beautiful as goddesses.

"You were made to live in those days. A creature of your calibre would have deserved a monseigneur."

Rosanette thought the compliments he paid her very pretty. The day was fixed for the next sitting. Frederick took it on himself to bring the accessories.

As the heat of the stove had stupefied her a little, they went home on foot through the Rue du Bac, and reached the Pont Royal.

It was fine weather, piercingly bright and warm. Some windows of houses in the city shone in the distance, like plates of gold, whilst behind them at the right the turrets of Nôtre Dame showed their outlines in black against the blue sky, softly bathed at the horizon in grey vapours.

The wind began to swell; and Rosanette, having declared that she felt hungry, they entered the "Patisserie Anglaise."

Young women with their children stood eating in front of the marble buffet, where plates of little cakes had glass covers pressed down on them. Rosanette swallowed two cream-tarts. The powdered sugar formed moustaches at the sides of her mouth. From time to time, in order to wipe it, she drew out her handkerchief from her muff, and her face, under her green silk hood, resembled a full-blown rose in the midst of its leaves.

They resumed their walk. In the Rue de la Paix she stood before a goldsmith's shop to look at a bracelet. Frederick wished to make her a present of it.

"No!" said she; "keep your money!"

He was hurt by these words.

"What's the matter now with the ducky? We are melancholy?"

And, the conversation having been renewed, he began making the same protestations of love to her as usual.

"You know well 'tis impossible!"

"Why?"

"Ah! because——"

They went on side by side, she leaning on his arm, and the flounces of her gown kept flapping against his legs. Then, he recalled to mind one winter twilight when on the same footpath Madame Arnoux walked thus by his side, and he became so much absorbed in this recollection that he no longer saw Rosanette, and did not bestow a thought upon her.

She kept looking straight before her in a careless fashion, lagging a little, like a lazy child. It was the hour when people had just come back from their promenade, and equipages were making their way at a quick trot over the hard pavement.

Pellerin's flatteries having probably recurred to her mind, she heaved a sigh.

"Ah! there are some lucky women in the world. Decidedly, I was made for a rich man!"

He replied, with a certain brutality in his tone:

"You have one, in the meantime!" for M. Oudry was looked upon as a man that could count a million three times over.

She asked for nothing better than to get free from him.

"What prevents you from doing so?" And he gave utterance to bitter jests about this old bewigged citizen, pointing out to her that such an intrigue was unworthy of her, and that she ought to break it off.

"Yes," replied the Maréchale, as if talking to herself. "'Tis what I shall end by doing, no doubt!"

Frederick was charmed by this disinterestedness. She slackened her pace, and he fancied that she was fatigued. She obstinately refused to let him take a cab, and she parted with him at her door, sending him a kiss with her finger-tips.

"Ah! what a pity! and to think that imbeciles take me for a man of wealth!"

He reached home in a gloomy frame of mind.

Hussonnet and Deslauriers were awaiting him. The Bohemian, seated before the table, made sketches of Turks' heads; and the advocate, in dirty boots, lay asleep on the sofa.

"Ha! at last," he exclaimed. "But how sullen you look! Will you listen to me?"

His vogue as a tutor had fallen off, for he crammed his pupils with theories unfavourable for their examinations. He had appeared in two or three cases in which he had been unsuccessful, and each new disappointment flung him back with greater force on the dream of his earlier days—a journal in which he could show himself off, avenge himself, and spit forth his bile and his opinions. Fortune and reputation, moreover, would follow as a necessary consequence. It was in this hope that he had got round the Bohemian, Hussonnet happening to be the possessor of a press.

At present, he printed it on pink paper. He invented hoaxes, composed rebuses, tried to engage in polemics, and even intended, in spite of the situation of the premises, to get up concerts. A year's subscription was to give a right to a place in the orchestra in one of the principal theatres of Paris. Besides, the board of management took on itself to furnish foreigners with all necessary information, artistic and otherwise. But the printer gave vent to threats; there were three quarters' rent due to the landlord. All sorts of embarrassments arose; and Hussonnet would have allowed *L'Art* to perish, were it not for the exhortations of the advocate, who kept every day exciting his mind. He had brought the other with him, in order to give more weight to the application he was now making.

"We've come about the journal," said he.

"What! are you still thinking about that?" said Frederick, in an absent tone.

"Certainly, I am thinking about it!"

And he explained his plan anew. By means of the Bourse returns, they would get into communication with financiers, and would thus obtain the hundred thousand francs indispensable as security. But, in order that the print might be transformed into a political journal, it was necessary beforehand to have a large *clientèle*, and for that purpose to make up their minds to go to some expense — so much for the cost of paper and printing, and for outlay at the office; in short, a sum of about fifteen thousand francs.

"I have no funds," said Frederick.

"And what are we to do, then?" said Deslauriers, with folded arms.

Frederick, hurt by the attitude which Deslauriers was assuming, replied:

"Is that my fault?"

"Ah! very fine. A man has wood in his fire, truffles on his table, a good bed, a library, a carriage, every kind of comfort. But let another man shiver under the slates, dine at twenty sous, work like a convict, and sprawl through want in the mire — is it the rich man's fault?"

And he repeated, "Is it the rich man's fault?" with a Ciceronian irony which smacked of the law-courts.

Frederick tried to speak.

"However, I understand one has certain wants — aristocratic wants; for, no doubt, some woman ——"

"Well, even if that were so? Am I not free ——?"

"Oh! quite free!"

And, after a minute's silence:

"Promises are so convenient!"

"Good God! I don't deny that I gave them!" said Frederick.

The advocate went on:

"At college we take oaths; we are going to set up a phalanx; we are going to imitate Balzac's Thirteen. Then, on meeting a friend after a separation: 'Good night, old fellow! Go about your business!' For he who might help the other carefully keeps everything for himself alone.'

"How is that?"

"Yes, you have not even introduced me to the Dambreuses."

Frederick cast a scrutinising glance at him. With his shabby frock-coat, his spectacles of rough glass, and his sallow face, that advocate seemed to him such a typical specimen of the penniless pedant that he could not prevent his lips from curling with a disdainful smile.

Deslauriers perceived this, and reddened.

He had already taken his hat to leave. Hussonnet, filled with uneasiness, tried to mollify him with appealing looks, and, as Frederick was turning his back on him:

"Look here, my boy, become my Mæcenas! Protect the arts!"

Frederick, with an abrupt movement of resignation, took a sheet of paper, and, having scrawled some lines on it, handed it to him. The Bohemian's face lighted up.

Then, passing across the sheet of paper to Deslauriers:

"Apologise, my fine fellow!"

Their friend begged his notary to send him fifteen thousand francs as quickly as possible.

"Ah! I recognise you in that," said Deslauriers.

"On the faith of a gentleman," added the Bohemian, "you are a noble fellow, you'll be placed in the gallery of useful men!"

The advocate remarked:

"You'll lose nothing by it, 'tis an excellent speculation."

"Faith," exclaimed Hussonnet, "I'd stake my head at the scaffold on its success!"

And he said so many foolish things, and promised so many wonderful things, in which perhaps he believed, that Frederick did not know whether he did this in order to laugh at others or at himself.

The same evening he received a letter from his mother. She expressed astonishment at not seeing him yet a minister, while indulging in a little banter at his expense. Then she spoke of her health, and informed him that M. Roque had now become one of her visitors.

"Since he is a widower, I thought there would be no objection to inviting him to the house. Louise is greatly changed for the better." And in a postscript: "You have told me nothing about your fine acquaintance, M. Dambreuse; if I were you, I would make use of him."

Why not? His intellectual ambitions had left him, and his fortune (he saw it clearly) was insufficient, for when his debts had been paid, and the sum agreed on remitted to the others, his income would be diminished by four thousand at least! Moreover, he felt the need of giving up this sort of life, and attaching himself to some pursuit. So, next day, when dining at Madame Arnoux's, he said that his mother was tormenting him in order to make him take up a profession.

"But I was under the impression," she said, "that M. Dambreuse was going to get you into the Council of State? That would suit you very well."

So, then, she wished him to take this course. He regarded her wish as a command.

The banker, as on the first occasion, was seated at his desk, and, with a gesture, intimated that he desired Frederick to wait a few minutes; for a gentleman who was standing at the door with his back turned had been discussing some serious topic with him.

The subject of their conversation was the proposed amalgamation of the different coal-mining companies.

On each side of the glass hung portraits of General Foy and Louis Philippe. Cardboard shelves rose along the panels up to the ceiling, and there were six straw chairs, M. Dambreuse not requiring a more fashionably-furnished apartment for the transaction of business. It resembled those gloomy kitchens in which great banquets are prepared.

Frederick noticed particularly two chests of prodigious size which stood in the corners. He asked himself how many millions they might contain. The banker unlocked one of them, and as the iron plate revolved, it disclosed to view nothing inside but blue paper books full of entries.

At last, the person who had been talking to M. Dambreuse passed in front of Frederick. It was Père Oudry. The two saluted one another, their faces colouring — a circumstance which surprised M. Dam-

breuse. However, he exhibited the utmost affability,
observing that nothing would be easier than to re-
commend the young man to the Keeper of the Seals.
They would be too happy to have him, he added,
concluding his polite attentions by inviting him to an
evening party which he would be giving in a few
days.

Frederick was stepping into a brougham on his
way to this party when a note from the Maréchale
reached him. By the light of the carriage-lamps he
read:

"Darling, I have followed your advice: I have just
expelled my savage. After to-morrow evening, liberty! Say whether I am not brave!"

Nothing more. But it was clearly an invitation to
him to take the vacant place. He uttered an exclamation, squeezed the note into his pocket, and set
forth.

Two municipal guards on horseback were stationed
in the street. A row of lamps burned on the two
front gates, and some servants were calling out in the
courtyard to have the carriages brought up to the
end of the steps before the house under the marquée.

Then suddenly the noise in the vestibule ceased.

Large trees filled up the space in front of the staircase. The porcelain globes shed a light which waved
like white moiré satin on the walls.

Frederick rushed up the steps in a joyous frame
of mind. An usher announced his name. M. Dambreuse extended his hand. Almost at the very same
moment, Madame Dambreuse appeared. She wore a
mauve dress trimmed with lace. The ringlets of her
hair were more abundant than usual, and not a single
jewel did she display.

5—16

She complained of his coming to visit them so rarely, and seized the opportunity to exchange a few confidential words with him.

The guests began to arrive. In their mode of bowing they twisted their bodies on one side or bent in two, or merely lowered their heads a little. Then, a married pair, a family passed in, and all scattered themselves about the drawing-room, which was already filled. Under the chandelier in the centre, an enormous ottoman-seat supported a stand, the flowers of which, bending forward, like plumes of feathers, hung over the heads of the ladies seated all around in a ring, while others occupied the easy-chairs, which formed two straight lines symmetrically interrupted by the large velvet curtains of the windows and the lofty bays of the doors with their gilded lintels.

The crowd of men who remained standing on the floor with their hats in their hands seemed, at some distance, like one black mass, into which the ribbons in the button-holes introduced red points here and there, and rendered all the more dull the monotonous whiteness of their cravats. With the exception of the very young men with the down on their faces, all appeared to be bored. Some dandies, with an expression of sullenness on their countenances, were swinging on their heels. There were numbers of men with grey hair or wigs. Here and there glistened a bald pate; and the visages of many of these men, either purple or exceedingly pale, showed in their worn aspect the traces of immense fatigues: for they were persons who devoted themselves either to political or commercial pursuits. M. Dambreuse had also invited a number of scholars and magistrates,

two or three celebrated doctors, and he depre-
cated with an air of humility the eulogies which they
pronounced on his entertainment and the allusions to
his wealth.

An immense number of men-servants, with fine
gold-laced livery, kept moving about on every side.
The large branched candlesticks, like bouquets of
flame, threw a glow over the hangings. They were
reflected in the mirrors; and at the bottom of the
dining-room, which was adorned with a jessamine
treillage, the side-board resembled the high altar of a
cathedral or an exhibition of jewellery, there were so
many dishes, bells, knives and forks, silver and silver-
gilt spoons in the midst of crystal ware glittering
with iridescence.

The three other reception-rooms overflowed with
artistic objects — landscapes by great masters on the
walls, ivory and porcelain at the sides of the tables,
and Chinese ornaments on the brackets. Lacquered
screens were displayed in front of the windows, clus-
ters of camelias rose above the mantel-shelves, and a
light music vibrated in the distance, like the hum-
ming of bees.

The quadrilles were not numerous, and the dancers, judged by the indifferent fashion in which they
dragged their pumps after them, seemed to be going
through the performance of a duty.

Frederick heard some phrases, such as the following:

"Were you at the last charity fête at the Hôtel
Lambert, Mademoiselle?" "No, Monsieur." "It will
soon be intolerably warm here." "Oh! yes, indeed;
quite suffocating!" "Whose polka, pray, is this?"
"Good heavens, Madame, I don't know!"

And, behind him, three greybeards, who had posted themselves in the recess of a window, were whispering some *risqué* remarks. A sportsman told a hunting story, while a Legitimist carried on an argument with an Orléanist. And, wandering about from one group to another, he reached the card-room, where, in the midst of grave-looking men gathered in a circle, he recognised Martinon, now attached to the Bar of the capital.

His big face, with its waxen complexion, filled up the space encircled by his collar-like beard, which was a marvel with its even surface of black hair; and, observing the golden mean between the elegance which his age might yearn for and the dignity which his profession exacted from him, he kept his thumbs stuck under his armpits, according to the custom of beaux, and then put his hands into his waistcoat pockets after the manner of learned personages. Though his boots were polished to excess, he kept his temples shaved in order to have the forehead of a thinker.

After he had addressed a few chilling words to Frederick, he turned once more towards those who were chatting around him. A land-owner was saying: "This is a class of men that dreams of upsetting society."

"They are calling for the organisation of labour," said another: "Can this be conceived?"

"What could you expect," said a third, "when we see M. de Genoude giving his assistance to the *Siècle*?"

"And even Conservatives style themselves Progressives. To lead us to what? To the Republic! as if such a thing were possible in France!"

Everyone declared that the Republic was impossible in France.

"No matter!" remarked one gentleman in a loud tone. "People take too much interest in the Revolution. A heap of histories, of different kinds of works, are published concerning it!"

"Without taking into account," said Martinon, "that there are probably subjects of far more importance which might be studied."

A gentleman occupying a ministerial office laid the blame on the scandals associated with the stage:

"Thus, for instance, this new drama of *La Reine Margot* really goes beyond the proper limits. What need was there for telling us about the Valois? All this exhibits loyalty in an unfavourable light. 'Tis just like your press! There is no use in talking, the September laws are altogether too mild. For my part, I would like to have court-martials, to gag the journalists! At the slightest display of insolence, drag them before a council of war, and then make an end of the business!"

"Oh, take care, Monsieur! take care!" said a professor. "Don't attack the precious boons we gained in 1830! Respect our liberties!" It would be better, he contended, to adopt a policy of decentralisation, and to distribute the surplus populations of the towns through the country districts.

"But they are gangrened!" exclaimed a Catholic. "Let religion be more firmly established!"

Martinon hastened to observe:

"As a matter of fact, it is a restraining force."

All the evil lay in this modern longing to rise above one's class and to possess luxuries.

"However," urged a manufacturer, "luxury aids commerce. Therefore, I approve of the Duc de Ne-

mours' action in insisting on having short breeches at
his evening parties."

"M. Thiers came to one of them in a pair of
trousers. You know his joke on the subject?"

"Yes; charming! But he turned round to the
demagogues, and his speech on the question of in-
compatibilities was not without its influence in bringing about the attempt of the **twelfth of May.**"

"Oh, pooh!"

"Ay, ay!"

The circle had to make a little opening to give a
passage to a man-servant carrying a tray, who was
trying to make his way into the card-room.

Under the green shades of the wax-lights the
tables were covered with two rows of cards and
gold coins. Frederick stopped beside one corner of
the table, lost the fifteen napoleons which he had in
his pocket, whirled lightly about, and found himself
on the threshold of the boudoir in which Madame Dambreuse happened to be at that moment.

It was filled with women sitting close to one another in little groups on seats without backs. Their
long skirts, swelling round them, seemed like waves,
from which their waists emerged; and their breasts
were clearly outlined by the slope of their corsages,
Nearly every one of them had a bouquet of violets in
her hand. The dull shade of their gloves showed off
the whiteness of their arms, which formed a contrast
with its human flesh tints. Over the shoulders of
some of them hung fringe or mourning-weeds, and,
every now and then, as they quivered with emotion,
it seemed as if their bodices were about to fall down.

But the decorum of their countenances tempered,
the exciting effect of their costumes. Several of them

had a placidity almost like that of animals; and this resemblance to the brute creation on the part of half-nude women made him think of the interior of a harem — indeed, a grosser comparison suggested itself to the young man's mind.

Every variety of beauty was to be found there — some English ladies, with the profile familiar in "keepsakes"; an Italian, whose black eyes shot forth lava-like flashes, like a Vesuvius; three sisters, dressed in blue; three Normans, fresh as April apples; a tall red-haired girl, with a set of amethysts. And the bright scintillation of diamonds, which trembled in aigrettes worn over their hair, the luminous spots of precious stones laid over their breasts, and the delightful radiance of pearls which adorned their foreheads mingled with the glitter of gold rings, as well as with the lace, powder, the feathers, the vermilion of dainty mouths, and the mother-of-pearl hue of teeth. The ceiling, rounded like a cupola, gave to the boudoir the form of a flower-basket, and a current of perfumed air circulated under the flapping of their fans.

Frederick, planting himself behind them, put up his eyeglass and scanned their shoulders, not all of which did he consider irreproachable. He thought about the Maréchale, and this dispelled the temptations that beset him or consoled him for not yielding to them.

He gazed, however, at Madame Dambreuse, and he considered her charming, in spite of her mouth being rather large and her nostrils too dilated. But she was remarkably graceful in appearance. There was, as it were, an expression of passionate languor in the ringlets of her hair, and her forehead, which was like agate, seemed to cover a great deal, and indicated a masterful intelligence.

She had placed beside her her husband's niece, a rather plain-looking young person. From time to time she left her seat to receive those who had just come in; and the murmur of feminine voices, made, as it were, a cackling like that of birds.

They were talking about the Tunisian ambassadors and their costumes. One lady had been present at the last reception of the Academy. Another referred to the *Don Juan* of Molière, which had recently been performed at the Théâtre Français.

But with a significant glance towards her niece, Madame Dambreuse laid a finger on her lips, while the smile which escaped from her contradicted this display of austerity.

Suddenly, Martinon appeared at the door directly in front of her. She arose at once. He offered her his arm. Frederick, in order to watch the progress of these gallantries on Martinon's part, walked past the card-table, and came up with them in the large drawing-room. Madame Dambreuse very soon quitted her cavalier, and began chatting with Frederick himself in a very familiar tone.

She understood that he did not play cards, and did not dance.

"Young people have a tendency to be melancholy!" Then, with a single comprehensive glance around:

"Besides, this sort of thing is not amusing — at least for certain natures!"

And she drew up in front of the row of armchairs, uttering a few polite remarks here and there, while some old men with double eyeglasses came to pay court to her.   She introduced Frederick to some of them.   M. Dambreuse touched him lightly on the elbow, and led him out on the terrace.

He had seen the Minister.   The thing was not easy to manage.   Before he could be qualified for the post of auditor to the Council of State, he should pass an examination.   Frederick, seized with an unaccountable self-confidence, replied that he had a knowledge of the subjects prescribed for it.

The financier was not surprised at this, after all the eulogies M. Roque had pronounced on his abilities.

At the mention of this name, a vision of little Louise, her house and her room, passed through his mind, and he remembered how he had on nights like this stood at her window listening to the wagoners driving past.   This recollection of his griefs brought back the thought of Madame Arnoux, and he relapsed into silence as he continued to pace up and down the terrace.   The windows shone amid the darkness like slabs of flame.   The buzz of the ball gradually grew fainter; the carriages were beginning to leave.

"Why in the world," M. Dambreuse went on, "are you so anxious to be attached to the Council of State?"

And he declared, in the tone of a man of broad views, that the public functions led to nothing — he could speak with some authority on that point — business was much better.

Frederick urged as an objection the difficulty of grappling with all the details of business.

"Pooh! I could post you up well in them in a very short time."

Would he like to be a partner in any of his own undertakings?

The young man saw, as by a lightning-flash, an enormous fortune coming into his hands.

"Let us go in again," said the banker. "You are staying for supper with us, are you not?"

It was three o'clock. They left the terrace.

In the dining-room, a table at which supper was served up awaited the guests.

M. Dambreuse perceived Martinon, and, drawing near his wife, in a low tone:

"Is it you who invited him?"

She answered dryly:

"Yes, of course."

The niece was not present.

The guests drank a great deal of wine, and laughed very loudly; and risky jokes did not give any offence, all present experiencing that sense of relief which follows a somewhat prolonged period of constraint.

Martinon alone displayed anything like gravity. He refused to drink champagne, as he thought this good form, and, moreover, he assumed an air of tact and politeness, for when M. Dambreuse, who had a contracted chest, complained of an oppression, he made repeated enquiries about that gentleman's health, and then let his blue eyes wander in the direction of Madame Dambreuse.

She questioned Frederick in order to find out which of the young ladies he liked best. He had noticed none of them in particular, and besides, he preferred the women of thirty.

"There, perhaps, you show your sense," she returned.

Then, as they were putting on their pelisses and paletots, M. Dambreuse said to him:

"Come and see me one of these mornings and we'll have a chat."

Martinon, at the foot of the stairs, was lighting a cigar, and, as he puffed it, he presented such a heavy profile that his companion allowed this remark to escape from him:

"Upon my word, you have a fine head!"

"It has turned a few other heads," replied the young magistrate, with an air of mingled self-complacency and annoyance.

As soon as Frederick was in bed, he summed up the main features of the evening party. In the first place, his own toilet (he had looked at himself several times in the mirrors), from the cut of his coat to the knot of his pumps left nothing to find fault with. He had spoken to influential men, and seen wealthy ladies at close quarters. M. Dambreuse had shown himself to be an admirable type of man, and Madame Dambreuse an almost bewitching type of woman. He weighed one by one her slightest words, her looks, a thousand things incapable of being analysed. It would be a right good thing to have such a mistress. And, after all, why should he not? He would have as good a chance with her as any other man. Perhaps she was not so hard to win? Then Martinon came back to his recollection; and, as he fell asleep, he smiled with pity for this worthy fellow.

He woke up with the thought of the Maréchale in his mind. Those words of her note, "After tomorrow evening," were in fact an appointment for the very same day.

He waited until nine o'clock, and then hurried to her house.

Some one who had been going up the stairs before him shut the door. He rang the bell; Delphine came out and told him that "Madame" was not there.

Frederick persisted, begging of her to admit him. He had something of a very serious nature to communicate to her; only a word would suffice. At length, the hundred-sous-piece argument proved successful, and the maid let him into the anteroom.

Rosanette appeared. She was in a negligée, with her hair loose, and, shaking her head, she waved her arms when she was some paces away from him to indicate that she could not receive him now.

Frederick descended the stairs slowly. This caprice was worse than any of the others she had indulged in. He could not understand it at all.

In front of the porter's lodge Mademoiselle Vatnaz stopped him.

"Has she received you?"

"No."

"You've been put out?"

"How do you know that?"

"'Tis quite plain. But come on; let us go away. I am suffocating!"

She made him accompany her along the street; she panted for breath; he could feel her thin arm trembling on his own. Suddenly, she broke out:

"Ah! the wretch!"

"Who, pray?"

"Why, he — he — Delmar!"

This revelation humiliated Frederick. He next asked:

"Are you quite sure of it?"

"Why, when I tell you I followed him!" exclaimed the Vatnaz. "I saw him going in! Now do you understand? I ought to have expected it for that matter—'twas I, in my stupidity, that introduced him to her. And if you only knew all; my God! Why, I picked him up, supported him, clothed him! And then all the paragraphs I got into the newspapers about him! I loved him like a mother!"

Then, with a sneer:

"Ha! Monsieur wants velvet robes! You may be sure 'tis a speculation on his part. And as for her!—to think that I knew her to earn her living as a seamstress! If it were not for me, she would have fallen into the mire twenty times over! But I will plunge her into it yet! I'll see her dying in a hospital—and everything about her will be known!"

And, like a torrent of dirty water from a vessel full of refuse, her rage poured out in a tumultuous fashion into Frederick's ear the recital of her rival's disgraceful acts.

"She lived with Jumillac, with Flacourt, with little Allard, with Bertinaux, with Saint-Valéry, the pockmarked fellow! No, 'twas the other! They are two brothers—it makes no difference. And when she was in difficulties, I settled everything. She is so avaricious! And then, you will agree with me, 'twas nice and kind of me to go to see her, for we are not persons of the same grade! Am I a fast woman —I? Do I sell myself? Without taking into account that she is as stupid as a head of cabbage. She writes 'category' with a 'th.' After all, they are well met. They make a precious couple, though he styles himself an artist and thinks himself a man of genius. But, my God! if he had only intelligence, he

would not have done such an infamous thing! Men
don't, as a rule, leave a superior woman for a hussy!
What do I care about him after all? He is becoming
ugly. I hate him! If I met him, mind you, I'd spit
in his face." She spat out as she uttered the words.
"Yes, this is what I think about him now. And
Arnoux, eh? Isn't it abominable? He has forgiven
her so often! You can't conceive the sacrifices he
has made for her. She ought to kiss his feet! He is
so generous, so good!"

Frederick was delighted at hearing Delmar disparaged. He had taken sides with Arnoux. This
perfidy on Rosanette's part seemed to him an abnor-
mal and inexcusable thing; and, infected with this elderly spinster's emotion, he felt a sort of tenderness
towards her. Suddenly he found himself in front of
Arnoux's door. Mademoiselle Vatnaz, without his attention having been drawn to it, had led him down
towards the Rue Poissonnière.

"Here we are!" said she. "As for me, I can't go
up; but you, surely there is nothing to prevent you?"

"From doing what?"

"From telling him everything, faith!"

Frederick, as if waking up with a start, saw the
baseness towards which she was urging him.

"Well?" she said after a pause.

He raised his eyes towards the second floor. Madame Arnoux's lamp was burning. In fact there was
nothing to prevent him from going up.

"I am going to wait for you here. Go on, then!"

This direction had the effect of chilling him, and
he said:

"I shall be a long time up there; you would do
better to return home. I will call on you to-morrow."

"No, no!" replied the Vatnaz, stamping with her foot. "Take him with you! Bring him there! Let him catch them together!"

"But Delmar will no longer be there."

She hung down her head.

"Yes; that's true, perhaps."

And she remained without speaking in the middle of the street, with vehicles all around her; then, fixing on him her wild-cat's eyes:

"I may rely on you, may I not? There is now a sacred bond between us. Do what you say, then; we'll talk about it to-morrow."

Frederick, in passing through the lobby, heard two voices responding to one another.

Madame Arnoux's voice was saying:

"Don't lie! don't lie, pray!"

He went in. The voices suddenly ceased.

Arnoux was walking from one end of the apartment to the other, and Madame was seated on the little chair near the fire, extremely pale and staring straight before her. Frederick stepped back, and was about to retire, when Arnoux grasped his hand, glad that some one had come to his rescue.

"But I am afraid——" said Frederick.

"Stay here, I beg of you!" he whispered in his ear.

Madame remarked:

"You must make some allowance for this scene, Monsieur Moreau. Such things sometimes unfortunately occur in households."

"They do when we introduce them there ourselves," said Arnoux in a jolly tone. "Women have crotchets, I assure you. This, for instance, is not a bad one—see! No; quite the contrary. Well, she has been amusing herself for the last hour by teasing me with a heap of idle stories."

"They are true," retorted Madame Arnoux, losing patience; "for, in fact, you bought it yourself."

"I?"

"Yes, you yourself, at the Persian House."

"The cashmere," thought Frederick.

He was filled with a consciousness of guilt, and got quite alarmed.

She quickly added:

"It was on Saturday, the fourteenth."

"The fourteenth," said Arnoux, looking up, as if he were searching in his mind for a date.

"And, furthermore, the clerk who sold it to you was a fair-haired young man."

"How could I remember what sort of man the clerk was?"

"And yet it was at your dictation he wrote the address, 18 Rue de Laval."

"How do you know?" said Arnoux in amazement.

She shrugged her shoulders.

"Oh! 'tis very simple: I went to get my cashmere altered, and the superintendent of the millinery department told me that they had just sent another of the same sort to Madame Arnoux."

"Is it my fault if there is a Madame Arnoux in the same street?"

"Yes; but not Jacques Arnoux," she returned.

Thereupon, he began to talk in an incoherent fashion, protesting that he was innocent. It was some misapprehension, some accident, one of those things that happen in some way that is utterly unaccountable. Men should not be condemned on mere suspicion, vague probabilities; and he referred to the case of the unfortunate Lesurques.

"In short, I say you are mistaken. Do you want me to take my oath on it?"

"'Tis not worth while."

"Why?"

She looked him straight in the face without saying a word, then stretched out her hand, took down the little silver chest from the mantelpiece, and handed him a bill which was spread open.

Arnoux coloured up to his ears, and his swollen and distorted features betrayed his confusion.

"But," he said in faltering tones, "what does this prove?"

"Ah!" she said, with a peculiar ring in her voice, in which sorrow and irony were blended. "Ah!"

Arnoux held the bill in his hands, and turned it round without removing his eyes from it, as if he were going to find in it the solution of a great problem.

"Ah! yes, yes; I remember," said he at length. "'Twas a commission. You ought to know about that matter, Frederick." Frederick remained silent. "A commission that Père Oudry entrusted to me."

"And for whom?"

"For his mistress."

"For your own!" exclaimed Madame Arnoux, springing to her feet and standing erect before him.

"I swear to you!"

"Don't begin over again. I know everything."

"Ha! quite right. So you're spying on me!"

She returned coldly:

"Perhaps that wounds your delicacy?"

"Since you are in a passion," said Arnoux, looking for his hat, "and can't be reasoned with——"

5—17

Then, with a big sigh:

"Don't marry, my poor friend, don't, if you take my advice!"

And he took himself off, finding it absolutely necessary to get into the open air.

Then there was a deep silence, and it seemed as if everything in the room had become more motionless than before. A luminous circle above the lamp whitened the ceiling, while at the corners stretched out bits of shade resembling pieces of black gauze placed on top of one another. The ticking of the clock and the crackling of the fire were the only sounds that disturbed the stillness.

Madame Arnoux had just seated herself in the armchair at the opposite side of the chimney-piece. She bit her lip and shivered. She drew her hands up to her face; a sob broke from her, and she began to weep.

He sat down on the little couch, and in the soothing tone in which one addresses a sick person:

"You don't suspect me of having anything to do with ——?"

She made no reply. But, continuing presently to give utterance to her own thoughts:

"I leave him perfectly free! There was no necessity for lying on his part!"

"That is quite true," said Frederick. "No doubt," he added, "it was the result of Arnoux's habits; he had acted thoughtlessly, but perhaps in matters of a graver character ——"

"What do you see, then, that can be graver?"

"Oh, nothing!"

Frederick bent his head with a smile of acquiescence. Nevertheless, he urged, Arnoux possessed certain good qualities; he was fond of his children.

"Ay, and he does all he can to ruin them!"

Frederick urged that this was due to an excessively easy-going disposition, for indeed he was a good fellow.

She exclaimed:

"But what is the meaning of that — a good fellow?"

And he proceeded to defend Arnoux in the vaguest kind of language he could think of, and, while expressing his sympathy with her, he rejoiced, he was delighted, at the bottom of his heart. Through retaliation or need of affection she would fly to him for refuge. His love was intensified by the hope which had now grown immeasurably stronger in his breast.

Never had she appeared to him so captivating, so perfectly beautiful. From time to time a deep breath made her bosom swell. Her two eyes, gazing fixedly into space, seemed dilated by a vision in the depths of her consciousness, and her lips were slightly parted, as if to let her soul escape through them. Sometimes she pressed her handkerchief over them tightly. He would have liked to be this dainty little piece of cambric moistened with her tears. In spite of himself, he cast a look at the bed at the end of the alcove, picturing to himself her head lying on the pillow, and so vividly did this present itself to his imagination that he had to restrain himself to keep from clasping her in his arms. She closed her eyelids, and now she appeared quiescent and languid. Then he drew closer to her, and, bending over her, he eagerly scanned her face. At that moment, he heard the noise of boots in the lobby outside — it was the other. They heard him shutting the door of his own room. Frederick made a sign to Madame Arnoux to ascertain from her whether he ought to go there.

She replied "Yes," in the same voiceless fashion, and this mute exchange of thoughts between them was, as it were, an assent — the preliminary step in adultery.

Arnoux was just taking off his coat to go to bed. "Well, how is she going on?"

"Oh! better," said Frederick; "this will pass off." But Arnoux was in an anxious state of mind.

"You don't know her; she has got hysterical now! Idiot of a clerk! This is what comes of being too good. If I had not given that cursed shawl to Rosanette!"

"Don't regret having done so a bit. Nobody could be more grateful to you than she is."

"Do you really think so?"

Frederick had not a doubt of it. The best proof of it was her dismissal of Père Oudry.

"Ah! poor little thing!"

And in the excess of his emotion, Arnoux wanted to rush off to her forthwith.

"'Tisn't worth while. I am calling to see her. She is unwell."

"All the more reason for my going."

He quickly put on his coat again, and took up his candlestick. Frederick cursed his own stupidity, and pointed out to him that for decency's sake he ought to remain this night with his wife. He could not leave her; it would be very nasty.

"I tell you candidly you would be doing wrong. There is no hurry over there. You will go tomorrow. Come; do this for my sake."

Arnoux put down his candlestick, and, embracing him, said:

"You are a right good fellow!"

CHAPTER IX.

THE FRIEND OF THE FAMILY.

HEN began for Frederick an existence of misery. He became the parasite of the house.

If anyone were indisposed, he called three times a day to know how the patient was, went to the piano-tuner's, contrived to do a thousand acts of kindness; and he endured with an air of contentment Mademoiselle Marthe's poutings and the caresses of little Eugène, who was always drawing his dirty hands over the young man's face. He was present at dinners at which Monsieur and Madame, facing each other, did not exchange a word, unless it happened that Arnoux provoked his wife with the absurd remarks he made. When the meal was over, he would play about the room with his son, conceal himself behind the furniture, or carry the little boy on his back, walking about on all fours, like the Bearnais.* At last, he would go out, and she would at once plunge into the eternal subject of complaint — Arnoux.

---

* Henry IV. — TRANSLATOR.

It was not his misconduct that excited her indignation, but her pride appeared to be wounded, and she did not hide her repugnance towards this man, who showed an absence of delicacy, dignity, and honour.

"Or rather, he is mad!" she said.

Frederick artfully appealed to her to confide in him. Ere long he knew all the details of her life. Her parents were people in a humble rank in life at Chartres. One day, Arnoux, while sketching on the bank of the river (at this period he believed himself to be a painter), saw her leaving the church, and made her an offer of marriage. On account of his wealth, he was unhesitatingly accepted. Besides, he was desperately in love with her. She added:

"Good heavens! he loves me still, after his fashion!"

They spent the few months immediately after their marriage in travelling through Italy.

Arnoux, in spite of his enthusiasm at the sight of the scenery and the masterpieces, did nothing but groan over the wine, and, to find some kind of amusement, organised picnics along with some English people. The profit which he had made by reselling some pictures tempted him to take up the fine arts as a commercial speculation. Then, he became infatuated about pottery. Just now other branches of commerce attracted him; and, as he had become more and more vulgarised, he contracted coarse and extravagant habits. It was not so much for his vices she had to reproach him as for his entire conduct. No change could be expected in him, and her unhappiness was irreparable.

Frederick declared that his own life in the same way was a failure.

He was still a young man, however. Why should
he despair? And she gave him good advice: "Work!
and marry!" He answered her with bitter smiles;
for in place of giving utterance to the real cause of
his grief, he pretended that it was of a different character, a sublime feeling, and he assumed the part of
an Antony to some extent, the man accursed by
fate — language which did not, however, change very
materially the complexion of his thoughts.

For certain men action becomes more difficult as
desire becomes stronger. They are embarrassed by
self-distrust, and terrified by the fear of making themselves disliked. Besides, deep attachments resemble
virtuous women: they are afraid of being discovered,
and pass through life with downcast eyes.

Though he was now better acquainted with Madame Arnoux (for that very reason perhaps), he was
still more faint-hearted than before. Each morning he
swore in his own mind that he would take a bold
course. He was prevented from doing so by an un-
conquerable feeling of bashfulness; and he had no
example to guide him, inasmuch as she was different
from other women. From the force of his dreams, he
had placed her outside the ordinary pale of humanity. At her side he felt himself of less importance in
the world than the sprigs of silk that escaped from
her scissors.

Then he thought of some monstrous and absurd
devices, such as surprises at night, with narcotics
and false keys — anything appearing easier to him
than to face her disdain.

Besides, the children, the two servant-maids, and
the relative position of the rooms caused insurmount-
able obstacles. So then he made up his mind to

possess her himself alone, and to bring her to live with him far away in the depths of some solitude. He even asked himself what lake would be blue enough, what seashore would be delightful enough for her, whether it would be in Spain, Switzerland, or the East; and expressly fixing on days when she seemed more irritated than usual, he told her that it would be necessary for her to leave the house, to find out some ground to justify such a step, and that he saw no way out of it but a separation. However, for the sake of the children whom she loved, she would never resort to such an extreme course. So much virtue served to increase his respect for her.

He spent each afternoon in recalling the visit he had paid the night before, and in longing for the evening to come in order that he might call again. When he did not dine with them, he posted himself about nine o'clock at the corner of the street, and, as soon as Arnoux had slammed the hall-door behind him, Frederick quickly ascended the two flights of stairs, and asked the servant-girl in an ingenuous fashion:

"Is Monsieur in?"

Then he would exhibit surprise at finding that Arnoux was gone out.

The latter frequently came back unexpectedly. Then Frederick had to accompany him to the little café in the Rue Sainte-Anne, which Regimbart now frequented.

The Citizen began by giving vent to some fresh grievance which he had against the Crown. Then they would chat, pouring out friendly abuse on one another, for the earthenware manufacturer took Regimbart for a thinker of a high order, and, vexed at see-

ing him neglecting so many chances of winning
distinction, teased the Citizen about his laziness. It
seemed to Regimbart that Arnoux was a man full of
heart and imagination, but decidedly of lax morals,
and therefore he was quite unceremonious towards a
personage he respected so little, refusing even to dine
at his house on the ground that "such formality was
a bore."

Sometimes, at the moment of parting, Arnoux
would be seized with hunger. He found it necessary to order an omelet or some roasted apples;
and, as there was never anything to eat in the establishment, he sent out for something. They waited.
Regimbart did not leave, and ended by consenting in
a grumbling fashion to have something himself. He
was nevertheless gloomy, for he remained for hours
seated before a half-filled glass. As Providence did
not regulate things in harmony with his ideas, he
was becoming a hypochondriac, no longer cared even
to read the newspapers, and at the mere mention of
England's name began to bellow with rage. On one
occasion, referring to a waiter who attended on him
carelessly, he exclaimed:

"Have we not enough of insults from the for-
eigner?"

Except at these critical periods he remained taci-
turn, contemplating "an infallible stroke of business
that would burst up the whole shop."

Whilst he was lost in these reflections, Arnoux in
a monotonous voice and with a slight look of intoxication, related incredible anecdotes in which he always shone himself, owing to his assurance; and
Frederick (this was, no doubt, due to some deep-
rooted resemblances) felt more or less attracted towards

him. He reproached himself for this weakness, believing that on the contrary he ought to hate this
man.

Arnoux, in Frederick's presence, complained of his
wife's ill-temper, her obstinacy, her unjust accusa-
tions. She had not been like this in former days.

"If I were you," said Frederick, "I would make
her an allowance and live alone."

Arnoux made no reply; and the next moment he
began to sound her praises. She was good, devoted,
intelligent, and virtuous; and, passing to her personal
beauty, he made some revelations on the subject
with the thoughtlessness of people who display their
treasures at taverns.

His equilibrium was disturbed by a catastrophe.

He had been appointed one of the Board of Superintendence in a kaolin company. But placing reliance
on everything that he was told, he had signed inac-
curate reports and approved, without verification, of
the annual inventories fraudulently prepared by the
manager. The company had now failed, and Arnoux,
being legally responsible, was, along with the others
who were liable under the guaranty, condemned to pay
damages, which meant a loss to him of thirty thousand
francs, not to speak of the costs of the judgment.

Frederick read the report of the case in a newspaper, and at once hurried off to the Rue de Paradis.

He was ushered into Madame's apartment. It was
breakfast-time. A round table close to the fire was
covered with bowls of *café au lait*. Slippers trailed
over the carpet, and clothes over the armchairs. Arnoux was attired in trousers and a knitted vest, with
his eyes bloodshot and his hair in disorder. Little
Eugène was crying at the pain caused by an attack

of mumps, while nibbling at a slice of bread and butter. His sister was eating quietly. Madame Arnoux, a little paler than usual, was attending on all three of them.

"Well," said Arnoux, heaving a deep sigh, "you know all about it?"

And, as Frederick gave him a pitying look: "There, you see, I have been the victim of my own trustfulness!"

Then he relapsed into silence, and so great was his prostration, that he pushed his breakfast away from him. Madame Arnoux raised her eyes with a shrug of the shoulders. He passed his hand across his forehead.

"After all, I am not guilty. I have nothing to reproach myself with. 'Tis a misfortune. It will be got over — ay, and so much the worse, faith!"

He took a bite of a cake, however, in obedience to his wife's entreaties.

That evening, he wished that she should go and dine with him alone in a private room at the Maison d'Or. Madame Arnoux did not at all understand this emotional impulse, taking offence, in fact, at being treated as if she were a light woman. Arnoux, on the contrary, meant it as a proof of affection. Then, as he was beginning to feel dull, he went to pay the Maréchale a visit in order to amuse himself.

Up to the present, he had been pardoned for many things owing to his reputation for good-fellowship. His lawsuit placed him amongst men of bad character. No one visited his house.

Frederick, however, considered that he was bound in honour to go there more frequently than ever.

He hired a box at the Italian opera, and brought them there with him every week. Meanwhile, the pair had reached that period in unsuitable unions when an invincible lassitude springs from concessions which people get into the habit of making, and which render existence intolerable. Madame Arnoux restrained her pent-up feelings from breaking out; Arnoux became gloomy; and Frederick grew sad at witnessing the unhappiness of these two ill-fated beings.

She had imposed on him the obligation, since she had given him her confidence, of making enquiries as to the state of her husband's affairs. But shame prevented him from doing so. It was painful to him to reflect that he coveted the wife of this man, at whose dinner-table he constantly sat. Nevertheless, he continued his visits, excusing himself on the ground that he was bound to protect her, and that an occasion might present itself for being of service to her.

Eight days after the ball, he had paid a visit to M. Dambreuse. The financier had offered him twenty shares in a coal-mining speculation; Frederick did not go back there again. Deslauriers had written letters to him, which he left unanswered. Pellerin had invited him to go and see the portrait; he always put it off. He gave way, however, to Cisy's persistent appeals to be introduced to Rosanette.

She received him very nicely, but without springing on his neck as she used to do formerly. His comrade was delighted at being received by a woman of easy virtue, and above all at having a chat with an actor. Delmar was there when he called. A drama in which he appeared as a peasant lecturing Louis XIV. and prophesying the events of '89 had made him so conspicuous, that the same part was continually assigned to him; and now his function consisted of attacks on the monarchs of all nations. As an English brewer, he inveighed against Charles I.; as a student at Salamanca, he cursed Philip II.; or, as a sensitive father, he expressed indignation against the Pompadour — this was the most beautiful bit of acting! The brats of the street used to wait at the door leading to the side-scenes in order to see him; and his biography, sold between the acts, described him as taking care of his aged mother, reading the Bible, assisting the poor, in fact, under the aspect of a Saint Vincent de Paul together with a dash of Brutus and Mirabeau. People spoke of him as "Our Delmar." He had a mission; he became another Christ.

All this had fascinated Rosanette; and she had got rid of Père Oudry, without caring one jot about consequences, as she was not of a covetous disposition.

Arnoux, who knew her, had taken advantage of the state of affairs for some time past to spend very little money on her. M. Roque had appeared on the scene, and all three of them carefully avoided anything like a candid explanation. Then, fancying that she had got rid of the other solely on his account, Arnoux increased her allowance, for she was living at a very expensive rate. She had even sold her cashmere in her anxiety to pay off her old debts, as she said; and he was continually giving her money, while she bewitched him and imposed upon him pitilessly. Therefore, bills and stamped paper rained all over the house. Frederick felt that a crisis was approaching.

One day he called to see Madame Arnoux. She had gone out. Monsieur was at work below stairs in the shop. In fact, Arnoux, in the midst of his Japanese vases, was trying to take in a newly-married pair who happened to be well-to-do people from the provinces. He talked about wheel-moulding and fine-moulding, about spotted porcelain and glazed porcelain; the others, not wishing to appear utterly ignorant of the subject, listened with nods of appro-bation, and made purchases.

When the customers had gone out, he told Fred-erick that he had that very morning been engaged in a little altercation with his wife. In order to obviate any remarks about expense, he had declared that the Maréchale was no longer his mistress. "I even told her that she was yours."

Frederick was annoyed at this; but to utter re-proaches might only betray him. He faltered: "Ah! you were in the wrong — greatly in the wrong!"

"What does that signify?" said Arnoux. "Where is the disgrace of passing for her lover? I am really so myself. Would you not be flattered at being in that position?"

Had she spoken? Was this a hint? Frederick hastened to reply:

"No! not at all! on the contrary!"

"Well, what then?"

"Yes, 'tis true; it makes no difference so far as that's concerned."

Arnoux next asked: "And why don't you call there oftener?"

Frederick promised that he would make it his business to go there again.

"Ah! I forgot! you ought, when talking about Rosanette, to let out in some way to my wife that you are her lover. I can't suggest how you can best do it, but you'll find out that. I ask this of you as a special favour — eh?"

The young man's only answer was an equivocal grimace. This calumny had undone him. He even called on her that evening, and swore that Arnoux's accusation was false.

"Is that really so?"

He appeared to be speaking sincerely, and, when she had taken a long breath of relief, she said to him:

"I believe you," with a beautiful smile. Then she hung down her head, and, without looking at him:

"Besides, nobody has any claim on you!"

So then she had divined nothing; and she despised him, seeing that she did not think he could love her well enough to remain faithful to her! Frederick, forgetting his overtures while with the other, looked on the permission accorded to him as an insult to himself.

After this she suggested that he ought now and then to pay Rosanette a visit, to get a little glimpse of what she was like.

Arnoux presently made his appearance, and, five minutes later, wished to carry him off to Rosanette's abode.

The situation was becoming intolerable.

His attention was diverted by a letter from a notary, who was going to send him fifteen thousand francs the following day; and, in order to make up for his neglect of Deslauriers, he went forthwith to tell him this good news.

The advocate was lodging in the Rue des Trois-Maries, on the fifth floor, over a courtyard. His study, a little tiled apartment, chilly, and with a grey paper on the walls, had as its principal decoration a gold medal, the prize awarded him on the occasion of taking out his degree as a Doctor of Laws, which was fixed in an ebony frame near the mirror. A mahogany bookcase enclosed under its glass front a hundred volumes, more or less. The writing-desk, covered with sheep-leather, occupied the centre of the apartment. Four old armchairs upholstered in green velvet were placed in the corners; and a heap of shavings made a blaze in the fireplace, where there was always a bundle of sticks ready to be lighted as soon as he rang the bell. It was his consultation-hour, and the advocate had on a white cravat.

The announcement as to the fifteen thousand francs (he had, no doubt, given up all hope of getting the amount) made him chuckle with delight.

"That's right, old fellow, that's right — that's quite right!"

He threw some wood into the fire, sat down again, and immediately began talking about the journal. The first thing to do was to get rid of Hussonnet.

"I'm quite tired of that idiot! As for officially professing opinions, my own notion is that the most equitable and forcible position is to have no opinions at all."

Frederick appeared astonished.

"Why, the thing is perfectly plain. It is time that politics should be dealt with scientifically. The old men of the eighteenth century began it when Rousseau and the men of letters introduced into the political sphere philanthropy, poetry, and other fudge, to the great delight of the Catholics — a natural alliance, however, since the modern reformers (I can prove it) all believe in Revelation. But, if you sing high masses for Poland, if, in place of the God of the Dominicans, who was an executioner, you take the God of the Romanticists, who is an upholsterer, if, in fact, you have not a wider conception of the Absolute than your ancestors, Monarchy will penetrate underneath your Republican forms, and your red cap will never be more than the headpiece of a priest. The only difference will be that the cell system will take the place of torture, the outrageous treatment of Religion that of sacrilege, and the European Concert that of the Holy Alliance; and in this beautiful order which we admire, composed of the wreckage of the followers of Louis XIV., the last remains of the Voltaireans, with some Imperial whitewash on top, and some fragments of the British Constitution, you will see the municipal councils trying to give annoyance to the Mayor, the general councils to their Prefect, the Chambers to the King, the Press to Power, and the Administration to everybody. But simple-minded people get enraptured about the Civil Code, a work fabricated — let them say what they like — in a mean and tyrannical spirit, for the legislator, in place of doing his duty to the State, which simply means to observe customs in a regular fashion, claims to model society like another Lycurgus. Why does the law impede fathers of families with regard to the making of wills? Why does it place shackles on the compulsory sale of real estate? Why does it punish as a misdemeanour vagrancy, which ought not even to be regarded as a technical contravention of the Code. And there are other things! I know all about them! and so I am

5—18

going to write a little novel, entitled 'The History of the Idea of Justice,' which will be amusing. But I am infernally thirsty! And you?"

He leaned out through the window, and called to the porter to go and fetch them two glasses of grog from the public-house over the way.

"To sum up, I see three parties — no! three groups — in none of which do I take the slightest interest: those who have, those who have nothing, and those who are trying to have. But all agree in their idiotic worship of Authority! For example, Mably recommends that the philosophers should be prevented from publishing their doctrines; M. Wronsky, the geometrician, describes the censorship as the 'critical expression of speculative spontaneity'; Père Enfantin gives his blessing to the Hapsburgs for having passed a hand across the Alps in order to keep Italy down; Pierre Leroux wishes people to be compelled to listen to an orator; and Louis Blanc inclines towards a State religion — so much rage for government have these vassals whom we call the people! Nevertheless, there is not a single legitimate government, in spite of their sempiternal principles. But 'principle' signifies 'origin.' It is always necessary to go back to a revolution, to an act of violence, to a transitory fact. Thus, our principle is the national sovereignty embodied in the Parliamentary form, though the Parliament does not assent to this! But in what way could the sovereignty of the people be more sacred than the Divine Right? They are both fictions. Enough of metaphysics; no more phantoms! There is no need of dogmas in order to get the streets swept! It will be said that I am turning society upside down. Well, after all, where would be the harm of that? It is, indeed, a nice thing — this society of yours."

Frederick could have given many answers. But, seeing that his theories were far less advanced than those of Sénécal, he was full of indulgence towards Deslauriers. He contented himself with arguing that such a system would make them generally hated.

"On the contrary, as we should have given to each party a pledge of hatred against his neighbour, all will reckon on us. You are about to enter into it yourself, and to furnish us with some transcendent criticism!"

It was necessary to attack accepted ideas — the Academy, the Normal School, the Conservatoire, the Comédie Française, everything that resembled an institution. It was in that way that they would give uniformity to the doctrines taught in their review. Then, as soon as it had been thoroughly well-established, the journal would suddenly be converted into a daily publication. Thereupon they could find fault with individuals.

"And they will respect us, you may be sure!"

Deslauriers touched upon that old dream of his — the position of editor-in-chief, so that he might have the unutterable happiness of directing others, of entirely cutting down their articles, of ordering them to be written or declining them. His eyes twinkled under his goggles; he got into a state of excitement, and drank a few glasses of brandy, one after the other, in an automatic fashion.

"You'll have to stand me a dinner once a week. That's indispensable, even though you should have to squander half your income on it. People would feel pleasure in going to it; it would be a centre for the others, a lever for yourself; and by manipulating public opinion at its two ends — literature and politics — you will see how, before six months have passed, we shall occupy the first rank in Paris."

Frederick, as he listened to Deslauriers, experienced a sensation of rejuvenescence, like a man who, after having been confined in a room for a long time, is suddenly transported into the open air. The enthusiasm of his friend had a contagious effect upon him.

"Yes, I have been an idler, an imbecile — you are right!"

"All in good time," said Deslauriers. "I have found my Frederick again!"

And, holding up his jaw with closed fingers:

"Ah! you have made me suffer! Never mind, I am fond of you all the same."

They stood there gazing into each other's faces, both deeply affected, and were on the point of embracing each other.

A woman's cap appeared on the threshold of the anteroom.

"What brings you here?" said Deslauriers.

It was Mademoiselle Clémence, his mistress.

She replied that, as she happened to be passing, she could not resist the desire to go in to see him, and in order that they might have a little repast together, she had brought some cakes, which she laid on the table.

"Take care of my papers!" said the advocate, sharply. "Besides, this is the third time that I have forbidden you to come at my consultation-hours."

She wished to embrace him.

"All right! Go away! Cut your stick!"

He repelled her; she heaved a great sigh.

"Ah! you are plaguing me again!"

"'Tis because I love you!"

"I don't ask you to love me, but to oblige me!"

This harsh remark stopped Clémence's tears. She took up her station before the window, and remained there motionless, with her forehead against the pane.

Her attitude and her silence had an irritating effect on Deslauriers.

"When you have finished, you will order your carriage, will you not?"

She turned round with a start.

"You are sending me away?"

"Exactly."

She fixed on him her large blue eyes, no doubt as a last appeal, then drew the two ends of her tartan across each other, lingered for a minute or two, and went away.

"You ought to call her back," said Frederick.

"Come, now!"

And, as he wished to go out, Deslauriers went into the kitchen, which also served as his dressing-room. On the stone floor, beside a pair of boots, were to be seen the remains of a meagre breakfast, and a mattress with a coverlid was rolled up on the floor in a corner.

"This will show you," said he, "that I receive few marchionesses. 'Tis easy to get enough of them, ay, faith! and some others, too! Those who cost nothing take up your time — 'tis money under another form. Now, I'm not rich! And then they are all so silly, so silly! Can you chat with a woman yourself?"

As they parted, at the corner of the Pont Neuf, Deslauriers said: "It's agreed, then; you'll bring the thing to me to-morrow as soon as you have it!"

"Agreed!" said Frederick.

When he awoke next morning, he received through the post a cheque on the bank for fifteen thousand francs.

This scrap of paper represented to him fifteen big bags of money; and he said to himself that, with such a sum he could, first of all, keep his carriage for three years instead of selling it, as he would soon be forced to do, or buy for himself two beautiful damaskeened pieces of armour, which he had seen on the Quai Voltaire, then a quantity of other things, pictures, books and what a quantity of bouquets of flowers, presents for Madame Arnoux! anything, in short, would have been preferable to risking losing everything in that journal! Deslauriers seemed to him presumptuous, his insensibility on the night before having chilled Frederick's affection for him; and the young man was indulging in these feelings of regret, when he was quite surprised by the sudden appearance of Arnoux, who sat down heavily on the side of the bed, like a man overwhelmed with trouble.

"What is the matter now?"

"I am ruined!"

He had to deposit that very day at the office of Maître Beaumont, notary, in the Rue Saint-Anne, eighteen thousand francs lent him by one Vanneroy.

"'Tis an unaccountable disaster. I have, however, given him a mortgage, which ought to keep him quiet. But he threatens me with a writ if it is not paid this afternoon promptly."

"And what next?"

"Oh! the next step is simple enough; he will take possession of my real estate.   Once the thing is publicly announced, it means ruin to me—that's all! Ah! if I could find anyone to advance me this cursed sum, he might take Vanneroy's place, and I should be saved!   You don't chance to have it yourself?"

The cheque had remained on the night-table near a book.   Frederick took up a volume, and placed it on the cheque, while he replied:

"Good heavens, my dear friend , no!"

But it was painful to him to say "no" to Arnoux.

"What, don't you know anyone who would——?"

"Nobody! and to think that in eight days I should be getting in money!   There is owing to me probably fifty thousand francs at the end of the month!"

"Couldn't you ask some of the persons that owe you money to make you an advance?"

"Ah! well, so I did!"

"But have you any bills or promissory notes?"

"Not one!"

"What is to be done?" said Frederick.

"That's what I'm asking myself," said Arnoux. "'Tisn't for myself, my God! but for my children and my poor wife!"

Then, letting each phrase fall from his lips in a broken fashion:

"In fact—I could rough it—I could pack off all I have—and go and seek my fortune—I don't know where!"

"Impossible!" exclaimed Frederick.

Arnoux replied with an air of calmness:

"How do you think I could live in Paris now?"

There was a long silence.   Frederick broke it by saying:

"When could you pay back this money?"

Not that he had it; quite the contrary! But there was nothing to prevent him from seeing some friends, and making an application to them.

And he rang for his servant to get himself dressed. Arnoux thanked him.

"The amount you want is eighteen thousand francs —isn't it?"

"Oh! I could manage easily with sixteen thousand! For I could make two thousand five hundred out of it, or get three thousand on my silver plate, if Vanneroy meanwhile would give me till to-morrow; and, I repeat to you, you may inform the lender, give him a solemn undertaking, that in eight days, perhaps even in five or six, the money will be reimbursed. Besides, the mortgage will be security for it. So there is no risk, you understand?"

Frederick assured him that he thoroughly understood the state of affairs, and added that he was going out immediately.

He would be sure on his return to bestow hearty maledictions on Deslauriers, for he wished to keep his word, and in the meantime, to oblige Arnoux.

"Suppose I applied to M. Dambreuse? But on what pretext could I ask for money? 'Tis I, on the contrary, that should give him some for the shares I took in his coal-mining company. Ah! let him go hang himself—his shares! I am really not liable for them!"

And Frederick applauded himself for his own independence, as if he had refused to do some service for M. Dambreuse.

"Ah, well," said he to himself afterwards, "since I'm going to meet with a loss in this way—for with fifteen thousand francs I might gain a hundred thousand! such things sometimes happen on the Bourse— well, then, since I am breaking my promise to one of them, am I not free? Besides, when Deslauriers might wait? No, no; that's wrong; let us go there."

He looked at his watch.

"Ah! there's no hurry. The bank does not close till five o'clock."

And, at half-past four, when he had cashed the cheque:

"'Tis useless now; I should not find him in. I'll go this evening." Thus giving himself the opportunity of changing his mind, for there always remain in the conscience some of those sophistries which we pour into it ourselves. It preserves the after-taste of them, like some unwholesome liquor.

He walked along the boulevards, and dined alone at the restaurant. Then he listened to one act of a play at the Vaudeville, in order to divert his thoughts. But his bank-notes caused him as much embarrassment as if he had stolen them. He would not have been very sorry if he had lost them.

When he reached home again he found a letter containing these words:

"What news? My wife joins me, dear friend, in the hope, etc.—Yours."

And then there was a flourish after his signature.

"His wife! She appeals to me!"

At the same moment Arnoux appeared, to have an answer as to whether he had been able to obtain the sum so sorely needed.

"Wait a moment; here it is," said Frederick.

And, twenty-four hours later, he gave this reply to Deslauriers:

"I have no money."

The advocate came back three days, one after the other, and urged Frederick to write to the notary. He even offered to take a trip to Havre in connection with the matter.

At the end of the week, Frederick timidly asked the worthy Arnoux for his fifteen thousand francs. Arnoux put it off till the following day, and then till the day after. Frederick ventured out late at night, fearing lest Deslauriers might come on him by surprise.

One evening, somebody knocked against him at the corner of the Madeleine. It was he.

And Deslauriers accompanied Frederick as far as the door of a house in the Faubourg Poissonnière.

"Wait for me!"

He waited. At last, after three quarters of an hour, Frederick came out, accompanied by Arnoux, and made signs to him to have patience a little longer. The earthenware merchant and his companion went up the Rue de Hauteville arm-in-arm, and then turned down the Rue de Chabrol.

The night was dark, with gusts of tepid wind. Arnoux walked on slowly, talking about the Galleries of Commerce — a succession of covered passages which would have led from the Boulevard Saint-Denis to the Châtelet, a marvellous speculation, into which he was very anxious to enter; and he stopped from time to time in order to have a look at the grisettes' faces in front of the shop-windows, and then, raising his head again, resumed the thread of his discourse.

Frederick heard Deslauriers' steps behind him like reproaches, like blows falling on his conscience. But he did not venture to claim his money, through a feeling of bashfulness, and also through a fear that it would be fruitless. The other was drawing nearer. He made up his mind to ask.

Arnoux, in a very flippant tone, said that, as he had not got in his outstanding debts, he was really unable to pay back the fifteen thousand francs.

"You have no need of money, I fancy?"

At that moment Deslauriers came up to Frederick, and, taking him aside:

"Be honest. Have you got the amount? Yes or no?"

"Well, then, no," said Frederick; "I've lost it."

"Ah! and in what way?"

"At play."

Deslauriers, without saying a single word in reply, made a very low bow, and went away. Arnoux had taken advantage of the opportunity to light a cigar in a tobacconist's shop. When he came back, he wanted to know from Frederick "who was that young man?"

"Oh! nobody—a friend."

Then, three minutes later, in front of Rosanette's door:

"Come on up," said Arnoux; "she'll be glad to see you. What a savage you are just now!"

A gas-lamp, which was directly opposite, threw its light on him; and, with his cigar between his white teeth and his air of contentment, there was something intolerable about him.

"Ha! now that I think of it, my notary has been at your place this morning about that mortgage-registry business. 'Tis my wife reminded me about it."

"A wife with brains!" returned Frederick automatically.

"I believe you."

And once more Arnoux began to sing his wife's praises. There was no one like her for spirit, tenderness, and thrift; he added in a low tone, rolling his eyes about: "And a woman with so many charms, too!"

"Good-bye!" said Frederick.

Arnoux made a step closer to him.

"Hold on! Why are you going?" And, with his hand half-stretched out towards Frederick, he stared at the young man, quite abashed by the look of anger in his face.

Frederick repeated in a dry tone, "Good-bye!"

He hurried down the Rue de Bréda like a stone rolling headlong, raging against Arnoux, swearing in his own mind that he would never see the man again, nor her either, so broken-hearted and desolate did he feel. In place of the rupture which he had anticipated, here was the other, on the contrary, exhibiting towards her a most perfect attachment from the ends of her hair to the inmost depths of her soul. Frederick was exasperated by the vulgarity of this man. Everything, then, belonged to him! He would meet Arnoux again at his mistress's door; and the mortification of a rupture would be added to rage at his own powerlessness. Besides, he felt humiliated by the other's display of integrity in offering him guaranties for his money. He would have liked to strangle him, and over the pangs of disappointment floated in his conscience, like a fog, the sense of his baseness towards his friend. Rising tears nearly suffocated him.

Deslauriers descended the Rue des Martyrs, swearing aloud with indignation; for his project, like an obelisk that has fallen, now assumed extraordinary proportions. He considered himself robbed, as if he had suffered a great loss. His friendship for Frederick was dead, and he experienced a feeling of joy at it — it was a sort of compensation to him! A hatred of all rich people took possession of him. He leaned towards Sénécal's opinions, and resolved to make every effort to propagate them.

All this time, Arnoux was comfortably seated in an easy-chair near the fire, sipping his cup of tea, with the Maréchale on his knees.

Frederick did not go back there; and, in order to distract his attention from his disastrous passion, he determined to write a "History of the Renaissance." He piled up confusedly on his table the humanists, the philosophers, and the poets, and he went to inspect some engravings of Mark Antony, and tried to understand Machiavelli. Gradually, the serenity of intellectual work had a soothing effect upon him. While his mind was steeped in the personality of others, he lost sight of his own — which is the only way, perhaps, of getting rid of suffering.

One day, while he was quietly taking notes, the door opened, and the man-servant announced Madame Arnoux.

It was she, indeed! and alone? Why, no! for she was holding little Eugène by the hand, followed by a nurse in a white apron. She sat down, and after a preliminary cough:

"It is a long time since you came to see us."

As Frederick could think of no excuse at the moment, she added:

"It was delicacy on your part!"

He asked in return:

"Delicacy about what?"

"About what you have done for Arnoux!" said she.

Frederick made a significant gesture. "What do I care about him, indeed? It was for your sake I did it!"

She sent off the child to play with his nurse in the drawing-room. Two or three words passed between them as to their state of health; then the conversation hung fire.

She wore a brown silk gown, which had the colour of Spanish wine, with a paletot of black velvet bordered with sable. This fur made him yearn to pass his hand over it; and her headbands, so long and so exquisitely smooth, seemed to draw his lips towards them. But he was agitated by emotion, and, turning his eyes towards the door:

"'Tis rather warm here!"

Frederick understood what her discreet glance meant.

"Ah! excuse me! the two leaves of the door are merely drawn together."

"Yes, that's true!"

And she smiled, as much as to say:

"I'm not a bit afraid!"

He asked her presently what was the object of her visit.

"My husband," she replied with an effort, "has urged me to call on you, not venturing to take this step himself!"

"And why?"

"You know M. Dambreuse, don't you?"

"Yes, slightly."

"Ah! slightly."

She relapsed into silence.

"No matter! finish what you were going to say."

Thereupon she told him that, two days before, Arnoux had found himself unable to meet four bills of a thousand francs, made payable at the banker's order and with his signature attached to them. She felt sorry for having compromised her children's fortune. But anything was preferable to dishonour; and, if M. Dambreuse stopped the proceedings, they would certainly pay him soon, for she was going to sell a little house which she had at Chartres.

"Poor woman!" murmured Frederick. "I will go. Rely on me!"

"Thanks!"

And she arose to go.

"Oh! there is nothing to hurry you yet."

She remained standing, examining the trophy of Mongolian arrows suspended from the ceiling, the bookcase, the bindings, all the utensils for writing. She lifted up the bronze bowl which held his pens. Her feet rested on different portions of the carpet. She had visited Frederick several times before, but always accompanied by Arnoux. They were now alone together — alone in his own house. It was an extraordinary event — almost a successful issue of his love.

She wished to see his little garden. He offered her his arm to show her his property — thirty feet of ground enclosed by some houses, adorned with shrubs at the corners and flower-borders in the middle. The early days of April had arrived. The leaves of the lilacs were already showing their borders of green. A breath of pure air was diffused around, and the little birds chirped, their song alternating with the distant sound that came from a coachmaker's forge.

Frederick went to look for a fire-shovel; and, while they walked on side by side, the child kept making sand-pies in the walk.

Madame Arnoux did not believe that, as he grew older, he would have a great imagination; but he had a winning disposition. His sister, on the other hand, possessed a caustic humour that sometimes wounded her.

"That will change," said Frederick. "We must never despair."

She returned:

"We must never despair!"

This automatic repetition of the phrase he had used appeared to him a sort of encouragement; he plucked a rose, the only one in the garden.

"Do you remember a certain bouquet of roses one evening, in a carriage?"

She coloured a little; and, with an air of bantering pity:

"Ah, I was very young then!"

"And this one," went on Frederick, in a low tone, "will it be the same way with it?"

She replied, while turning about the stem between her fingers, like the thread of a spindle:

"No, I will preserve it."

She called over the nurse, who took the child in her arms; then, on the threshold of the door in the street, Madame Arnoux inhaled the odour of the flower, leaning her head on her shoulder with a look as sweet as a kiss.

When he had gone up to his study, he gazed at the armchair in which she had sat, and every object which she had touched. Some portion of her was diffused around him. The caress of her presence lingered there still.

"So, then, she came here," said he to himself.

And his soul was bathed in the waves of infinite tenderness.

Next morning, at eleven o'clock, he presented himself at M. Dambreuse's house. He was received in the dining-room. The banker was seated opposite his wife at breakfast. Beside her sat his niece, and at the other side of the table appeared the governess, an English woman, strongly pitted with small-pox.

M. Dambreuse invited his young friend to take his place among them, and when he declined:

"What can I do for you? I am listening to whatever you have to say to me."

Frederick confessed, while affecting indifference, that he had come to make a request in behalf of one Arnoux.

"Ha! ha! the ex-picture-dealer," said the banker, with a noiseless laugh which exposed his gums. "Oudry formerly gave security for him; he has given a lot of trouble."

And he proceeded to read the letters and newspapers which lay close beside him on the table.

Two servants attended without making the least noise on the floor; and the loftiness of the apartment, which had three portières of richest tapestry, and two white marble fountains, the polish of the chafing-dish, the arrangement of the side-dishes, and even the rigid folds of the napkins, all this sumptuous comfort impressed Frederick's mind with the contrast between it and another breakfast at the Arnouxs' house. He did not take the liberty of interrupting M. Dambreuse.

Madame noticed his embarrassment.

"Do you occasionally see our friend Martinon?"

5—19

"He will be here this evening," said the young girl in a lively tone.

"Ha! so you know him?" said her aunt, fixing on her a freezing look.

At that moment one of the men-servants, bending forward, whispered in her ear.

"Your dressmaker, Mademoiselle — Miss John!"

And the governess, in obedience to this summons, left the room along with her pupil.

M. Dambreuse, annoyed at the disarrangement of the chairs by this movement, asked what was the matter.

"'Tis Madame Regimbart."

"Wait a moment! Regimbart! I know that name. I have come across his signature."

Frederick at length broached the question. Arnoux deserved some consideration; he was even going, for the sole purpose of fulfilling his engagements, to sell a house belonging to his wife.

"She is considered very pretty," said Madame Dambreuse.

The banker added, with a display of good-nature:

"Are you on friendly terms with them — on intimate terms?"

Frederick, without giving an explicit reply, said that he would be very much obliged to him if he considered the matter.

"Well, since it pleases you, be it so; we will wait. I have some time to spare yet; suppose we go down to my office. Would you mind?"

They had finished breakfast. Madame Dambreuse bowed slightly towards Frederick, smiling in a singular fashion, with a mixture of politeness and irony. Frederick had no time to reflect about it, for M. Dambreuse, as soon as they were alone:

"You did not come to get your shares?"

And, without permitting him to make any excuses:

"Well! well! 'tis right that you should know a little more about the business."

He offered Frederick a cigarette, and began his statement.

The General Union of French Coal Mines had been constituted. All that they were waiting for was the order for its incorporation. The mere fact of the amalgamation had diminished the cost of superintendence, and of manual labour, and increased the profits. Besides, the company had conceived a new idea, which was to interest the workmen in its undertaking. It would erect houses for them, healthful dwellings; finally, it would constitute itself the purveyor of its *employés,* and would have everything supplied to them at net prices.

"And they will be the gainers by it, Monsieur: there's true progress! that's the way to reply effectively to certain Republican brawlings. We have on our Board"—he showed the prospectus—"a peer of France, a scholar who is a member of the Institute, a retired field-officer of genius. Such elements reassure the timid capitalists, and appeal to intelligent capitalists!"

The company would have in its favour the sanction of the State, then the railways, the steam service, the metallurgical establishments, the gas companies, and ordinary households.

"Thus we heat, we light, we penetrate to the very hearth of the humblest home. But how, you will say to me, can we be sure of selling? By the aid of protective laws, dear Monsieur, and we shall get them!—that is a matter that concerns us! For my part, however, I am a downright prohibitionist! The country before anything!"

He had been appointed a director; but he had no time to occupy himself with certain details, amongst other things with the editing of their publications.

"I find myself rather muddled with my authors. I have forgotten my Greek. I should want some one who could put my ideas into shape."

And suddenly: "Will you be the man to perform those duties, with the title of general secretary?"

Frederick did not know what reply to make.

"Well, what is there to prevent you?"

His functions would be confined to writing a report every year for the shareholders. He would find himself day after day in communication with the most notable men in Paris. Representing the company with the workmen, he would ere long be worshipped by them as a natural consequence, and by this means he would be able, later, to push him into the General Council, and into the position of a deputy.

Frederick's ears tingled. Whence came this good-will? He got confused in returning thanks. But it was not necessary, the banker said, that he should be dependent on anyone. The best course was to take some shares, "a splendid investment besides, for your capital guarantees your position, as your position does your capital."

"About how much should it amount to?" said Frederick.

"Oh, well! whatever you please — from forty to sixty thousand francs, I suppose."

This sum was so trifling in M. Dambreuse's eyes,

and his authority was so great, that the young man resolved immediately to sell a farm.

He accepted the offer. M. Dambreuse was to select one of his disengaged days for an appointment in order to finish their arrangements.

"So I can say to Jacques Arnoux ——— ?"

"Anything you like — the poor chap — anything you like!"

Frederick wrote to the Arnouxs' to make their minds easy, and he despatched the letter by a manservant, who brought back the letter: "All right!" His action in the matter deserved better recognition. He expected a visit, or, at least, a letter. He did not receive a visit, and no letter arrived.

Was it forgetfulness on their part, or was it intentional? Since Madame Arnoux had come once, what was to prevent her from coming again? The species of confidence, of avowal, of which she had made him the recipient on the occasion, was nothing better, then, than a manœuvre which she had executed through interested motives.

"Are they playing on me? and is she an accomplice of her husband?" A sort of shame, in spite of his desire, prevented him from returning to their house.

One morning (three weeks after their interview), M. Dambreuse wrote to him, saying that he expected him the same day in an hour's time.

On the way, the thought of Arnoux oppressed him once more, and, not having been able to discover any reason for his conduct, he was seized with a feeling of wretchedness, a melancholy presentiment. In order to shake it off, he hailed a cab, and drove to the Rue de Paradis.

Arnoux was away travelling.

"And Madame?"

"In the country, at the works."

"When is Monsieur coming back?"

"To-morrow, without fail."

He would find her alone; this was the opportune moment. Something imperious seemed to cry out in the depths of his consciousness: "Go, then, and meet her!"

But M. Dambreuse? "Ah! well, so much the worse. I'll say that I was ill."

He rushed to the railway-station, and, as soon as he was in the carriage:

"Perhaps I have done wrong. Pshaw! what does it matter?"

Green plains stretched out to the right and to the left. The train rolled on. The little station-houses glistened like stage-scenery, and the smoke of the locomotive kept constantly sending forth on the same side its big fleecy masses, which danced for a little while on the grass, and were then dispersed.

Frederick, who sat alone in his compartment, gazed at these objects through sheer weariness, lost in that languor which is produced by the very excess of impatience. But cranes and warehouses presently appeared. They had reached Creil.

The town, built on the slopes of two low-lying hills (the first of which was bare, and the second crowned by a wood), with its church-tower, its houses of unequal size, and its stone bridge, seemed to him to present an aspect of mingled gaiety, reserve, and propriety. A long flat barge descended to the edge of the water, which leaped up under the lash of the wind.

Fowl perched on the straw at the foot of the cru-
cifix erected on the spot; a woman passed with
some wet linen on her head.

After crossing the bridge, he found himself in an
isle, where he beheld on his right the ruins of an
abbey. A mill with its wheels revolving barred up
the entire width of the second arm of the Oise, over
which the manufactory projected. Frederick was
greatly surprised by the imposing character of this
structure. He felt more respect for Arnoux on account of it. Three paces further on, he turned up an
alley, which had a grating at its lower end.

He went in. The doorkeeper called him back, exclaiming:

"Have you a permit?"

"For what purpose?"

"For the purpose of visiting the establishment."

Frederick said in a rather curt tone that he had
come to see M. Arnoux.

"Who is M. Arnoux?"

"Why, the chief, the master, the proprietor, in
fact!"

"No, monsieur! These are MM. Lebœuf and Mil-
liet's works!"

The good woman was surely joking! Some workmen arrived; he came up and spoke to two or three
of them. They gave the same response.

Frederick left the premises, staggering like a
drunken man; and he had such a look of perplexity,
that on the Pont de la Boucherie an inhabitant of the
town, who was smoking his pipe, asked whether he
wanted to find out anything. This man knew where
Arnoux's manufactory was. It was situated at Mon-
tataire.

Frederick asked whether a vehicle was to be got. He was told that the only place where he could find one was at the station. He went back there. A shaky-looking calash, to which was yoked an old horse, with torn harness hanging over the shafts, stood all alone in front of the luggage office. An urchin who was looking on offered to go and find Père Pilon. In ten minutes' time he came back, and announced that Père Pilon was at his breakfast. Frederick, unable to stand this any longer, walked away. But the gates of the thoroughfare across the line were closed. He would have to wait till two trains had passed. At last, he made a dash into the open country.

The monotonous greenery made it look like the cover of an immense billiard-table. The scoriæ of iron were ranged on both sides of the track, like heaps of stones. A little further on, some factory chimneys were smoking close beside each other. In front of him, on a round hillock, stood a little turreted château, with the quadrangular belfry of a church. At a lower level, long walls formed irregular lines past the trees; and, further down again, the houses of the village spread out.

They had only a single story, with staircases consisting of three steps made of uncemented blocks. Every now and then the bell in front of a grocery-shop could be heard tinkling. Heavy steps sank into the black mire, and a light shower was falling, which cut the pale sky with a thousand hatchings.

Frederick pursued his way along the middle of the street. Then, he saw on his left, at the opening of a pathway, a large wooden arch, whereon was traced, in letters of gold, the word "Faïences."

It was not without an object that Jacques Arnoux had selected the vicinity of Creil. By placing his works as close as possible to the other works (which had long enjoyed a high reputation), he had created a certain confusion in the public mind, with a favourable result so far as his own interests were concerned.

The main body of the building rested on the same bank of a river which flows through the meadowlands. The master's house, surrounded by a garden, could be distinguished by the steps in front of it, adorned with four vases, in which cactuses were bristling.

Heaps of white clay were drying under sheds. There were others in the open air; and in the midst of the yard stood Sénécal with his everlasting blue paletot lined with red.

The ex-tutor extended towards Frederick his cold hand.

"You've come to see the master?   He's not there."

Frederick, nonplussed, replied in a stupefied fashion:

"I knew it." But the next moment, correcting himself:

"'Tis about a matter that concerns Madame Arnoux. Can she receive me?"

"Ha! I have not seen her for the last three days," said Sénécal.

And he broke into a long string of complaints. When he accepted the post of manager, he understood that he would have been allowed to reside in Paris, and not be forced to bury himself in this country district, far from his friends, deprived of newspapers. No matter! he had overlooked all that. But Arnoux appeared to pay no heed to his merits. He was, moreover, shallow and retrograde — no one could be more ignorant. In place of seeking for artistic improvements, it would have been better to introduce firewood instead of coal and gas. The shop-keeping spirit *thrust itself in* —— Sénécal laid stress on the last words. In short, he disliked his present occupation, and he all but appealed to Frederick to say a word in his behalf in order that he might get an increase of salary.

"Make your mind easy," said the other.

He met nobody on the staircase. On the first floor, he pushed his way head-foremost into an empty room. It was the drawing-room. He called out at the top of his voice. There was no reply. No doubt, the cook had gone out, and so had the housemaid. At length, having reached the second floor, he pushed a door open. Madame Arnoux was alone in this room, in front of a press with a mirror attached. The belt of her dressing-gown hung down her hips; one entire half of her hair fell in a dark wave over her right shoulder; and she had raised both arms in order to hold up her chignon with one hand and to put a pin through it with the other. She broke into an exclamation and disappeared.

Then, she came back again properly dressed. Her waist, her eyes, the rustle of her dress, her entire appearance, charmed him. Frederick felt it hard to keep from covering her with kisses.

"I beg your pardon," said she, "but I could not——"

He had the boldness to interrupt her with these words:

"Nevertheless — you looked very nice — just now."

She probably thought this compliment a little coarse, for her cheeks reddened. He was afraid that he might have offended her. She went on:

"What lucky chance has brought you here?"

He did not know what reply to make; and, after a slight chuckle, which gave him time for reflection:

"If I told you, would you believe me?"

"Why not?"

Frederick informed her that he had had a frightful dream a few nights before.

"I dreamt that you were seriously ill — near dying."

"Oh! my husband and I are never ill."

"I have dreamt only of you," said he.

She gazed at him calmly: "Dreams are not always realised."

Frederick stammered, sought to find appropriate words to express himself in, and then plunged into a flowing period about the affinity of souls. There existed a force which could, through the intervening bounds of space, bring two persons into communication with each other, make known to each the other's feelings, and enable them to reunite.

She listened to him with downcast face, while she smiled with that beautiful smile of hers. He watched her out of the corner of his eye with delight, and poured out his love all the more freely through the easy channel of a commonplace remark.

She offered to show him the works; and, as she persisted, he made no objection.

In order to divert his attention with something of an amusing nature, she showed him the species of museum that decorated the staircase. The specimens, hung up against the wall or laid on shelves, bore witness to the efforts and the successive fads of Arnoux. After seeking vainly for the red of Chinese copper, he had wished to manufacture majolicas, faïence, Etruscan and Oriental ware, and had, in fact, attempted all the improvements which were realised at a later period.

So it was that one could observe in the series big vases covered with figures of mandarins, porringers of shot reddish-brown, pots adorned with Arabian inscriptions, drinking-vessels in the style of the Renaissance, and large plates on which two personages were outlined as it were on bloodstone, in a delicate, aërial fashion. He now made letters for signboards and wine-labels; but his intelligence was not high enough to attain to art, nor commonplace enough to look merely to profit, so that, without satisfying anyone, he had ruined himself.

They were both taking a view of these things when Mademoiselle Marthe passed.

"So, then, you did not recognise him?" said her mother to her.

"Yes, indeed," she replied, bowing to him, while her clear and sceptical glance—the glance of a virgin— seemed to say in a whisper: "What are you coming here for?" and she rushed up the steps with her head slightly bent over her shoulder.

Madame Arnoux led Frederick into the yard attached to the works, and then explained to him in a grave tone how different clays were ground, cleaned, and sifted.

"The most important thing is the preparation of pastes."

And she introduced him into a hall filled with vats, in which a vertical axis with horizontal arms kept turning. Frederick felt some regret that he had not flatly declined her offer a little while before.

"These things are merely the slobberings," said she.

He thought the word grotesque, and, in a measure, unbecoming on her lips.

Wide straps ran from one end of the ceiling to the other, so as to roll themselves round the drums, and everything kept moving continuously with a provoking mathematical regularity.

They left the spot, and passed close to a ruined hut, which had formerly been used as a repository for gardening implements.

"It is no longer of any use," said Madame Arnoux.

He replied in a tremulous voice:

"Happiness may have been associated with it!"

The clacking of the fire-pump drowned his words, and they entered the workshop where rough drafts were made.

Some men, seated at a narrow table, placed each in front of himself on a revolving disc a piece of paste. Then each man with his left hand scooped out the insides of his own piece while smoothing its surface with the right; and vases could be seen bursting into shape like blossoming flowers.

Madame Arnoux had the moulds for more difficult works shown to him.

In another portion of the building, the threads, the necks, and the projecting lines were being formed. On the floor above, they removed the seams, and stopped up with plaster the little holes that had been left by the preceding operations.

At every opening in the walls, in corners, in the middle of the corridor, everywhere, earthenware vessels had been placed side by side.

Frederick began to feel bored.

"Perhaps these things are tiresome to you?" said she.

Fearing lest it might be necessary to terminate his visit there and then, he affected, on the contrary, a tone of great enthusiasm. He even expressed regret at not having devoted himself to this branch of industry.

She appeared surprised.

"Certainly! I would have been able to live near you."

And as he tried to catch her eye, Madame Arnoux, in order to avoid him, took off a bracket little balls of paste, which had come from abortive readjustments, flattened them out into a thin cake, and pressed her hand over them.

"Might I carry these away with me?" said Frederick.

"Good heavens! are you so childish?"

He was about to reply when in came Sénécal.

The sub-manager, on the threshold, had noticed a breach of the rules. The workshops should be swept every week. This was Saturday, and, as the workmen had not done what was required, Sénécal announced that they would have to remain an hour longer.

"So much the worse for you!"

They stooped over the work assigned to them unmurmuringly, but their rage could be divined by the hoarse sounds which came from their chests. They were, moreover, very easy to manage, having all been dismissed from the big manufactory. The Republican had shown himself a hard taskmaster to them. A mere theorist, he regarded the people only in the mass, and exhibited an utter absence of pity for individuals.

Frederick, annoyed by his presence, asked Madame Arnoux in a low tone whether they could have an opportunity of seeing the kilns. They descended to the ground-floor; and she was just explaining the use of caskets, when Sénécal, who had followed close behind, placed himself between them.

He continued the explanation of his own motion, expatiated on the various kinds of combustibles, the process of placing in the kiln, the pyroscopes, the cylindrical furnaces; the instruments for rounding, the lustres, and the metals, making a prodigious display of chemical terms, such as "chloride," "sulphuret," "borax," and "carbonate." Frederick did not understand a single one of them, and kept turning round every minute towards Madame Arnoux.

"You are not listening," said she. "M. Sénécal, however, is very clear. He knows all these things much better than I."

The mathematician, flattered by this eulogy, proposed to show the way in which colours were laid on. Frederick gave Madame Arnoux an anxious, questioning look. She remained impassive, not caring to be alone with him, very probably, and yet unwilling to leave him.

He offered her his arm.

"No—many thanks! the staircase is too narrow!" And, when they had reached the top, Sénécal opened the door of an apartment filled with women.

They were handling brushes, phials, shells, and plates of glass. Along the cornice, close to the wall, extended boards with figures engraved on them; scraps of thin paper floated about, and a melting-stove sent forth fumes that made the temperature oppressive, while there mingled with it the odour of turpentine.

The workwomen had nearly all sordid costumes. It was noticeable, however, that one of them wore a

Madras handkerchief, and long earrings. Of slight frame, and, at the same time, plump, she had large black eyes and the fleshy lips of a negress. Her ample bosom projected from under her chemise, which was fastened round her waist by the string of her petticoat; and, with one elbow on the board of the work-table and the other arm hanging down, she gazed vaguely at the open country, a long distance away. Beside her were a bottle of wine and some pork chops.

The regulations prohibited eating in the work-shops, a rule intended to secure cleanliness at work and to keep the hands in a healthy condition.

Sénécal, through a sense of duty or a longing to exercise despotic authority, shouted out to her ere he had come near her, while pointing towards a framed placard:

"I say, you girl from Bordeaux over there! read out for me Article 9!"

"Well, what then?"

"What then, mademoiselle? You'll have to pay a fine of three francs."

She looked him straight in the face in an impudent fashion.

"What does that signify to me? The master will take off your fine when he comes back! I laugh at you, my good man!"

Sénécal, who was walking with his hands behind his back, like an usher in the study-room, contented himself with smiling.

"Article 13, insubordination, ten francs!"

The girl from Bordeaux resumed her work. Madame Arnoux, through a sense of propriety, said nothing; but her brows contracted. Frederick murmured:

"Ha! you are very severe for a democrat!"

The other replied in a magisterial tone:

"Democracy is not the unbounded license of individualism. It is the equality of all belonging to the same community before the law, the distribution of work, order."

"You are forgetting humanity!" said Frederick.

Madame Arnoux took his arm. Sénécal, perhaps, offended by this mark of silent approbation, went away.

Frederick experienced an immense relief. Since morning he had been looking out for the opportunity to declare itself; now it had arrived. Besides, Madame Arnoux's spontaneous movements seemed to him to contain promises; and he asked her, as if on the pretext of warming their feet, to come up to her room. But, when he was seated close beside her, he began once more to feel embarrassed. He was at a loss for a starting-point. Sénécal, luckily, suggested an idea to his mind.

"Nothing could be more stupid," said he, "than this punishment!"

Madame Arnoux replied: "There are certain severe measures which are indispensable!"

"What! you who are so good! Oh! I am mistaken, for you sometimes take pleasure in making other people suffer!"

"I don't understand riddles, my friend!"

And her austere look, still more than the words she used, checked him. Frederick was determined to go on. A volume of De Musset chanced to be on the chest of drawers; he turned over some pages, then began to talk about love, about his hopes and his transports.

5-2v

All this, according to Madame Arnoux, was criminal or factitious. The young man felt wounded by
this negative attitude with regard to his passion, and,
in order to combat it, he cited, by way of proof, the
suicides which they read about every day in the
newspapers, extolled the great literary types, Phèdre,
Dido, Romeo, Desgrieux. He talked as if he meant
to do away with himself.

The fire was no longer burning on the hearth; the
rain lashed against the window-panes. Madame Arnoux, without stirring, remained with her hands resting on the sides of her armchair. The flaps of her
cap fell like the fillets of a sphinx. Her pure profile
traced out its clear-cut outlines in the midst of the
shadow.

He was anxious to cast himself at her feet. There
was a creaking sound in the lobby, and he did not
venture to carry out his intention.

He was, moreover, restrained by a kind of religious awe. That robe, mingling with the surrounding shadows, appeared to him boundless, infinite,
incapable of being touched; and for this very reason his
desire became intensified. But the fear of doing too
much, and, again, of not doing enough, deprived him
of all judgment.

"If she dislikes me," he thought, "let her drive
me away; if she cares for me, let her encourage me."

He said, with a sigh:

"So, then, you don't admit that a man may love
—a woman?"

Madame Arnoux replied:

"Assuming that she is at liberty to marry, he
may marry her; when she belongs to another, he
should keep away from her."

"So happiness is impossible?"

"No! But it is never to be found in falsehood, mental anxiety, and remorse."

"What does it matter, if one is compensated by the enjoyment of supreme bliss?"

"The experience is too costly."

Then he sought to assail her with irony.

"Would not virtue in that case be merely cowardice?"

"Say rather, clear-sightedness. Even for those women who might forget duty or religion, simple good sense is sufficient. A solid foundation for wisdom may be found in self-love."

"Ah, what shopkeeping maxims these are of yours!"

"But I don't boast of being a fine lady."

At that moment the little boy rushed in.

"Mamma, are you coming to dinner?"

"Yes, in a moment."

Frederick arose. At the same instant, Marthe made her appearance.

He could not make up his mind to go away, and, with a look of entreaty:

"These women you speak of are very unfeeling, then?"

"No, but deaf when it is necessary to be so."

And she remained standing on the threshold of her room with her two children beside her. He bowed without saying a word. She mutely returned his salutation.

What he first experienced was an unspeakable astonishment. He felt crushed by this mode of impressing on him the emptiness of his hopes. It seemed to him as if he were lost, like a man who has fallen to the bottom of an abyss and knows that no help will come to him, and that he must die. He walked on, however, but at random, without looking before him. He knocked against stones; he mistook his way. A clatter of wooden shoes sounded close to his ear; it was caused by some of the working-girls who were leaving the foundry. Then he realised where he was.

The railway lamps traced on the horizon a line of flames. He arrived just as the train was starting, let himself be pushed into a carriage, and fell asleep.

An hour later on the boulevards, the gaiety of Paris by night made his journey all at once recede into an already far-distant past. He resolved to be strong, and relieved his heart by vilifying Madame Arnoux with insulting epithets.

"She is an idiot, a goose, a mere brute; let us not bestow another thought on her!"

When he got home, he found in his study a letter of eight pages on blue glazed paper, with the initials "R. A."

It began with friendly reproaches.

"What has become of you, my dear? I am getting quite bored."

But the handwriting was so abominable, that Frederick was about to fling away the entire bundle of sheets, when he noticed in the postscript the following words:

"I count on you to come to-morrow and drive me to the races."

What was the meaning of this invitation? Was it another trick of the Maréchale? But a woman does not make a fool of the same man twice without some object; and, seized with curiosity, he read the letter over again attentively.

Frederick was able to distinguish "Misunderstanding — to have taken a wrong path — disillusions — poor children that we are! — like two rivers that join each other!" etc.

He kept the sheets for a long time between his fingers. They had the odour of orris; and there was in the form of the characters and the irregular spaces between the lines something suggestive, as it were, of a disorderly toilet, that fired his blood.

"Why should I not go?" said he to himself at length. "But if Madame Arnoux were to know about it? Ah! let her know! So much the better! and let her feel jealous over it! In that way I shall be avenged!"

CHAPTER X.

AT THE RACES.

HE Maréchale was prepared for his visit, and had been awaiting him.

"This is nice of you!" she said, fixing a glance of her fine eyes on his face, with an expression at the same time tender and mirthful.

When she had fastened her bonnet-strings, she sat down on the divan, and remained silent.

"Shall we go?" said Frederick. She looked at the clock on the mantelpiece.

"Oh, no! not before half-past one!" as if she had imposed this limit to her indecision.

At last, when the hour had struck:

"Ah! well, *andiamo, caro mio!*" And she gave a final touch to her headbands, and left directions for Delphine.

"Is Madame coming home to dinner?"

"Why should we, indeed? We shall dine together somewhere — at the Café Anglais, wherever you wish."

"Be it so!"

Her little dogs began yelping around her.

"We can bring them with us, can't we?"

Frederick carried them himself to the vehicle. It was a hired berlin with two post-horses and a postilion. He had put his man-servant in the back seat. The Maréchale appeared satisfied with his attentions. Then, as soon as she had seated herself, she asked him whether he had been lately at the Arnouxs'.

"Not for the past month," said Frederick.

"As for me, I met him the day before yesterday. He would have even come to-day, but he has all sorts of troubles — another lawsuit — I don't know what. What a queer man!"

Frederick added with an air of indifference:

"Now that I think of it, do you still see — what's that his name is? — that ex-vocalist — Delmar?"

She replied dryly:

"No; that's all over."

So it was clear that there had been a rupture between them. Frederick derived some hope from this circumstance.

They descended the Quartier Bréda at an easy pace. As it happened to be Sunday, the streets were deserted, and some citizens' faces presented themselves at the windows. The carriage went on more rapidly. The noise of wheels made the passers-by turn round; the leather of the hood, which had slid down, was glittering. The man-servant doubled himself up, and the two Havanese, beside one another, seemed like two ermine muffs laid on the cushions. Frederick let himself jog up and down with the rocking of the carriage-straps. The Maréchale turned her head to the right and to the left with a smile on her face.

Her straw hat of mother-of-pearl colour was trimmed with black lace. The hood of her bournous floated in the wind, and she sheltered herself from the rays of the sun under a parasol of lilac satin pointed at the top like a pagoda.

"What loves of little fingers!" said Frederick, softly taking her other hand, her left being adorned with a gold bracelet in the form of a curb-chain.

"I say! that's pretty! Where did it come from?"

"Oh! I've had it a long time," said the Maréchale.

The young man did not challenge this hypocritical answer in any way. He preferred to profit by the circumstance. And, still keeping hold of the wrist, he pressed his lips on it between the glove and the cuff.

"Stop! People will see us!"

"Pooh! What does it signify?"

After passing by the Place de la Concorde, they drove along the Quai de la Conférence and the Quai de Billy, where might be noticed a cedar in a garden. Rosanette believed that Lebanon was situated in China; she laughed herself at her own ignorance, and asked Frederick to give her lessons in geography. Then, leaving the Trocadéro at the right, they crossed the Pont de Jéna, and drew up at length in the middle of the Champ de Mars, near some other vehicles already drawn up in the Hippodrome.

The grass hillocks were covered with common people. Some spectators might be seen on the balcony of the Military School; and the two pavilions outside the weighing-room, the two galleries contained within its enclosure, and a third in front of that of the king, were filled with a fashionably dressed crowd whose deportment showed their regard for this as yet novel form of amusement.

The public around the course, more select at this period, had a less vulgar aspect. It was the era of trouser-straps, velvet collars, and white gloves. The ladies, attired in showy colours, displayed gowns with long waists; and seated on the tiers of the stands, they formed, so to speak, immense groups of flowers, spotted here and there with black by the men's costumes. But every glance was directed towards the celebrated Algerian Bou-Maza, who sat, impassive, between two staff officers in one of the private galleries. That of the Jockey Club contained none but grave-looking gentlemen.

The more enthusiastic portion of the throng were seated underneath, close to the track, protected by two lines of sticks which supported ropes. In the immense oval described by this passage, cocoanut-sellers were shaking their rattles, others were selling programmes of the races, others were hawkiug cigars, with loud cries. On every side there was a great murmur. The municipal guards passed to and fro. A bell, hung from a post covered with figures, began ringing, Five horses appeared, and the spectators in the galleries resumed their seats.

Meanwhile, big clouds touched with their winding outlines the tops of the elms opposite. Rosanette was afraid that it was going to rain.

"I have umbrellas," said Frederick, "and everything that we need to afford ourselves diversion," he added, lifting up the chest, in which there was a stock of provisions in a basket.

"Bravo! we understand each other!"

"And we'll understand each other still better, shall we not?"

"That may be," she said, colouring.

The jockeys, in silk jackets, were trying to draw up their horses in order, and were holding them back with both hands. Somebody lowered a red flag. Then the entire five bent over the bristling manes, and off they started. At first they remained pressed close to each other in a single mass; this presently stretched out and became cut up. The jockey in the yellow jacket was near falling in the middle of the first round; for a long time it was uncertain whether Filly or Tibi should take the lead; then Tom Pouce appeared in front. But Clubstick, who had been in the rear since the start, came up with the others and outstripped them, so that he was the first to reach the winning-post, beating Sir Charles by two lengths. It was a surprise. There was a shout of applause; the planks shook with the stamping of feet.

"We are amusing ourselves," said the Maréchale. "I love you, darling!"

Frederick no longer doubted that his happiness was secure. Rosanette's last words were a confirmation of it.

A hundred paces away from him, in a four-wheeled cabriolet, a lady could be seen. She stretched her head out of the carriage-door, and then quickly drew it in again. This movement was repeated several times. Frederick could not distinguish her face. He had a strong suspicion, however, that it was Madame Arnoux. And yet this seemed impossible! Why should she have come there?

He stepped out of his own vehicle on the pretence of strolling into the weighing-room.

"You are not very gallant!" said Rosanette.

He paid no heed to her, and went on. The four-wheeled cabriolet, turning back, broke into a trot.

Frederick at the same moment, found himself button-holed by Cisy.

"Good-morrow, my dear boy! how are you going on? Hussonnet is over there! Are you listening to me?"

Frederick tried to shake him off in order to get up with the four-wheeled cabriolet. The Maréchale beckoned to him to come round to her. Cisy perceived her, and obstinately persisted in bidding her good-day.

Since the termination of the regular period of mourning for his grandmother, he had realised his ideal, and succeeded in "getting the proper stamp." A Scotch plaid waistcoat, a short coat, large bows over the pumps, and an entrance-card stuck in the ribbon of his hat; nothing, in fact, was wanting to produce what he described himself as his *chic* — a *chic* characterised by Anglomania and the swagger of the musketeer. He began by finding fault with the Champ de Mars, which he referred to as an "execrable turf," then spoke of the Chantilly races, and the droll things that had occurred there, swore that he could drink a dozen glasses of champagne while the clock was striking the midnight hour, offered to make a bet with the Maréchale, softly caressed her two lapdogs; and, leaning against the carriage-door on one elbow, he kept talking nonsense, with the handle of his walking-stick in his mouth, his legs wide apart, and his back stretched out. Frederick, standing beside him, was smoking, while endeavouring to make out what had become of the cabriolet.

The bell having rung, Cisy took himself off, to the great delight of Rosanette, who said he had been boring her to death.

The second race had nothing special about it; neither had the third, save that a man was thrown over the shaft of a cart while it was taking place. The fourth, in which eight horses contested the City Stakes, was more interesting.

The spectators in the gallery had clambered to the top of their seats. The others, standing up in the vehicles, followed with opera-glasses in their hands the movements of the jockeys. They could be seen starting out like red, yellow, white, or blue spots across the entire space occupied by the crowd that had gathered around the ring of the hippodrome. At a distance, their speed did not appear to be very great; at the opposite side of the Champ de Mars, they seemed even to be slackening their pace, and to be merely slipping along in such a way that the horses' bellies touched the ground without their outstretched legs bending at all. But, coming back at a more rapid stride, they looked bigger; they cut the air in their wild gallop. The sun's rays quivered; pebbles went flying about under their hoofs. The wind, blowing out the jockeys' jackets, made them flutter like veils. Each of them lashed the animal he rode with great blows of his whip in order to reach the winning-post—that was the goal they aimed at. One swept away the figures, another was hoisted off his saddle, and, in the midst of a burst of applause, the victorious horse dragged his feet to the weighing-room, all covered with sweat, his knees stiffened, his neck and shoulders bent down, while his rider, looking as if he were expiring in his saddle, clung to the animal's flanks.

The final start was retarded by a dispute which had arisen. The crowd, getting tired, began to scatter. Groups of men were chatting at the lower end of each gallery. The talk was of a free-and-easy description. Some fashionable ladies left, scandalised by seeing fast women in their immediate vicinity.

There were also some specimens of the ladies who appeared at public balls, some light-comedy actresses of the boulevards, and it was not the best-looking portion of them that got the most appreciation. The elderly Georgine Aubert, she whom a writer of vaudevilles called the Louis XI. of her profession, horribly painted, and giving vent every now and then to a laugh resembling a grunt, remained reclining at full length in her big calash, covered with a sable furtippet, as if it were midwinter. Madame de Remoussat, who had become fashionable by means of a notorious trial in which she figured, sat enthroned on the seat of a brake in company with some Americans; and Thérèse Bachelu, with her look of a Gothic virgin, filled with her dozen furbelows the interior of a trap which had, in place of an apron, a flower-stand filled with roses. The Maréchale was jealous of these magnificent displays. In order to attract attention, she began to make vehement gestures and to speak in a very loud voice.

Gentlemen recognised her, and bowed to her. She returned their salutations while telling Frederick their names. They were all counts, viscounts, dukes, and marquises, and carried a high head, for in all eyes he could read a certain respect for his good fortune.

Cisy had a no less happy air in the midst of the circle of mature men that surrounded them. Their faces wore cynical smiles above their cravats, as if they were laughing at him. At length he gave a tap in the hand of the oldest of them, and made his way towards the Maréchale.

She was eating, with an affectation of gluttony, a slice of *pâté de foie gras*. Frederick, in order to make himself agreeable to her, followed her example, with a bottle of wine on his knees.

The four-wheeled cabriolet reappeared. It *was* Madame Arnoux! Her face was startlingly pale.

"Give me some champagne," said Rosanette.

And, lifting up her glass, full to the brim, as high as possible, she exclaimed:

"Look over there! Look at my protector's wife, one of the virtuous women!"

There was a great burst of laughter all round her; and the cabriolet disappeared from view. Frederick tugged impatiently at her dress, and was on the point of flying into a passion. But Cisy was there, in the same attitude as before, and, with increased assurance, he invited Rosanette to dine with him that very evening.

"Impossible!" she replied; "we're going together to the Café Anglais."

Frederick, as if he had heard nothing, remained silent; and Cisy quitted the Maréchale with a look of disappointment on his face.

While he had been talking to her at the right-hand door of the carriage, Hussonnet presented himself at the opposite side, and, catching the words "Café Anglais":

"It's a nice establishment; suppose we had a pick there, eh?"

"Just as you like," said Frederick, who, sunk down in the corner of the berlin, was gazing at the horizon as the four-wheeled cabriolet vanished from his sight, feeling that an irreparable thing had happened, and that there was an end of his great love. And the other woman was there beside him, the gay and easy love! But, worn out, full of conflicting desires, and no longer even knowing what he wanted, he was possessed by a feeling of infinite sadness, a longing to die.

A great noise of footsteps and of voices made him raise his head. The little ragamuffins assembled round the track sprang over the ropes and came to stare at the galleries. Thereupon their occupants rose to go. A few drops of rain began to fall. The crush of vehicles increased, and Hussonnet got lost in it.

"Well! so much the better!" said Frederick.

"We like to be alone better — don't we?" said the Maréchale, as she placed her hand in his.

Then there swept past him with a glitter of copper and steel a magnificent landau to which were yoked four horses driven in the Daumont style by two jockeys in velvet vests with gold fringes. Madame Dambreuse was by her husband's side, and Martinon was on the other seat facing them. All three of them gazed at Frederick in astonishment.

"They have recognised me!" said he to himself.

Rosanette wished to stop in order to get a better view of the people driving away from the course. Madame Arnoux might again make her appearance! He called out to the postilion:

"Go on! go on! forward!" And the berlin dashed towards the Champs-Élysées in the midst of the other vehicles — calashes, britzkas, wurths, tandems, tilburies, dog-carts, tilted carts with leather curtains, in which workmen in a jovial mood were singing, or one-horse chaises driven by fathers of families. In victorias

crammed with people some young fellows seated on
the others' feet let their legs both hang down.   Large
broughams, which had their seats lined with cloth,
carried dowagers fast asleep, or else a splendid ma-
chine passed with a seat as simple and coquettish as
a dandy's black coat.

The shower grew heavier. Umbrellas, parasols,
and mackintoshes were put into requisition. People
cried out at some distance away: "Good-day!" "Are
you quite well?" "Yes!" "No!" "Bye-bye!" — and
the faces succeeded each other with the rapidity of
Chinese shadows.

Frederick and Rosanette did not say a word to
each other, feeling a sort of dizziness at seeing all
these wheels continually revolving close to them.

At times, the rows of carriages, too closely pressed
together, stopped all at the same time in several lines.
Then they remained side by side, and their occupants
scanned one another. Over the sides of panels adorned
with coats-of-arms indifferent glances were cast on the
crowd. Eyes full of envy gleamed from the interiors of hackney-coaches. Depreciatory smiles responded to the haughty manner in which some
people carried their heads. Mouths gaping wide expressed idiotic admiration; and, here and there, some
lounger, in the middle of the road, fell back with a
bound, in order to avoid a rider who had been gal-
loping through the midst of the vehicles, and had
succeeded in getting away from them. Then, everything set itself in motion once more; the coachmen
let go the reins, and lowered their long whips; the
horses, excited, shook their curb-chains, and flung
foam around them; and the cruppers and the harness
getting moist, were smoking with the watery evapo-

ration, through which struggled the rays of the sink-
ing sun.   Passing under the Arc de Triomphe, there
stretched out at the height of a man, a reddish light,
which shed a glittering lustre on the naves of the
wheels, the handles of the carriage-doors, the ends of
the shafts, and the rings of the carriage-beds; and on
the two sides of the great avenue—like a river in
which manes, garments, and human heads were undulating—the trees, all glittering with rain, rose up
like two green walls.   The blue of the sky overhead,
reappearing in certain places, had the soft hue of satin.

Then, Frederick recalled the days, already far
away, when he yearned for the inexpressible happiness of finding himself in one of these carriages
by the side of one of these women.   He had attained
to this bliss, and yet he was not thereby one jot the
happier.

The rain had ceased falling.   The pedestrians, who
had sought shelter between the columns of the Public
Storerooms, took their departure.   Persons who had
been walking along the Rue Royale, went up again
towards the boulevard.   In front of the residence of
the Minister of Foreign Affairs a group of boobies had
taken up their posts on the steps.

When it had got up as high as the Chinese Baths,
as there were holes in the pavement, the berlin
slackened its pace.   A man in a hazel-coloured paletot was walking on the edge of the footpath.   A
splash, spurting out from under the springs, showed
itself on his back.   The man turned round in a rage.
Frederick grew pale; he had recognised Deslauriers.

At the door of the Café Anglais he sent away the
carriage.   Rosanette had gone in before him while he
was paying the postilion.

He found her subsequently on the stairs chatting with a gentleman. Frederick took her arm; but in the lobby a second gentleman stopped her.

"Go on," said she; "I am at your service."

And he entered the private room alone. Through the two open windows people could be seen at the casements of the other houses opposite. Large watery masses were quivering on the pavement as it began to dry, and a magnolia, placed on the side of a balcony, shed a perfume through the apartment. This fragrance and freshness had a relaxing effect on his nerves. He sank down on the red divan underneath the glass.

The Maréchale here entered the room, and, kissing him on the forehead:

"Poor pet! there's something annoying you!"

"Perhaps so," was his reply.

"You are not alone; take heart!"—which was as much as to say: "Let us each forget our own concerns in a bliss which we shall enjoy in common."

Then she placed the petal of a flower between her lips and extended it towards him so that he might peck at it. This movement, full of grace and of almost voluptuous gentleness, had a softening influence on Frederick.

"Why do you give me pain?" said he, thinking of Madame Arnoux.

"I give you pain?"

And, standing before him, she looked at him with her lashes drawn close together and her two hands resting on his shoulders.

All his virtue, all his rancour gave way before the utter weakness of his will.

He continued:

"Because you won't love me," and he took her on his knees.

She gave way to him. He pressed his two hands round her waist. The crackling sound of her silk dress inflamed him.

"Where are they?" said Hussonnet's voice in the lobby outside.

The Maréchale arose abruptly, and went across to the other side of the room, where she sat down with her back to the door.

She ordered oysters, and they seated themselves at table.

Hussonnet was not amusing. By dint of writing every day on all sorts of subjects, reading many newspapers, listening to a great number of discussions, and uttering paradoxes for the purpose of dazzling people, he had in the end lost the exact idea of things, blinding himself with his own feeble fireworks. The embarrassments of a life which had formerly been frivolous, but which was now full of difficulty, kept him in a state of perpetual agitation; and his impotency, which he did not wish to avow, rendered him snappish and sarcastic. Referring to a new ballet entitled *Oƶaï,* he gave a thorough blowing-up to the dancing, and then, when the opera was in question, he attacked the Italians, now replaced by a company of Spanish actors, "as if people had not quite enough of Castilles * already!" Frederick was shocked at this, owing to his romantic attachment to Spain, and, with a view to diverting the conversation into a new channel, he enquired about the College of France,

* This pun of Hussonnet turns on the double sense of the word "Castille," which not only means a place in Spain, but also an altercation.—TRANSLATOR.

where Edgar Quinet and Mickiewicz had attended. But Hussonnet, an admirer of M. de Maistre, declared himself on the side of Authority and Spiritualism. Nevertheless, he had doubts about the most well-established facts, contradicted history, and disputed about things whose certainty could not be questioned; so that at mention of the word "geometry," he exclaimed: "What fudge this geometry is!" All this he intermingled with imitations of actors. Sainville was specially his model.

Frederick was quite bored by these quibbles. In an outburst of impatience he pushed his foot under the table, and pressed it on one of the little dogs.

Thereupon both animals began barking in a horrible fashion.

"You ought to get them sent home!" said he, abruptly.

Rosanette did not know anyone to whom she could intrust them.

Then, he turned round to the Bohemian:

"Look here, Hussonnet; sacrifice yourself!"

"Oh! yes, my boy! That would be a very obliging act!"

Hussonnet set off, without even requiring to have an appeal made to him.

In what way could they repay him for his kindness? Frederick did not bestow a thought on it. He was even beginning to rejoice at finding himself alone with her, when a waiter entered.

"Madame, somebody is asking for you!"

"What! again?"

"However, I must see who it is," said Rosanette.

He was thirsting for her; he wanted her. This disappearance seemed to him an act of prevarication, almost a piece of rudeness. What, then, did she mean? Was it not enough to have insulted Madame Arnoux? So much for the latter, all the same! Now he hated all women; and he felt the tears choking him, for his love had been misunderstood and his desire eluded.

The Maréchale returned, and presented Cisy to him.

"I have invited Monsieur. I have done right, have I not?"

"How is that! Oh! certainly."

Frederick, with the smile of a criminal about to be executed, beckoned to the gentleman to take a seat.

The Maréchale began to run her eye through the bill of fare, stopping at every fantastic name.

"Suppose we eat a turban of rabbits *à la Richelieu* and a pudding *à la d'Orléans?*"*

"Oh! not Orléans, pray!" exclaimed Cisy, who was a Legitimist, and thought of making a pun.

"Would you prefer a turbot *à la* Chambord?" she next asked.

Frederick was disgusted with this display of politeness.

The Maréchale made up her mind to order a simple fillet of beef cut up into steaks, some crayfishes, truffles, a pine-apple salad, and vanilla ices.

"We'll see what next. Go on for the present! Ah! I was forgetting! Bring me a sausage!—not with garlic!"

And she called the waiter "young man," struck her glass with her knife, and flung up the crumbs of

---

* The word "Orleans" means light woollen cloth, and possibly Cisy's pun might be rendered: "Oh! no cloth pudding, please."
—TRANSLATOR.

her bread to the ceiling. She wished to drink some
Burgundy immediately.

"It is not taken in the beginning," said Frederick.

This was sometimes done, according to the
Vicomte.

"Oh! no. Never!"

"Yes, indeed; I assure you!"

"Ha! you see!"

The look with which she accompanied these
words meant: "This is a rich man — pay attention to
what he says!"

Meantime, the door was opening every moment;
the waiters kept shouting; and on an infernal piano in
the adjoining room some one was strumming a waltz.
Then the races led to a discussion about horseman-
ship and the two rival systems. Cisy was upholding
Baucher and Frederick the Comte d'Aure when Rosanette shrugged her shoulders:

"Enough — my God! — he is a better judge of
these things than you are — come now!"

She kept nibbling at a pomegranate, with her elbow resting on the table. The wax-candles of the
candelabrum in front of her were flickering in the
wind. This white light penetrated her skin with
mother-of-pearl tones, gave a pink hue to her lids,
and made her eyeballs glitter. The red colour of the
fruit blended with the purple of her lips; her thin
nostrils heaved; and there was about her entire person an air of insolence, intoxication, and recklessness
that exasperated Frederick, and yet filled his heart
with wild desires.

Then, she asked, in a calm voice, who owned
that big landau with chestnut-coloured livery.

Cisy replied that it was "the Comtesse Dambreuse."

"They're very rich—aren't they?"

"Oh! very rich! although Madame Dambreuse, who was merely a Mademoiselle Boutron and the daughter of a prefect, had a very modest fortune."

Her husband, on the other hand, must have inherited several estates—Cisy enumerated them: as he visited the Dambreuses, he knew their family history.

Frederick, in order to make himself disagreeable to the other, took a pleasure in contradicting him. He maintained that Madame Dambreuse's maiden name was De Boutron, which proved that she was of a noble family.

"No matter! I'd like to have her equipage!" said the Maréchale, throwing herself back on the armchair.

And the sleeve of her dress, slipping up a little, showed on her left wrist a bracelet adorned with three opals.

Frederick noticed it.

"Look here! why——"

All three looked into one another's faces, and reddened.

The door was cautiously half-opened; the brim of a hat could be seen, and then Hussonnet's profile exhibited itself.

"Pray excuse me if I disturb the lovers!"

But he stopped, astonished at seeing Cisy, and that Cisy had taken his own seat.

Another cover was brought; and, as he was very hungry, he snatched up at random from what remained of the dinner some meat which was in a dish, fruit out of a basket, and drank with one hand while he helped himself with the other, all the time telling them the result of his mission. The two bow-wows had been taken home. Nothing fresh at the house. He had found the cook in the company of a soldier — a fictitious story which he had especially invented for the sake of effect.

The Maréchale took down her cloak from the window-screw. Frederick made a rush towards the bell, calling out to the waiter, who was some distance away:

"A carriage!"

"I have one of my own," said the Vicomte.

"But, Monsieur!"

"Nevertheless, Monsieur!"

And they stared into each other's eyes, both pale and their hands trembling.

At last, the Maréchale took Cisy's arm, and pointing towards the Bohemian seated at the table:

"Pray mind him! He's choking himself. I wouldn't care to let his devotion to my pugs be the cause of his death."

The door closed behind him.

"Well?" said Hussonnet.

"Well, what?"

"I thought——"

"What did you think?"

"Were you not——?"

He completed the sentence with a gesture.

"Oh! no — never in all my life!"

Hussonnet did not press the matter further.

He had an object in inviting himself to dinner. His journal,— which was no longer called *L'Art,* but *Le Flambart,** with this epigraph, "Gunners, to your cannons!"— not being at all in a flourishing condition, he had a mind to change it into a weekly review,

* *The Blazer.*

conducted by himself, without any assistance from Deslauriers. He again referred to the old project and explained his latest plan.

Frederick, probably not understanding what he was talking about, replied with some vague words. Hussonnet snatched up several cigars from the tables, said "Good-bye, old chap," and disappeared.

Frederick called for the bill. It had a long list of items; and the waiter, with his napkin under his arm, was expecting to be paid by Frederick, when another, a sallow-faced individual, who resembled Martinon, came and said to him:

"Beg pardon; they forgot at the bar to add in the charge for the cab."

"What cab?"

"The cab the gentleman took a short time ago for the little dogs."

And the waiter put on a look of gravity, as if he pitied the poor young man. Frederick felt inclined to box the fellow's ears. He gave the waiter the twenty francs' change as a *pour-boire*.

"Thanks, Monseigneur," said the man with the napkin, bowing low.